# THE HUTCHINSON
# TREASURY OF CHILDREN'S
# LITERATURE

# The Hutchinson
# Treasury
# of Children's
# Literature

## Edited by Alison Sage

### Foreword by Quentin Blake

Hutchinson
LONDON SYDNEY AUCKLAND JOHANNESBURG

With special thanks to Klaus Flugge
and the authors and illustrators of Andersen Press for their
generous contribution to this anthology

Design: Paul Welti
Chief Editor: Pilar Jenkins
Assistant Editor: Madeleine Nicklin
Typesetting: Peter Howard

First published in 1995

1 3 5 7 9 10 8 6 4 2

First published in the United Kingdom in 1995 by Hutchinson Children's Books, Random House UK Limited
20 Vauxhall Bridge Road London SWlV 2SA

Random House Australia (Pty) Limited, 20 Alfred Street, Milsons Point, Sydney, New South Wales 2061, Australia

Random House New Zealand Limited, 18 Poland Road, Glenfield, Auckland 10, New Zealand

Random House South Africa (Pty) Limited, P0 Box 337, Bergvlei, South Africa

Random House UK Limited Reg. No. 954009

A CIP catalogue record for this book is available from the British Library

ISBN 0 09 176144 1

Printed and bound in Singapore by
Tien Wah Press [Pte] Ltd

# CONTENTS

Foreword by Quentin Blake 10

## PART ONE
*Youngest Picture Books & Rhymes*

NURSERY RHYMES *Nicola Bayley* . . . . . . . . . . . . . . . . . . . . . . . . . . 14

THE QUEEN OF HEARTS *Randolph Caldecott* . . . . . . . . . . . . . . . . . . 18

NURSERY RHYME BOOK *Quentin Blake* . . . . . . . . . . . . . . . . . . . . . 22

NURSERY RHYME CLASSICS *Kate Greenaway* . . . . . . . . . . . . . . . . . . 26

MOTHER GOOSE *Arthur Rackham* . . . . . . . . . . . . . . . . . . . . . . . . . 32

I WANT MY POTTY *Tony Ross* . . . . . . . . . . . . . . . . . . . . . . . . . . . 36

A DARK, DARK TALE *Ruth Brown* . . . . . . . . . . . . . . . . . . . . . . . . . 43

PAT-A-CAKE, PAT-A-CAKE *Sarah Pooley* . . . . . . . . . . . . . . . . . . . . 47

HALLO! HOW ARE YOU? *Shigeo Watanabe* Illustrated by Yasuo Ohtomo . . . . . . . 48

SING A SONG OF SIXPENCE *Randolph Caldecott* . . . . . . . . . . . . . . . . . 52

KING ROLLO AND THE NEW SHOES *David McKee* . . . . . . . . . . . . . . . . 53

MR GUMPY'S OUTING *John Burningham* . . . . . . . . . . . . . . . . . . . . . 60

ALFIE'S FEET *Shirley Hughes* . . . . . . . . . . . . . . . . . . . . . . . . . . . 70

HICKORY, DICKORY, DOCK *Sarah Pooley* . . . . . . . . . . . . . . . . . . . . . 78

IN THE ATTIC *Hiawyn Oram* Illustrated by Satoshi Kitamura . . . . . . . . . 79

THE SNOWY DAY *Ezra Jack Keats* . . . . . . . . . . . . . . . . . . . . . . . . . 88

TWINKLE, TWINKLE, LITTLE STAR *Sarah Pooley* . . . . . . . . . . . . . . . . 97

THE WIND BLEW *Pat Hutchins* . . . . . . . . . . . . . . . . . . . . . . . . . . 98

I'M A LITTLE TEAPOT *Sarah Pooley* . . . . . . . . . . . . . . . . . . . . . . . 103

WILLY AND HUGH *Anthony Browne* . . . . . . . . . . . . . . . . . . . . . . . . . . . . . .104

GRANNY GRANNY PLEASE COMB MY HAIR *Grace Nichols* . . . . . . . . . . . . . .111

MR RABBIT AND THE LOVELY PRESENT *Charlotte Zolotow*

Illustrated by Maurice Sendak . . . . . . . . . . . . . . . . . . . . . . . . . . . . . . . . . .112

IT'S YOUR TURN, ROGER! *Susanna Gretz* . . . . . . . . . . . . . . . . . . . . . . . . .120

THE SILENT SHIP *Colin West* . . . . . . . . . . . . . . . . . . . . . . . . . . . . . . . . . .131

THE VELVETEEN RABBIT *Margery Williams* Illustrated by Maggie Glen . . . . . . . . . .132

DR XARGLE'S BOOK OF EARTHLETS *Jeanne Willis* Illustrated by Tony Ross . . . . . .146

GERALDINE GIRAFFE *Colin West* . . . . . . . . . . . . . . . . . . . . . . . . . . . . . . .159

# PART TWO

*Older Picture Books, Poems, Fairy Tales & Stories*

OLD BEAR *Jane Hissey* . . . . . . . . . . . . . . . . . . . . . . . . . . . . . . . . . . . . . .162

WHAT IS PINK? *Christina Rossetti* . . . . . . . . . . . . . . . . . . . . . . . . . . . . . . .170

THE WHALES' SONG *Dyan Sheldon* Illustrated by Gary Blythe . . . . . . . . . . . . . .171

JESUS' CHRISTMAS PARTY *Nicholas Allan* . . . . . . . . . . . . . . . . . . . . . . . . . .178

THE WINTER HEDGEHOG *Ann and Reg Cartwright* . . . . . . . . . . . . . . . . . . . .192

CARRY GO BRING COME *Vyanne Samuels* Illustrated by Jennifer Northway . . . . . . .200

DOCTOR DE SOTO *William Steig* . . . . . . . . . . . . . . . . . . . . . . . . . . . . . . .204

THUMBELINA *Hans Christian Andersen* Retold by James Riordan

Illustrated by Wayne Anderson . . . . . . . . . . . . . . . . . . . . . . . . . . . . . . . . . .210

THE TALE OF MRS TIGGY-WINKLE *Beatrix Potter* . . . . . . . . . . . . . . . . . . . .220

THE POLAR EXPRESS *Chris Van Allsburg* . . . . . . . . . . . . . . . . . . . . . . . . . .226

PUGWASH AND THE BURIED TREASURE *John Ryan* . . . . . . . . . . . . . . . . . . .232

THE OWL AND THE PUSSY-CAT *Edward Lear* . . . . . . . . . . . . . . . . . . . . . . 238

SNOW-WHITE *Grimm Retold by Josephine Poole* Illustrated by Angela Barrett . . . . . . . 240

HOW TOM BEAT CAPTAIN NAJORK AND HIS HIRED SPORTSMEN *Russell Hoban*
Illustrated by Quentin Blake . . . . . . . . . . . . . . . . . . . . . . . . 252

BADGER'S PARTING GIFTS *Susan Varley* . . . . . . . . . . . . . . . . . . . . . 260

BUBBLE TROUBLE *Margaret Mahy* Illustrated by Tony Ross . . . . . . . . . . . 265

MRS PEPPERPOT AND THE SPRING CLEANING *Alf Prøysen*
Illustrated by Björn Berg . . . . . . . . . . . . . . . . . . . . . . . . . 272

DON'T PUT MUSTARD IN THE CUSTARD *Michael Rosen*
Illustrated by Quentin Blake . . . . . . . . . . . . . . . . . . . . . . . . 276

THE TWELVE DANCING PRINCESSES *Grimm Retold by Naomi Lewis*
Illustrated by Lidia Postma . . . . . . . . . . . . . . . . . . . . . . . . 280

HAPPY BIRTHDAY, DILROY! *John Agard* Illustrated by John Richardson . . . . . . . . . 285

## PART THREE

*Extracts from Younger Fiction, Poems & Traditional Stories*

THERE'S SOME SKY IN THIS PIE *Joan Aiken* Illustrated by Jan Pieńkowski . . . . . . . 288

MAMMY, SUGAR FALLING DOWN *Trish Cooke*
Illustrated by Alicia Garcia de Lynam . . . . . . . . . . . . . . . . . . . . 292

THE STORY OF DR DOLITTLE *Hugh Lofting* . . . . . . . . . . . . . . . . . . . . 296

THE DOG LOVERS *Spike Milligan* . . . . . . . . . . . . . . . . . . . . . . . 301

TEN IN A BED *Allan Ahlberg* Illustrated by André Amstutz . . . . . . . . . . . . . 302

A VISIT FROM ST NICHOLAS *Clement Clarke Moore* . . . . . . . . . . . . . . . 308

THE SILVER CURLEW *Eleanor Farjeon* Illustrated by E. H. Shepard . . . . . . . . . . . 310

THE BFG *Roald Dahl* Illustrated by Quentin Blake . . . . . . . . . . . . . . 314

OONA AND THE GIANT CUCHULAIN *James Riordan*

Illustrated by Angela Barrett . . . . . . . . . . . . . . . . . . . . . . . . . . . . . . . 318

THE WIZARD OF OZ *L. Frank Baum* Illustrated by W. W. Denslow . . . . . . . . . . . . 323

MATILDA *Hilaire Belloc* Illustrated by Posy Simmonds . . . . . . . . . . . . . . . . 328

PETER PAN *J. M. Barrie* Illustrated by Susie Jenkin-Pearce . . . . . . . . . . . . . . . 330

FIND THE WHITE HORSE *Dick King-Smith* Illustrated by Larry Wilkes . . . . . . . . . 334

THE STREAM THAT STOOD STILL *Beverley Nichols*

Illustrated by Richard Kennedy . . . . . . . . . . . . . . . . . . . . . . . . . . . . . . 340

THE FAIRIES *William Allingham* . . . . . . . . . . . . . . . . . . . . . . . . . . . . . 345

ALICE'S ADVENTURES IN WONDERLAND *Lewis Carroll*

Illustrated by Peter Weevers . . . . . . . . . . . . . . . . . . . . . . . . . . . . . . . 346

JABBERWOCKY *Lewis Carroll* . . . . . . . . . . . . . . . . . . . . . . . . . . . . . . 353

BRER RABBIT AND THE TAR BABY *Retold by Julius Lester*

Illustrated by Jerry Pinkney . . . . . . . . . . . . . . . . . . . . . . . . . . . . . . . 354

FAME WAS A CLAIM OF UNCLE ED'S *Ogden Nash*

Illustrated by Marjorie Priceman . . . . . . . . . . . . . . . . . . . . . . . . . . . . . 357

THE LION, THE WITCH AND THE WARDROBE *C. S. Lewis*

Illustrated by Pauline Baynes . . . . . . . . . . . . . . . . . . . . . . . . . . . . . . . 358

THE INCREDIBLE ADVENTURES OF PROFESSOR BRANESTAWM *Norman Hunter*

Illustrated by W. Heath Robinson . . . . . . . . . . . . . . . . . . . . . . . . . . . . . 364

P. C. PLOD AT THE PILLAR BOX *Roger McGough* . . . . . . . . . . . . . . . . . . . . 371

STIG OF THE DUMP *Clive King*

Illustrated by Dick van der Maat and Edward Ardizzone . . . . . . . . . . . . . . . . . 372

THE LISTENERS *Walter de la Mare* . . . . . . . . . . . . . . . . . . . . . . . . . . . . 377

THE PHOENIX AND THE CARPET *E. Nesbit*

Illustrated by Steve Braund and H. R. Millar . . . . . . . . . . . . . . . . . . . . . . . 378

SUPERFUDGE *Judy Blume* Illustrated by Susan Hellard . . . . . . . . . . . . . . . . . . 386

8

# PART FOUR

*Extracts from Older Fiction & Poems*

THE BORROWERS *Mary Norton* Illustrated by Diana Stanley . . . . . . . . . . . . . . . 394

BATTLE FOR THE PARK *Colin Dann* Illustrated by Frances Broomfield . . . . . . . . . . . 400

BALLET SHOES *Noel Streatfeild* Illustrated by Susie Jenkin-Pearce . . . . . . . . . . . . . . . 406

THE JUNGLE BOOK *Rudyard Kipling* Illustrated by Stuart Tresilian . . . . . . . . . . . . . 412

MOON-WIND *Ted Hughes* . . . . . . . . . . . . . . . . . . . . . . . . . . . . . . . . . . . . . 421

UNCLE *J. P. Martin* Illustrated by Quentin Blake . . . . . . . . . . . . . . . . . . . . . . . . 422

THE SECRET GARDEN *Frances Hodgson Burnett*
Illustrated by Charles Robinson . . . . . . . . . . . . . . . . . . . . . . . . . . . . . . . . . 428

THE WIND IN THE WILLOWS *Kenneth Grahame*
Illustrated by Arthur Rackham . . . . . . . . . . . . . . . . . . . . . . . . . . . . . . . . . . 436

EMIL AND THE DETECTIVES *Erich Kästner* Illustrated by Walter Trier . . . . . . . . . . . 442

A CHRISTMAS CAROL *Charles Dickens* . . . . . . . . . . . . . . . . . . . . . . . . . . . . . 445

SWALLOWS AND AMAZONS *Arthur Ransome*
Illustrated by Jack McCarthy . . . . . . . . . . . . . . . . . . . . . . . . . . . . . . . . . . . 448

THE RUNAWAYS *Ruth Thomas* Illustrated by Derek Brazell . . . . . . . . . . . . . . . . . 456

TOM'S MIDNIGHT GARDEN *Philippa Pearce* Illustrated by Louise Brierley . . . . . . . . 463

REDWALL *Brian Jacques* Illustrated by Pete Lyon . . . . . . . . . . . . . . . . . . . . . . . 470

TREASURE ISLAND *Robert Louis Stevenson* Illustrated by N. C. Wyeth . . . . . . . . . . . 476

THE TYGER *William Blake* . . . . . . . . . . . . . . . . . . . . . . . . . . . . . . . . . . . . . 483

THE SWORD IN THE STONE *T. H. White* Illustrated by Virginia Mayo . . . . . . . . . . . 484

LIMERICKS *Michael Palin* Illustrated by Tony Ross . . . . . . . . . . . . . . . . . . . . . . . 491

THE NARGUN AND THE STARS *Patricia Wrightson* Illustrated by Joan Saint . . . . . . . 492

OBJECTION *Kit Wright* Illustrated by Posy Simmonds . . . . . . . . . . . . . . . . . . . . 499

THE KINGDOM BY THE SEA *Robert Westall* Illustrated by Tony Kerins . . . . . . . . . . . 500

Acknowledgements 510

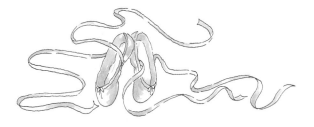

9

# FOREWORD

THE people who are publishing this book decided that someone had to come out in front and explain what it is about. Then they pointed at me and said: "You have volunteered." So here I am. I'll do my best.

You can see for yourself how big this book is. In it there are almost one hundred different pieces of writing. Some are complete books in themselves; some are extracts from larger books; some are poems. They are by a tremendous variety of writers: by writers of some of the most treasured children's books of the past, like J. M. Barrie, Robert Louis Stevenson and E. Nesbit; and by lots of well-known authors of today who are probably at work writing new books at this very minute. And there are illustrations too from dozens of artists, including many of my favourites, like Beatrix Potter, E. H. Shepard and Edward Ardizzone. All people whose books have been read and loved and looked at over and over again.

It's hardly surprising, then, if I feel a bit embarrassed about having to take on the job of saying something by way of introduction to all these extraordinary people. Of course, I also feel extremely pleased, and for all kinds of reasons. One reason – one that I'd like to tell you more about – is that there are stories here by several writers I have worked with and known as friends, and seeing their stories has helped to remind me of our meetings and our discussions. Roald Dahl is one. I can

remember going down to Gipsy House many times to talk to him about the drawings for his books; not in the celebrated shed in the garden – that was only for writing – but in the sitting room amongst the family. After we had looked at all the pictures there would be dinner, with our author sitting in his big chair at the head of the table, teasing the visitors (including me), and at the end of the meal handing round his box of assorted bars of chocolate, with Chopper, the little terrier, excitedly wagging his tail in expectation of his share.

Or going to see Joan Aiken: walking up five flights to her apartment tucked away at the top of an old building in New York; or driving down to Sussex, where we ate the chicken pie that she had made and walked in the peaceful wooded grounds of Petworth House amongst the deer. Joan Aiken is so compact and composed, and has such a calm way of talking, that you almost forget that she is the very person from whom have come so many amazing, funny, mysterious and sometimes frightening stories. But that is one of the things that is so wonderful about words.

And then visiting Russell Hoban in his writing-room in London, with the fog gathering amongst the trees in the park outside, and the lights of the underground trains flickering as they pass. That room always reminds me of a cave. It's full of books, maps, pictures, puppets and modern electronic equipment. In amongst all that, Russell

Hoban, with his trim beard and checked shirt and glinting spectacles, is like some twenty-first-century wizard, keyed in to the messages of the planet.

These are some of the meetings that these stories remind me of; and yet the strange thing is that what writers write (and artists draw) is even more interesting than they are themselves; the encounters that they offer us in their works are even more extraordinary.

This Treasury is a book to search in, and if you search in it you will find yourself in the most unexpected places and with the most unusual characters. With Mowgli, for instance, in the jungle, or with Mole, messing about in boats by the river bank; with Peter on a snowy day in the city, or Tom in the Midnight Garden; with Dorothy on the road to Oz, or with young King Arthur in the Forest Sauvage. You may meet Professor Branestawm, Peter Pan, Captain Pugwash or Doctor De Soto; Lord Salmon, the Winter Hedgehog or the Velveteen Rabbit. You may even see a beautiful but rather temperamental bird called the Phoenix reborn from the flames. And more besides.

One last thing. There are some books that tell you exactly what age of reader they are intended for. This is not one of those. Of course, if you are a young reader you may find some of these stories and poems difficult to understand; and if you are older you may think some of them already too young for you. But sometimes it's good to read things that are too difficult – it's possible to get the smell and the feel of a story even if you are not exactly sure of everything that's happening. And sometimes it's good to go back and read stories that look easy (they aren't always as simple as they seem). Good books are for everybody who likes words and pictures; it doesn't matter how old those people are. These are for you.

QUENTIN BLAKE

# PART ONE

# *Nicola Bayley*
# NURSERY RHYMES

Goosey, goosey, gander,
Whither shall I wander?
Upstairs and downstairs
And in my lady's chamber.
There I met an old man
Who would not say his prayers,
I took him by the left leg
And threw him down the stairs.

THIS little pig went to market,
This little pig stayed at home,
This little pig had roast beef,
And this little pig had none,
And this little pig went wee-wee-wee
all the way home.

THERE was an old woman
   Who lived in a shoe,
She had so many children
She didn't know what to do;
She gave them some broth
Without any bread,
And whipped them all soundly
And put them to bed.

THERE was a crooked man,
And he walked a crooked mile,
He found a crooked sixpence
Against a crooked stile;
He bought a crooked cat,
Which caught a crooked mouse,
And they all lived together
In a little crooked house.

# THE
# QUEEN OF HEARTS

*Illustrated by Randolph Caldecott*

THE Queen of Hearts,
She made some Tarts,

All on a Summer's Day:

The Knave of Hearts,

He stole those Tarts,
And took them right away.

The King of Hearts,
Called for those Tarts,
And beat the Knave full sore:

The Knave of Hearts,
Brought back those Tarts,

And vowed he'd steal no more.

# Quentin Blake
# NURSERY RHYME BOOK

LITTLE Jack Sprat
Once had a pig,
It was not very little,
Nor yet very big,
It was not very lean,
It was not very fat –
It's a good pig to grunt,
Said little Jack Sprat.

OINK

PUSSY Cat ate the dumplings,
Pussy Cat ate the dumplings,
Mama stood by,
And cried, Oh fie!
Why did you eat
the dumplings?

HANDY spandy, Jack-a-Dandy
Loves plum cake and sugar candy.
He bought some at a grocer's shop

And out he came,
hop, hop,
hop, hop!

# NURSERY RHYME CLASSICS

*Illustrated by Kate Greenaway*

MARY had a little lamb,
Its fleece was white as snow;
And everywhere that Mary went
The lamb was sure to go.

It followed her to school one day,
Which was against the rule;
It made the children laugh and play
To see a lamb at school.

And so the teacher sent it out,
But still it waited near;
And stood there patiently about
Till Mary did appear.

"Why does the lamb love Mary so?"
The eager children cry;
"Why, Mary loves the lamb, you know,"
The teacher did reply.

A dillar, a dollar,
  A ten o'clock scholar,
What makes you come so soon?
You used to come at ten o'clock
But now you come at noon.

ONE foot up and one foot down
This is the way to London Town.

JACK Sprat could eat no fat
His wife could eat no lean
And so between them both, you see,
They licked the platter clean.

RING-a-ring-a-roses
A pocket full of posies.
Atishoo! Atishoo!
We all fall down.

Picking up the daisies
Picking up the daisies.
Atishoo! Atishoo!
We all stand up.

"Pussy cat, pussy cat, where have you been?"
"I've been up to London to visit the Queen."
"Pussy cat, pussy cat, what did you there?"
"I frightened a little mouse under her chair."

# MOTHER GOOSE

*Illustrated by Arthur Rackham*

BAA, baa, black sheep,
Have you any wool?
"Yes, sir, yes, sir,
Three bags full:
One for my master,
And one for my dame,
And one for the little boy
Who lives in the lane."

Bye, baby bunting.
Daddy's gone a hunting,
To get a little rabbit's skin
To wrap the baby bunting in.

HERE we go round the mulberry bush,
The mulberry bush, the mulberry bush,
Here we go round the mulberry bush,
On a cold and frosty morning.

This is the way we wash our hands,
Wash our hands, wash our hands,
This is the way we wash our hands,
On a cold and frosty morning.

This is the way we wash our clothes,
Wash our clothes, wash our clothes,
This is the way we wash our clothes,
On a cold and frosty morning.

This is the way we go to school,
Go to school, go to school,
This is the way we go to school,
On a cold and frosty morning.

This is the way we come out of school,
Come out of school, come out of school,
This is the way we come out of school,
On a cold and frosty morning.

# Tony Ross
# I WANT MY POTTY

"NAPPIES ARE YUUECH!" said the little princess. "There MUST be something better!"

"The potty's the place," said the queen.

At first the little princess thought the potty was worse.

"THE POTTY'S THE PLACE!" said the queen.

So…the little princess had to learn.

Sometimes the little princess was a long way from the potty when she needed it most.

Sometimes the little princess played tricks on the potty...

...and sometimes the potty played tricks on the little princess.

Soon the potty was fun

and the little princess loved it.

Everybody said the little princess was clever and would grow up to be a wonderful queen.

"The potty's the place!" said the little princess proudly.

One day the little princess was playing at the top of the castle… when…

"I WANT MY POTTY!" she cried.

"She wants her potty," cried the maid.

"She wants her potty," cried the king.

"She wants her potty," cried the cook.

"She wants her potty," cried the gardener.

"She wants her potty," cried the general.

"I know where it is," cried the admiral.

So the potty was taken as quickly as possible to the little princess... just

…a little too late.

## Ruth Brown

# A DARK, DARK TALE

ONCE UPON A TIME there was a dark, dark moor. On the moor there was a dark, dark wood.

In the wood there was a dark, dark house.
At the front of the house there was a dark, dark door.

Behind the door there was a dark, dark hall.
In the hall there were some dark, dark stairs.

Up the stairs there was a dark, dark passage.
Across the passage was a dark, dark curtain.

Behind the curtain was a dark, dark room.
In the room was a dark, dark cupboard.

In the cupboard was a dark, dark corner.
In the corner was a dark, dark box.

And in the box there was ...                    **A MOUSE!**

# PAT-A-CAKE,
# PAT-A-CAKE

*Illustrated by Sarah Pooley*

Pat-a-cake, pat-a-cake,
Baker's man,
Bake me a cake
As fast as you can.
Pat it and prick it
And mark it with B,
And put it in the oven
For Baby and me.

## Shigeo Watanabe

# HALLO! HOW ARE YOU?

*Illustrated by Yasuo Ohtomo*

"HALLO, FLOWERS. How are you?"

"Hallo, sparrows. How are you?"

"Hallo, cat. How are you?"

"Hallo, dog.
How are you?"

"Hallo, Mr Milkman.
How are you?"

"Hallo, Mr Paperman.
How are you?"

"Hallo, Mr Postman.
How are you?"

"Hallo, Mama.
How are you?"

"What a funny
little bear you are."

"Wait. Wait!"

"Hallo, Papa.
How are you?"

"Hallo, Little Bear.
I'm very well, thank you.
How are you?"

51

# SING A
# SONG OF SIXPENCE

*Illustrated by Randolph Caldecott*

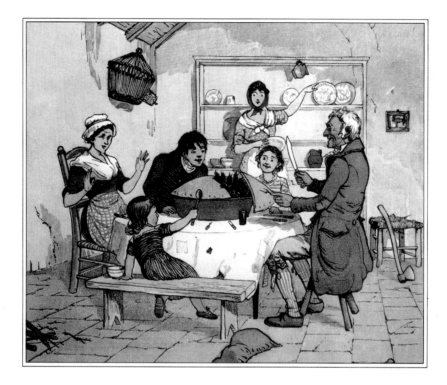

Sing a song of sixpence,
A pocket full of rye;
Four and twenty blackbirds,
Baked in a pie.

When the pie was opened,
The birds began to sing.
Wasn't that a dainty dish,
To set before the king?

The king was in the counting house,
Counting out his money;
The queen was in the parlour,
Eating bread and honey;

The maid was in the garden
Hanging out the clothes,
When down came a blackbird
And snapped off her nose.

But then there came a Jenny wren
And popped it on again.

*David McKee*

# KING ROLLO AND
# THE NEW SHOES

ONE DAY King Rollo visited the shoe shop.

He bought himself a new pair of shoes.

Of course, he already had shoes.

Kings have lots of shoes.

Lots and lots

and lots of shoes.

But King Rollo's new shoes were different.

His new shoes had laces.

King Rollo smiled and put on his new shoes.

"Do them up for me, please," he said to the magician.

"I can't always be around to do up your laces," said the magician.

"Make a magic spell to do them up," said King Rollo.

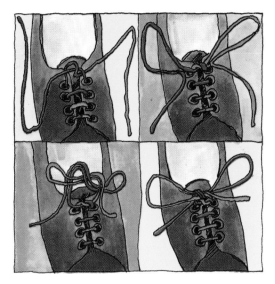

"A waste of magic. I'll show you how to do them up," said the magician.

"Left over right and under and pull. Make a little loop. Now make another. One loop goes over and under the other."

He repeated it with the other shoe.

"Just practise," said the magician, as King Rollo went into his room.

Soon strange noises came from the room. "Left over right and under and BLOW!"

And sometimes a sudden CRASH! like a thrown shoe.

"King Rollo has new shoes," the magician told the cook. "Lace-ups."

Later the noises were much quieter.

That afternoon Queen Gwen came to have tea with King Rollo.

The cook took her to King Rollo's room just as he came out.

"Oh," said Queen Gwen. "I do like your new shoes – they're lace-ups.

"Yes," smiled King Rollo, "and I did them up myself."

# John Burningham
# MR GUMPY'S OUTING

THIS is Mr Gumpy.

Mr Gumpy owned a boat and his house was by a river.

One day Mr Gumpy went out in his boat.
"May we come with you?" said the children.
"Yes," said Mr Gumpy, "if you don't squabble."
"Can I come along, Mr Gumpy?" said the rabbit.
"Yes, but don't hop about."
"I'd like a ride," said the cat.
"Very well," said Mr Gumpy. "But you're not to chase
the rabbit."

"Will you take me with you?" said the dog.
"Yes," said Mr Gumpy. "But don't tease the cat."
"May I come, please, Mr Gumpy?" said the pig.
"Very well, but don't muck about."
"Have you a place for me?" said the sheep.
"Yes, but don't keep bleating."

"Can we come too?" said the chickens.
"Yes, but don't flap," said Mr Gumpy.
"Can you make room for me?" said the calf.
"Yes, if you don't trample about."
"May I join you, Mr Gumpy?" said the goat.
"Very well, but don't kick."

For a little while they all went
along happily but then …

The goat kicked

The calf trampled

The chickens flapped

The sheep bleated

The pig mucked about

The dog teased the cat

The cat chased the rabbit

The rabbit hopped

The children squabbled

The boat tipped …

and into the water they fell.

Then Mr Gumpy and the goat and the calf and the chickens and the
sheep and the pig and the dog and the cat and the rabbit and the
children all swam to the bank and climbed out to dry in the hot sun.
"We'll walk home across the fields," said Mr Gumpy.
"It's time for tea."

"Goodbye," said Mr Gumpy. "Come for a ride another day."

# HICKORY, DICKORY, DOCK

*Illustrated by Sarah Pooley*

HICKORY, dickory, dock,
The mouse ran up the clock.
The clock struck one,
The mouse ran down,
Hickory, dickory, dock.
Tick tock, tick tock.

# Hiawyn Oram
# IN THE ATTIC

*Illustrated by Satoshi Kitamura*

I HAD A MILLION TOYS and I was bored.

I climbed into the attic.

I was there now. The attic was empty. Or was it?

I found a family of mice

and a colony of beetles and a cool, quiet place to rest and think.

I met a spider and we made a web.

I opened a window that opened other windows.

I found an old engine and I made it work.

I went out to look for someone to share what I had found

and found a friend. My friend and I

found a game that could go on forever because it kept changing.

I climbed out of the attic and
told my mother where I'd
been all day.

"But we don't have an attic," she said.

Well, she wouldn't know, would she?

She hasn't found the ladder.

# Ezra Jack Keats
# THE SNOWY DAY

ONE WINTER MORNING Peter woke up
and looked out of the window.
Snow had fallen during the night. It
covered everything as far as he could see.

After breakfast he put on his snowsuit and ran
outside. The snow was piled up very high
along the street to make a path for walking.

Crunch, crunch, crunch, his feet sank into the snow.
He walked with his toes pointing out, like this.

He walked with his toes pointing in, like that.
Then he dragged his feet s-l-o-w-l-y to make tracks.

And he found something sticking out
of the snow that made a new track. It was a stick

— a stick that was just right for
smacking a snow-covered tree.
Down fell the snow – plop!
– on top of Peter's head.

He thought it would be fun to join the big boys in their snowball fight, but he knew he wasn't old enough – not yet.

So he made a smiling snowman, and he made angels.

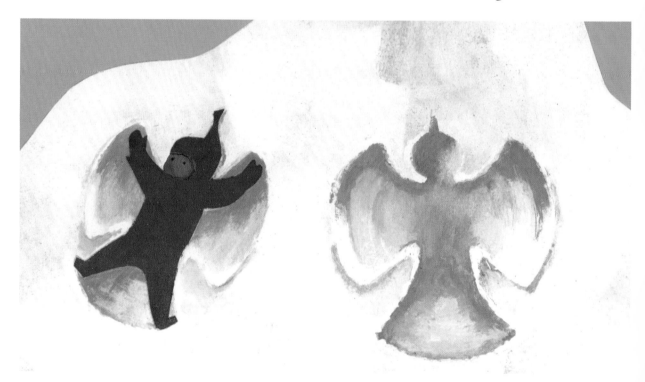

He pretended he was a mountain-climber.
He climbed up a great big tall heaping mountain of snow –

and slid all the way down.

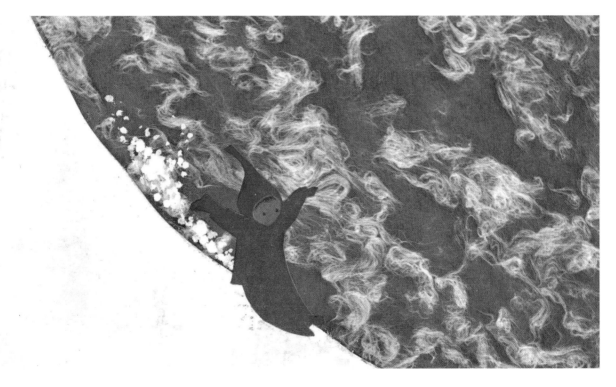

He picked up a handful of snow – and another, and still another. He packed it round and firm and put the snowball in his pocket for tomorrow. Then he went into his warm house.

He told his mother all about his adventures while she took off his wet socks.

And he thought and thought and thought about them.

Before he got into bed he looked in his pocket. His pocket was empty. The snowball wasn't there. He felt very sad.

While he slept, he dreamed that the sun had melted all the snow away.

But when he woke up his dream was gone. The snow was still everywhere. New snow was falling!

After breakfast he called to his friend from across the hall, and they went out together into the deep, deep snow.

# TWINKLE, TWINKLE, LITTLE STAR

*Illustrated by Sarah Pooley*

TWINKLE, twinkle, little star,
How I wonder what you are,
Up above the world so high,
Like a diamond in the sky.

## Pat Hutchins
# THE WIND BLEW

T<small>HE</small> <small>WIND</small> blew.

It took the umbrella from Mr White
and quickly turned it inside out.

It snatched the balloon from little Priscilla
and swept it up to join the umbrella.

98

And not content, it took a hat,
and still not satisfied with that,

it whipped a kite into the air
and kept it spinning round up there.

It grabbed a shirt left out to dry
and tossed it upward to the sky.

It plucked a hanky from a nose
and up and up and up it rose.

It lifted the wig from the judge's head
and didn't drop it back. Instead

it whirled the postman's letters up,
as if it hadn't done enough.

It blew so hard it quickly stole
a striped flag fluttering on a pole.

It pulled the new scarves from the twins
and tossed them to the other things.

It sent the newspapers fluttering round,
then, tired of the things it found,

it mixed them up and threw them down

and blew away to sea.

# I'M A
# LITTLE TEAPOT

*Illustrated by Sarah Pooley*

I'M a little teapot, short and stout;
Here's my handle, here's my spout.
When I see the tea-cups, hear me shout,
"Tip me up and pour me out."

# Anthony Browne
# WILLY AND HUGH

**W**ILLY WAS lonely.

Everyone seemed to have friends. Everyone except Willy.

No one let him join in any games; they all said he was useless.

One day Willy was walking in the park …

minding his own business …

and Hugh Jape was running …

they met.

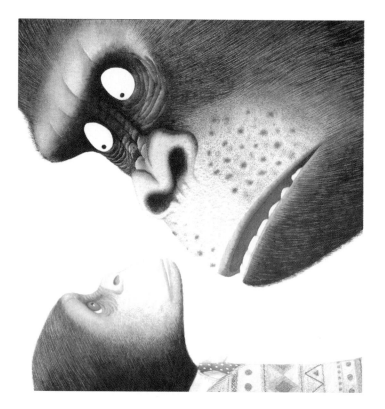

"Oh, I'm so sorry," said Hugh. Willy was amazed. "But *I'm* sorry," he said, "I wasn't watching where I was going." "No, it was *my* fault," said Hugh. "I wasn't looking where *I* was going. I'm sorry." Hugh helped Willy to his feet.

They sat down on a bench and watched the joggers.
"Looks like they're *really* enjoying themselves," said Hugh.
Willy laughed.

Buster Nose appeared. "I've been
looking for you, little wimp," he
sneered.

Hugh stood up. "Can *I* be of any
help?" he asked.
Buster left. Very quickly.

So Willy and Hugh
decided to go to the zoo.

Then they went
to the library,
and Willy read
to Hugh.

As they were leaving the library, Hugh
stopped suddenly …

He'd seen a
TERRIFYING CREATURE …

"Can *I* be of any
help?" asked Willy,
and he carefully
moved the spider
out of the way.

Willy felt quite pleased with himself.
"Shall we meet up tomorrow?" asked Hugh.
"Yes, that would be great," said Willy.

And it was.

*Grace Nichols*

# GRANNY GRANNY PLEASE COMB MY HAIR

GRANNY Granny
please comb my hair
you always take your time
you always take such care

You put me to sit on a cushion
between your knees
you rub a little coconut oil
parting gentle as a breeze

Mummy Mummy
she's always in a hurry – hurry
rush
she pulls my hair
sometimes she tugs

But Granny
you have all the time in the world
and when you're finished
you always turn my head and say
"Now who's a nice girl."

*Charlotte Zolotow*

# MR RABBIT AND THE LOVELY PRESENT

*Illustrated by Maurice Sendak*

"Mʀ Rᴀʙʙɪᴛ," said the little girl, "I want help."
"Help, little girl, I'll give you help if I can," said Mr Rabbit.
"Mr Rabbit," said the little girl, "it's about my mother."
"Your mother?" said Mr Rabbit.
"It's her birthday," said the little girl.
"Happy birthday to her then," said Mr Rabbit. "What are you giving her?"

"That's just it," said the little girl. "That's why I want help. I have nothing to give her."

"Nothing to give your mother on her birthday?" said Mr Rabbit. "Little girl, you really do want help."

"I would like to give her something that she likes," said the little girl.

"Something that she likes is a good present," said Mr Rabbit.

"But what?" said the little girl.

"Yes, what?" said Mr Rabbit.

"She likes red," said the little girl.

"Red," said Mr Rabbit. "You can't give her red."

"Something red, maybe," said the little girl.

"Oh, something red," said Mr Rabbit.

"What is red?" said the little girl.

"Well," said Mr Rabbit, "there's red underwear."

"No," said the little girl, "I can't give her that."

"There are red roofs," said Mr Rabbit.

"No, we have a roof," said the little girl. "I don't want to give her that."

"There are red birds," said Mr Rabbit, "red cardinals."

"No," said the little girl, "she likes birds in trees."

"There are red fire engines," said Mr Rabbit.

"No," said the little girl, "she doesn't like fire engines."

"Well," said Mr Rabbit, "there are apples."

"Good," said the little girl. "That's good. She likes apples. But I need something else."

"What else does she like?" said Mr Rabbit.

"Well, she likes yellow," said the little girl.

"Yellow," said Mr Rabbit. "You can't give her yellow."

"Something yellow, maybe," said the little girl.

"Oh, something yellow," said Mr Rabbit.

"What is yellow?" said the little girl.

"Well," said Mr Rabbit, "there are yellow taxicabs."

"I'm sure she doesn't want a taxicab," said the little girl.

"The sun is yellow," said Mr Rabbit.

"But I can't give her the sun," said the little girl, "though I would if I could."

"A canary bird is yellow," said Mr Rabbit.

"She likes birds in trees," the little girl said.

"That's right, you told me," said Mr Rabbit. "Well, butter is yellow. Does she like butter?"

"We have butter," said the little girl.

"Bananas are yellow," said Mr Rabbit.

"Oh, good. That's good," said the little girl. "She likes bananas. I need something else, though."

"What else does she like?" said Mr Rabbit.

"She likes green," said the little girl.

"Green," said Mr Rabbit. "You can't give her green."

"Something green, maybe," said the little girl.

"Emeralds," said the rabbit. "Emeralds make a lovely gift."

"I can't afford an emerald," said the little girl.

"Parrots are green," said Mr Rabbit, "but she likes birds in trees."

"No," said the little girl, "parrots won't do."

"Peas and spinach," said Mr Rabbit. "Peas are green. Spinach is green."

"No," said the little girl. "We have those for dinner all the time."

"Caterpillars," said Mr Rabbit. "Some of them are very green."

"She doesn't care for caterpillars," the little girl said.

"How about pears?" said Mr Rabbit. "Bartlett pears?"

"The very thing," said the little girl. "That's the very thing. Now I have apples and bananas and pears, but I need something else."

"What else does she like?" said Mr Rabbit.

"She likes blue," the little girl said.

"Blue. You can't give her blue," said Mr Rabbit.

"Something blue, maybe," said the little girl.

"Lakes are blue," said the rabbit.

"But I can't give her a lake, you know," said the little girl.

117

"Stars are blue."

"I can't give her stars," the little girl said, "but I would if I could."

"Sapphires make a lovely gift," said Mr Rabbit.

"But I can't afford sapphires, either," said the little girl.

"Bluebirds are blue, but she likes birds in trees," said Mr Rabbit.

"Right," said the little girl.

"How about blue grapes?" said Mr Rabbit.

"Yes," said the little girl. "That is good, very good. She likes grapes. Now I have apples and pears and bananas and grapes."

"That makes a good gift," said Mr Rabbit. "All you need now is a basket."

"I have a basket," said the little girl.

So she took her basket and she filled it with the green pears and the yellow bananas and the red apples and the blue grapes. It made a lovely present.

"Thank you for your help, Mr Rabbit," said the little girl.

"Not at all," said Mr Rabbit. "Very glad to help."

"Good-bye, now," said the little girl.

"Good-bye," said Mr Rabbit, "and a happy birthday and a happy basket of fruit to your mother."

# *Susanna Gretz*
# IT'S YOUR TURN, ROGER!

IN ALL THE FLATS in Roger's
house it's nearly supper time.

"Roger, it's your turn to set the table."
That's his sister calling.

"I see you, Roger!"
That's his little brother.

"Roger, you know we all take turns at helping."
That's Roger's dad.

"Roger, it's *your turn*."
That's Roger's uncle.

"ROGER!
You heard what Uncle Tim said.
I don't want to hear another
word about it...

...and that's final!"
That's Roger's mum.

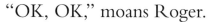

"OK, OK," moans Roger.

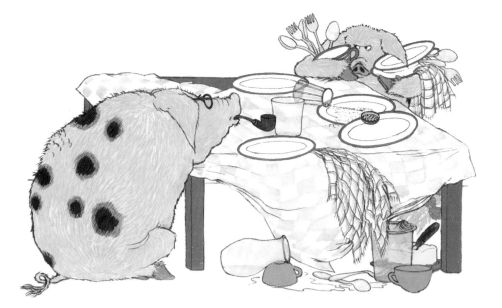

"In other families you don't have to help," Roger grumbles.
"Are you sure?" asks Uncle Tim. "Why don't you go and see?"

"All right, I *will*," says Roger.

He stomps out of the door...

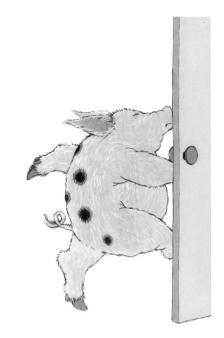

...and on upstairs.
"Come in, come in," says the family
on the first floor.
"Do I have to set the table?" asks Roger.
"Certainly not, you're a guest. Come in
and have some fishmeal soup."

What a fancy supper table, thinks Roger...but what *horrible* soup!

"Excuse me," says Roger, and he hops upstairs.

"Come in, come in," says the
family on the second floor.
"Do I have to set the table?"
asks Roger.
"Certainly not, you're a guest.
Come in and have some
mud pancakes."

What a messy table, thinks Roger…and what *dreadful* pancakes!

No one notices as he slips out.

"Come in, come in," says the
family on the third floor.
"Do I have to set the table?"
asks Roger.
"Certainly not, you're a guest.
Come in and have a little snack."

125

This family doesn't even *have* a table…Roots and snails – YUK!

Roger hurries away.

"Come in, come in," says the family
in the top flat.
"Do I have to set the table?"
asks Roger.
"Certainly not, you're a guest.
Come in and have some milky
mush."
"Well…" says Roger.
He *is* getting
hungry.

Everyone in the top flat is busy
getting the supper table ready.

Roger sits by himself and watches.
If I weren't a "guest",
I could help too, he thinks.

Supper time!

"What's a guest?" he asks someone.
"Well…guests don't really live here."
"Oh," says Roger. "Now where *I* live…"

Just then a special smell creeps all
the way upstairs to the top flat.

"Where *I* live," shouts Roger, "there's
something *good* for supper

– and it's my turn to help!"

"I took your turn for you," says Uncle Tim.
"I'll take your turn tomorrow," says Roger, between mouthfuls.

Worm pie for dessert – whoopee! Roger's favourite.

## *Colin West*
# THE SILENT SHIP

I sailed a ship as white as snow,
As soft as clouds on high,
Tall was the mast, broad was the beam,
And safe and warm was I.

I stood astern my stately ship
And felt so grand and high,
To see the lesser ships give way
As I went gliding by.

## Margery Williams
# THE VELVETEEN RABBIT

*Illustrated by Maggie Glen*

THERE WAS ONCE A VELVETEEN RABBIT, and in the beginning he was really splendid. He was fat and bunchy, as a rabbit should be; his coat was spotted brown and white, he had real thread whiskers, and his ears were lined with pink sateen. On Christmas morning, when he sat wedged in the top of the Boy's stocking, with a sprig of holly between his paws, the effect was charming.

There were other things in the stocking, nuts and oranges and a toy engine, and chocolate almonds and a clockwork mouse, but the Rabbit was quite the best of all. For at least two hours the Boy loved him, and then Aunts and Uncles came to dinner, and there was a great rustling of tissue paper and unwrapping of parcels, and in the excitement of looking at all the new presents the Velveteen Rabbit was forgotten.

For a long time he lived in the toy cupboard or on the nursery floor, and no one thought very much about him. He was naturally shy, and being only made of velveteen, some of the more expensive toys quite snubbed him. The only person who was kind to him at all was the Skin Horse.

The Skin Horse had lived longer in the nursery than any of the others. He was so old that his brown coat was bald in patches and showed the seams underneath, and most of the hairs in his tail had been pulled out to string bead necklaces. He was wise, for he had seen a long succession of mechanical toys arrive to boast and swagger, and by-and-by break their mainsprings and pass away, and he knew that they were only toys, and would never turn into anything else. For nursery magic is very strange and wonderful, and only those playthings that are old and wise and experienced like the Skin Horse understand all about it.

"What is REAL?" asked the Rabbit one day, when they were lying side by side near the nursery fender, before Nana came to tidy the room. "Does it mean having things that buzz inside you and a stick-out handle?"

"Real isn't how you are made," said the Skin Horse. "It's a thing that happens to you. When a child loves you for a long, long time, not just to play with, but REALLY loves you, then you become Real."

"Does it hurt?" asked the Rabbit.

"Sometimes," said the Skin Horse, for he was always truthful. "When you are Real you don't mind being hurt."

"Does it happen all at once, like being wound up," he asked, "or bit by bit?"

"It doesn't happen all at once," said the Skin Horse. "You become. It takes a long time. That's why it doesn't often happen to people who break easily, or have sharp edges, or who have to be carefully kept. Generally, by the time you are Real, most of your hair has been loved off, and your eyes drop out and you get loose in the joints and very shabby. But these things don't matter at all, because once you are Real you can't be ugly, except to people who don't understand."

"I suppose *you* are Real?" said the Rabbit. And then he wished he had not said it, for he thought the Skin Horse might be sensitive. But the Skin Horse only smiled.

"The Boy's Uncle made me Real," he said. "That was a great many years ago; but once you are Real you can't become unreal again. It lasts for always."

The Rabbit sighed. He thought it would be a long time before this magic called Real happened to him. He longed to become Real, to know what it felt like; and yet the idea of growing shabby and losing his eyes and whiskers was rather sad. He wished that he could become it without these uncomfortable things happening to him.

There was a person called Nana who ruled the nursery. Sometimes she took no notice of the playthings lying about, and sometimes, for no reason whatever, she went swooping about like a great wind and hustled them away in cupboards. She called this "tidying up", and the playthings all hated it, especially the tin ones. The Rabbit didn't mind it so much, for wherever he was thrown he came down soft.

One evening, when the Boy was going to bed, he couldn't find the china dog that always slept with him. Nana was in a hurry, and it was too much trouble to hunt for china dogs at bedtime, so she simply looked about her, and seeing that the toy cupboard door stood open, she made a swoop.

"Here," she said, "take your old Bunny! He'll do to sleep with you!" And she dragged the Rabbit out by one ear, and put him into the Boy's arms.

That night, and for many nights after, the Velveteen Rabbit slept in the Boy's bed. At first he found it rather uncomfortable, for the Boy hugged him very tight, and sometimes he rolled over on him, and sometimes he pushed him so far under the pillow that the Rabbit could scarcely breathe. And he missed, too, those long moonlight hours in the nursery, when all the house was silent, and his talks with the Skin Horse. But very soon he grew to like it, for the Boy used to talk to him, and made nice tunnels for him under the bedclothes that he said were like the burrows the real rabbits lived in. And they had splendid games together, in whispers, when Nana had gone away to her supper and left the nightlight burning on the mantelpiece. And when the Boy dropped off to sleep, the Rabbit would snuggle down close under his little warm chin and dream, with the Boy's hands clasped close round him all night long.

And so time went on, and the little Rabbit was very happy – so happy that he never noticed how his beautiful velveteen fur was getting shabbier and shabbier, and his tail coming unsewn, and all the pink rubbed off his nose where the Boy had kissed him.

Spring came, and they had long days in the garden, for wherever the Boy went the Rabbit went too. He had rides in the wheelbarrow, and picnics on the grass, and lovely fairy huts built for him under the raspberry canes behind the flower border. And once, when the Boy was

called away suddenly to go out to tea, the Rabbit was left out on the lawn until long after dusk, and Nana had to come and look for him with the candle because the Boy couldn't go to sleep unless he was there. He was wet through with the dew and quite earthy from diving into the burrows the Boy had made for him in the flower-bed, and Nana grumbled as she rubbed him off with a corner of her apron.

"You must have your old Bunny!" she said. "Fancy all that fuss for a toy!"

The Boy sat up in bed and stretched out his hands.

"Give me my Bunny!" he said. "You mustn't say that. He isn't a toy. He's REAL!"

When the little Rabbit heard that he was happy, for he knew that what the Skin Horse had said was true at last. The nursery magic had happened to him, and he was a toy no longer. He was Real. The Boy himself had said it.

That night he was almost too happy to sleep, and so much love stirred in his little sawdust heart that it almost burst. And into his boot-button eyes, that had long ago lost their polish, there came a look of wisdom and beauty, so that even Nana noticed it next morning when she picked him up, and said, "I declare if that old Bunny hasn't got quite a knowing expression!"

That was a wonderful Summer!

Near the house where they lived there was a wood, and in the long June evenings the Boy liked to go there after tea to play. He took the Velveteen Rabbit with him, and before he wandered off to pick flowers, or play at brigands among the trees, he always made the Rabbit a little nest somewhere among the bracken, where he would be quite cosy, for he was a kind-hearted little boy and he liked Bunny to be comfortable. One evening, while the Rabbit was lying there alone, watching the ants that ran to and fro between his velvet paws in the grass, he saw two strange beings creep out of the tall bracken near him.

They were rabbits like himself, but quite furry and brand-new. They must have been very well made, for their seams didn't show at all, and they changed shape in a queer way when they moved; one minute they were long and thin and the next minute fat and bunchy, instead of always staying the same like he did. Their feet padded softly on the ground, and they crept quite close to him, twitching their noses, while the Rabbit stared hard to see which side the clockwork stuck out, for he knew that people who jump generally have something to wind them up. But he couldn't see it. They were evidently a new kind of rabbit altogether.

They stared at him, and the little Rabbit stared back. And all the time their noses twitched.

"Why don't you get up and play with us?" one of them asked.

"I don't feel like it," said the Rabbit, for he didn't want to explain that he had no clockwork.

"Ho!" said the furry rabbit. "It's as easy as anything." And he gave a big hop sideways and stood on his hind legs.

"I don't believe you can!" he said.

"I can!" said the little Rabbit. "I can jump higher than anything!" He meant when the Boy threw him, but of course he didn't want to say so.

"Can you hop on your hind legs?" asked the furry rabbit.

That was a dreadful question, for the Velveteen Rabbit had no hind legs at all! The back of him was made all in one piece, like a pincushion. He sat still in the bracken, and hoped that the other rabbits wouldn't notice.

"I don't want to!" he said again.

But the wild rabbits have very sharp eyes. And this one stretched out his neck and looked.

"He hasn't got any hind legs!" he called out. "Fancy a rabbit without any hind legs!" And he began to laugh.

"I have!" cried the little Rabbit. "I have got hind legs! I am sitting on them!"

"Then stretch them out and show me, like this!" said the wild rabbit. And he began to whirl round and dance, till the little Rabbit got quite dizzy.

"I don't like dancing," he said. "I'd rather sit still!"

But all the while he was longing to dance, for a funny new tickly feeling ran through him, and he felt he would give anything in the world to be able to jump about like these rabbits did.

The strange rabbit stopped dancing, and came quite close. He came so close this time that his long whiskers brushed the Velveteen Rabbit's ear, and then he wrinkled his nose suddenly and flattened his ears and jumped backwards.

"He doesn't smell right!" he exclaimed. "He isn't a rabbit at all! He isn't real!"

"I *am* Real!" said the little Rabbit. "I am Real! The Boy said so!" And he nearly began to cry.

Just then there was a sound of footsteps, and the Boy ran past near them, and with a stamp of feet and a flash of white tails the two strange rabbits disappeared.

"Come back and play with me!" called the little Rabbit. "Oh, do come back! I *know* I am Real!"

But there was no answer, only the little ants ran to and fro, and the bracken swayed gently where the two strangers had passed. The Velveteen Rabbit was all alone.

"Oh, dear!" he thought. "Why did they run away like that? Why couldn't they stop and talk to me?"

For a long time he lay very still, watching the bracken, and hoping that they would come back. But they never returned, and presently the sun sank lower and the little white moths fluttered out, and the Boy came and carried him home.

Weeks passed, and the little Rabbit grew very old and shabby, but the Boy loved him just as much. He loved him so hard that he loved all his whiskers off, and the pink lining to his ears turned grey, and his brown spots faded. He even began to lose his shape, and he scarcely looked like a rabbit any more, except to the Boy. To him he was always beautiful, and that was all that the little Rabbit cared about. He didn't mind how he looked to other people, because the nursery magic had made him

Real, and when you are Real shabbiness doesn't matter.

And then, one day, the Boy was ill.

His face grew very flushed, and he talked in his sleep, and his little body was so hot that it burned the Rabbit when he held him close. Strange people came and went in the nursery, and a light burned all night and through it all the little Velveteen Rabbit lay there, hidden from sight under the bedclothes, and he never stirred, for he was afraid that if they found him someone might take him away, and he knew that the Boy needed him.

It was a long weary time, for the Boy was too ill to play, and the little Rabbit found it rather dull with nothing to do all day long. But he snuggled down patiently, and looked forward to the time when the Boy should be well again, and they would go out in the garden amongst the flowers and the butterflies and play splendid games in the raspberry thicket like they used to. All sorts of delightful things he planned, and while the Boy lay half asleep he crept up close to the pillow and whispered them in his ear. And presently the fever turned, and the Boy got better. He was able to sit up in bed and look at picture-books, while the little Rabbit cuddled close at his side. And one day, they let him get up and dress.

It was a bright, sunny morning, and the windows stood wide open. They had carried the Boy out on to the balcony, wrapped in a shawl, and the little Rabbit lay tangled up among the bedclothes, thinking.

The Boy was going to the seaside tomorrow. Everything was arranged, and now it only remained to carry out the doctor's orders. They talked about it all, while the little Rabbit lay under the bedclothes, with just his head peeping out, and listened. The room was to be disinfected, and all the books and toys that the Boy had played with in bed must be burnt.

"Hurrah!" thought the little Rabbit. "Tomorrow we shall go to the seaside!" For the Boy had often talked of the seaside, and he wanted very much to see the big waves coming in, and the tiny crabs, and the sand castles.

Just then Nana caught sight of him.

"How about his old Bunny?" she asked.

"*That?*" said the doctor. "Why, it's a mass of scarlet fever germs! — Burn it at once. What? Nonsense! Get him a new one. He mustn't have that any more!"

And so the little Rabbit was put into a sack with the old picture-books and a lot of rubbish, and carried out to the end of the garden behind the fowl-house. That was a fine place to make a bonfire, only the gardener was too busy just then to attend to it. He had the potatoes to dig and the green peas to gather, but next morning he promised to come quite early and burn the whole lot.

That night the Boy slept in a different bedroom, and he had a new bunny to sleep with him. It was a splendid bunny, all white plush with real glass eyes, but the Boy was too excited to care very much about it. For tomorrow he was going to the seaside, and that in itself was such a wonderful thing that he could think of nothing else.

And while the Boy was asleep, dreaming of the seaside, the little Rabbit lay among the old picture-books in the corner behind the fowl-house, and he felt very lonely. The sack had been left untied, and so by wriggling a bit he was able to get his head through the opening and look out. He was shivering a little, for he had always been used to sleeping in a proper bed, and by this time his coat had worn so thin and threadbare from hugging that it was no longer any protection to him. Nearby he could see the thicket of raspberry canes, growing tall and close like a tropical jungle, in whose shadow he had played with the Boy on bygone mornings. He thought of those long sunlit hours in the garden – how happy they were – and a great sadness came over him. He seemed to see them all pass before him, each more beautiful than the other, the fairy huts in the flower-bed, the quiet evenings in the wood when he lay in the bracken and the little ants ran over his paws; the wonderful day when he first knew that he was Real. He thought of the Skin Horse, so wise and gentle, and all that he had told him. Of what use was it to be loved and lose one's beauty and become Real if it all ended like this? And a tear, a real tear, trickled down his little shabby velvet nose and fell to the ground.

And then a strange thing happened. For where the tear had fallen a flower grew out of the ground, a mysterious flower, not at all like any that grew in the garden. It had slender green leaves the colour of emeralds, and in the centre of the leaves a blossom like a golden cup. It

was so beautiful that the little Rabbit forgot to cry, and just lay there watching it. And presently the blossom opened, and out of it there stepped a fairy.

She was quite the loveliest fairy in the whole world. Her dress was of pearl and dewdrops, and there were flowers round her neck and in her hair, and her face was like the most perfect flower of all. And she came close to the little Rabbit and gathered him up in her arms and kissed him on his velveteen nose that was all damp from crying.

"Little Rabbit," she said, "don't you know who I am?"

The Rabbit looked up at her, and it seemed to him that he had seen her face before, but he couldn't think where.

"I am the nursery magic Fairy," she said. "I take care of all the playthings that the children have loved. When they are old and worn out and the children don't need them any more, then I come and take them away with me and turn them into Real."

"Wasn't I Real before?" asked the little Rabbit.

"You were Real to the Boy," the Fairy said, "because he loved you. Now you shall be Real to everyone."

And she held the little Rabbit close in her arms and flew with him into the wood.

It was light now, for the moon had risen. All the forest was beautiful, and the fronds of the bracken shone like frosted silver. In the open glade between the tree-trunks the wild rabbits danced with their shadows on the velvet grass, but when they saw the Fairy they all stopped dancing and stood round in a ring to stare at her.

"I've brought you a new playfellow," the Fairy said. "You must be very kind to him and teach him all he needs to know in Rabbitland, for he is going to live with you for ever and ever!"

And she kissed the little Rabbit again and put him down on the grass.

"Run and play, little Rabbit!" she said.

But the little Rabbit sat quite still for a moment and never moved. For when he saw all the wild rabbits dancing around him he suddenly remembered about his hind legs, and he didn't want them to see that he was made all in one piece. He did not know that when the Fairy kissed him that last time she had changed him altogether. And he might have sat there a long time, too shy to move, if just then something hadn't tickled his nose, and before he thought what he was doing he lifted his hind toe to scratch it.

And he found that he actually had hind legs! Instead of dingy

velveteen he had brown fur, soft and shiny, his ears twitched by themselves, and his whiskers were so long that they brushed the grass. He gave one leap and the joy of using those hind legs was so great that he went springing about the turf on them, jumping sideways and whirling round as the others did, and he grew so excited that when at last he did stop to look for the Fairy she had gone.

He was a Real Rabbit at last, at home with the other rabbits.

Autumn passed and Winter, and in the Spring, when the days grew warm and sunny, the Boy went out to play in the wood behind the house. And while he was playing, two rabbits crept out from the bracken and peeped at him. One of them was brown all over, but the other had strange markings under his fur, as though long ago he had been spotted, and the spots still showed through. And about his little soft nose and his round black eyes there was something familiar, so that the Boy thought to himself:

"Why, he looks just like my old Bunny that was lost when I had scarlet fever!"

But he never knew that it really was his own Bunny, come back to look at the child who had first helped him to be Real.

# *Jeanne Willis*
# DR XARGLE'S BOOK OF EARTHLETS

*Illustrated by Tony Ross*

GOOD MORNING, class.

Today we are going to learn about Earthlets.

They come in four colours. Pink, brown, black or yellow ... but not green.

They have one head
and only two eyes, two
short tentacles with
pheelers on the end and
two long tentacles called
leggies.

They have square claws
which they use to
frighten off wild beasts
known as Tibbles and
Marmaduke.

Earthlets grow fur on their heads but not enough to keep them warm.

They must be wrapped in the hairdo of a sheep.

Very old Earthlings (or "Grannies") unravel the sheep and with two pointed sticks they make Earthlet wrappers in blue and white and pink.

Earthlets have no fangs
at birth.
For many days they
drink only milk through
a hole in their face.

When they have finished the milk they must be patted and squeezed to stop them exploding.

When they grow a fang, the parent Earthling takes the egg of a hen and mangles it with a prong.

After soaking, Earthlets must be dried carefully to stop them shrinking. Then they are sprinkled with dust to stop them sticking to things.

Earthlets can be recognised by their fierce cry, "WAAAAAAA!"

To stop them doing this, the Earthling daddy picks them up and flings them into the atmosphere.

Then he tries to catch them.

155

If they still cry, the Earthling mummy pulls their pheelers one by one and says "This little piggy went to market" until the Earthlet makes a "hee hee" noise.

If they still cry, they are sent to a place called beddybyes.

This is a swinging box with a soft lining in which there lives a small bear called Teddy.

That is the end of today's lesson.

If you are all very good and quiet we are going to put our disguises on and visit planet Earth to see some real Earthlets.

The spaceship leaves in five minutes.

## Colin West
# GERALDINE GIRAFFE

THE longest
ever
woolly
scarf
was
worn
by
Geraldine
Giraffe.
Around
her
neck
the
scarf
she
wound,
but
still
it
trailed
upon
the
ground.

# Jane Hissey
# OLD BEAR

IT WASN'T ANYBODY'S BIRTHDAY, but Bramwell Brown had a feeling that today was going to be a special day. He was sitting thoughtfully on the windowsill with his friends Duck, Rabbit and Little Bear when he suddenly remembered that someone wasn't there who should be.

A very long time ago, he had seen his good friend Old Bear being packed away in a box. Then he was taken up a ladder, through a trap door and into the attic. The children were being too rough with him and he needed somewhere safe to go for a while.

"Has he been forgotten, do you think?" Bramwell asked his friends.

"I think he might have been," said Rabbit.

"Well," said Little Bear, "isn't it time he came back down with us? The children are older now and would look after him properly. Let's go and get him!"

"What a marvellous idea!" said Bramwell. "But how can we rescue him? It's a long way up to the attic and we haven't got a ladder."

"We could build a tower of bricks," suggested Little Bear.

Rabbit collected all the bricks and the others set about building the tower. It grew very tall, and Little Bear was just putting on the last brick when the tower began to wobble.

circled the plane again, this time very close to the hole. Little Bear grabbed the edge and with a mighty heave he pulled himself inside.

He got out his torch and looked around. The attic was very dark and quiet; full of boxes, old clothes and dust. He couldn't see Old Bear at all.

"Any bears in here?" he whispered, and stood still to listen.

From somewhere quite near he heard a muffled "Grrrrr," followed by, "Did somebody say something?" Little Bear moved a few things aside and there, propped up against a cardboard box and covered in dust, was Old Bear.

Little Bear jumped up and down with excitement. "Old Bear! Old Bear! I've found Old Bear!" he shouted.

"So you have," said Old Bear.

"Have you been lonely?" asked Little Bear.

"Quite lonely," said Old Bear. "But I've been asleep a lot of the time."

"Well," said Little Bear kindly, "would you like to come back to the playroom with us now?"

"That would be lovely," replied Old Bear. "But how will we get down?"

"Don't worry about that," said Little Bear, "Bramwell has thought of everything. He's given us these handkerchiefs to use as parachutes."

"Good old Bramwell," said the old teddy. "I'm glad he didn't forget me." Old Bear stood up and shook the dust out of his fur and Little Bear helped him into his parachute. They went over to the hole in the ceiling.

"Ready," shouted Rabbit.

"Steady," shouted Duck.

"GO!" shouted Bramwell Brown.

The two bears leapt bravely from the hole in the ceiling. Their handkerchief parachutes opened out and they floated gently down...landing safely in the blanket.

"But how did they know you were there, Grandma?" asked Lilly. "How would they find you?"

Lilly's grandmother smiled. "Oh, you had to bring them something special. A perfect shell. Or a beautiful stone. And if they liked you the whales would take your gift and give you something in return."

"What would they give you, Grandma?" asked Lilly. "What did you get from the whales?"

Lilly's grandmother sighed. "Once or twice," she whispered, "once or twice I heard them sing."

Lilly's uncle Frederick stomped into the room. "You're nothing but a daft old fool!" he snapped. "Whales were important for their meat, and for their bones, and for their blubber. If you have to tell Lilly something, then tell her something useful. Don't fill her head with nonsense. Singing whales indeed!"

"There were whales here millions of years before there were ships, or cities, or even cavemen," continued Lilly's grandmother. "People used to say they were magical."

"People used to eat them and boil them down for oil!" grumbled Lilly's uncle Frederick. And he turned his back and stomped out to the garden.

Lilly dreamt about whales.

In her dreams she saw them, as large as mountains and bluer than the sky. In her dreams she heard them singing, their voices like the wind. In her dreams they leapt from the water and called her name.

Next morning Lilly went down to the ocean. She went where no one fished or swam or sailed their boats. She walked to the end of the old jetty, the water was empty and still. Out of her pocket she took a yellow flower and dropped it in the water.

"This is for you," she called into the air.

Lilly sat at the end of the jetty and waited.

She waited all morning and all afternoon.

Then, as dusk began to fall, Uncle Frederick came down the hill after her. "Enough of this foolishness," he said. "Come on home. I'll not have you dreaming your life away."

That night, Lilly awoke suddenly.

The room was bright with moonlight. She sat up and listened. The house was quiet. Lilly climbed out of bed and went to the window. She could hear something in the distance, on the far side of the hill.

She raced outside and down to the shore. Her heart was pounding as she reached the sea.

There, enormous in the ocean, were the whales.

They leapt and jumped and spun across the moon.

Their singing filled up the night.

Lilly saw her yellow flower dancing on the spray.

Minutes passed, or maybe hours. Suddenly Lilly felt the breeze rustle her nightdress and the cold nip at her toes. She shivered and rubbed her eyes. Then it seemed the ocean was still again and the night black and silent.

Lilly thought she must have been dreaming. She stood up and turned for home. Then from far, far away, on the breath of the wind she heard,

"Lilly!

Lilly!"

The whales were calling her name.

## Ann and Reg Cartwright
# THE WINTER HEDGEHOG

ONE COLD, MISTY AUTUMN AFTERNOON, the hedgehogs gathered in a wood. They were searching the undergrowth for leaves for their nests, preparing for the long sleep of winter.

All, that is, except one.

The smallest hedgehog had overheard two foxes talking about winter. "What is winter?" he had asked his mother.

"Winter comes when we are asleep," she had replied. "It can be beautiful, but it can also be dangerous, cruel and very, very cold. It's not for the likes of us. Now go to sleep."

But the smallest hedgehog couldn't sleep. As evening fell he slipped away to look for winter. When hedgehogs are determined they can move very swiftly, and soon the little hedgehog was far from home. An owl swooped down from high in a tree.

"Hurry home," he called. "It's time for your long sleep." But on and on went the smallest hedgehog until the sky turned dark and the trees were nothing but shadows.

The next morning, the hedgehog awoke to find the countryside covered in fog. "Who goes there?" called a voice, and a large rabbit emerged from the mist; amazed to see a hedgehog about with winter coming on.

"I'm looking for winter," replied the hedgehog. "Can you tell me where it is?"

"Hurry home," said the rabbit. "Winter is on its way and it's no time for hedgehogs."

But the smallest hedgehog wouldn't listen. He was determined to find winter.

Days passed. The little hedgehog found plenty of slugs and insects to eat, but he couldn't find winter anywhere.

Then one day the air turned icy cold. Birds flew home to their roosts and the animals hid in their burrows and warrens. The smallest hedgehog felt very lonely and afraid and wished he was asleep with the other hedgehogs. But it was too late to turn back now!

That night winter came. A frosty wind swept through the grass and blew the last straggling leaves from the trees. In the morning the whole countryside was covered in a carpet of snow.

"Winter!" cried the smallest hedgehog. "I've found it at last." And all the birds flew down from the trees to join him.

The trees were completely bare and the snow sparkled on the grass. The little hedgehog went to the river to drink, but it was frozen. He shivered, shook his prickles and stepped on to the ice. His feet began to slide and the faster he scurried, the faster he sped across it. "Winter is wonderful," he cried. At first he did not see the fox, like a dark shadow, slinking towards him.

"Hello! Come and join me," he called as the fox reached the riverbank. But the fox only heard the rumble of his empty belly. With one leap he pounced on to the ice. When the little hedgehog saw his sly yellow eyes he understood what the fox was about. But every time he tried to run away he slipped on the ice. He curled into a ball and spiked his prickles.

"Ouch!" cried the fox. The sharp prickles stabbed his paws and he reeled towards the centre of the river where he disappeared beneath the thin ice.

"That was close," the smallest hedgehog cried to himself. "Winter is beautiful, but it is also cruel, dangerous and very, very cold."

Winter was everywhere: in the

air, in the trees, on the ground and in the hedgerows. Colder and colder it grew until the snow froze under the hedgehog's feet. Then the snow came again and a cruel north wind picked it up and whipped it into a blizzard. The night fell as black as ink and he lost his way. "Winter is dangerous and cruel and very, very cold," moaned the little hedgehog.

Luck saved him. A hare scurrying home gave him shelter in his burrow. By morning the snow was still falling, but gently now, covering everything it touched in a soft white blanket.

The smallest hedgehog was enchanted as he watched the pattern his paws made. Reaching the top of a hill, he rolled into a ball and spun over and over, turning himself into a great white snowball as he went. Down and down he rolled until he reached the feet of two children building a snowman.

"Hey, look at this," said the little girl; "a perfect head for our snowman."

"I'm a hedgehog," he cried. But no one heard his tiny hedgehog voice.

The girl placed the hedgehog snowball on the snowman's body and the boy used a carrot for a nose and pebbles for the eyes. "Let me out," shouted the hedgehog. But the children just stood back and admired their work before going home for lunch.

When the children had gone, the cold and hungry hedgehog nibbled at the carrot nose. As he munched the sun came out and the snow began to melt. He blinked in the bright sunlight, tumbled down the snowman's body and was free.

Time went on. The hedgehog saw the world in its winter cloak. He saw

bright red berries disappear from the hedgerows as the birds collected them for their winter larders. And he watched children speed down the hill on their sleighs.

The winter passed. One day the air grew warmer and the river began to flow again. A stoat, who had

changed his coat to winter white, changed it back to brown. Then the little hedgehog found crocuses and snowdrops beneath the trees and he knew it was time to go home. Slowly he made his way back to the wood.

From out of every log, sleepy hedgehogs were emerging from their long sleep.

"Where have you been?" they called to the smallest hedgehog.

"I found winter," he replied.

"And what was it like?" asked his mother.

"It was wonderful and beautiful, but it was also..."

"Dangerous, cruel and very, very cold," finished his mother.

But she was answered by a yawn, a sigh and a snore and the smallest hedgehog was fast asleep.

# Vyanne Samuels
# CARRY GO
# BRING COME

*Illustrated by Jennifer Northway*

IT WAS SATURDAY MORNING at Leon's house. It was a big Saturday morning at Leon's house. It was Marcia's wedding day. Marcia was Leon's sister.

Everyone in the house was getting ready for the big Saturday morning. Everyone was getting ready for the big wedding.

Everyone that was except Leon, who was fast asleep downstairs.

"Wake up, Leon!" shouted his mother upstairs.

But Leon did not move.

"Wake up, Leon!" shouted his sister Marlene upstairs.

But Leon did not move.

Leon's mother and his sisters, Marlene and Marcia, were so busy taking big blue rollers out of their hair, that they forgot to shout at Leon to wake up again.

They were getting ready for the big day.

They were getting ready for Marcia's wedding.

"Wake up, Leon," said Grandma softly downstairs.

Leon's two eyes opened up immediately.

Leon was awake.

"Carry this up to your mother," said Grandma, handing him a pink silk flower.

Leon ran upstairs to the bedroom with the pink silk flower. But before he could knock on the door, his sister Marcia called to him:

"Wait a little," she said, and she handed him a white head-dress. "Carry this down to Grandma."

So, Leon put the flower between his teeth, head-dress in his two hands, and ran down the stairs to Grandma.

When he got to his grandma's door, she called to him before he could knock.

"Wait a little," she said. He waited.

"Carry these up to Marlene," she said, and she poked a pair of blue shoes out at him.

So, Leon put the head-dress on his head, kept the flower between his teeth and carried the shoes in his two hands.

He tripped upstairs to Marlene.

But when he got to the bedroom door, Marlene called to him before he could knock.

"Wait a little," she said, and she poked a pair of yellow gloves through the door. "Carry these down to Grandma."

So, Leon put the gloves on his hands, the shoes on his feet, the head-dress on his head and the pink silk flower between his teeth.

He wobbled downstairs to Grandma, who called to him before he could knock.

"Wait a little," she said. He waited.

"Carry this to Marcia," she said, and she poked a green bottle of perfume through the door.

"Mind how you go," she said.

So, Leon climbed the stairs holding carefully the green bottle of perfume, wearing carefully the yellow gloves, dragging carefully the blue shoes, balancing carefully the white head-dress, biting carefully the pink silk flower…when suddenly he could go no further and shouted:

"HELP!" from the middle of the stairs.

He nearly swallowed the flower.

His mother ran out of the room upstairs, his sister Marlene ran out of the room upstairs and Grandma rushed out of her room downstairs. There was a big silence. They all looked at Leon.

"Look 'pon his feet!" said his mother.

"Look 'pon his fingers and his hands!" said Marlene.

"Look 'pon his head!" said Grandma.

"Look 'pon his mouth!" said Marcia.

And they all let go a big laugh!

Leon looked like a bride!

One by one, Mother, Marcia, Marlene and Grandma took away the pink silk flower, the white head-dress, the green bottle of perfume, the blue shoes and the yellow gloves.

"When am I going to get dressed for the wedding?" asked Leon, wearing just his pyjamas now.

"Just wait a little!" said Grandma.

Leon's two eyes opened wide.

"YOU MEAN I HAVE TO WAIT A LITTLE!" he shrieked.

And before anyone could answer, he ran downstairs…and jumped straight back into his bed, without waiting even a little.

# William Steig
# DOCTOR DE SOTO

Doctor De Soto, the dentist, did very good work, so he had no end of patients. Those close to his own size – moles, chipmunks, et cetera – sat in the regular dentist's chair.

Larger animals sat on the floor, while Doctor De Soto stood on a ladder.

For extra-large animals, he had a special room. There Doctor De Soto was hoisted up to the patient's mouth by his assistant, who also happened to be his wife.

Doctor De Soto was especially popular with the big animals. He was able to work inside their mouths, wearing galoshes to keep his feet dry; and his fingers were so delicate, and his drill so dainty, they could hardly feel any pain.

Being a mouse, he refused to treat animals dangerous to mice, and it said so on his sign. When the doorbell rang, he and his wife would look out the window. They wouldn't admit even the most timid-looking cat.

One day, when they looked out, they saw a well-dressed fox with a flannel bandage around his jaw.

"I cannot treat you, sir!" Doctor De Soto shouted. "Sir! Haven't you read my sign?"

"Please!" the fox wailed. "Have mercy, I'm suffering!" And he wept so bitterly it was pitiful to see.

"Just a moment," said Doctor De Soto. "That poor fox," he whispered to his wife. "What shall we do?"

"Let's risk it," said Mrs De Soto. She pressed the buzzer and let the fox in.

He was up the stairs in a flash. "Bless your little hearts," he cried, falling to his knees. "I beg you, *do* something! My tooth is killing me."

"Sit on the floor, sir," said Doctor De Soto, "and remove the bandage, please."

Doctor De Soto climbed up the ladder and bravely entered the fox's mouth. "Ooo-wow!" he gasped. The fox had a rotten bicuspid and unusually bad breath.

"This tooth will have to come out," Doctor De Soto announced. "But we can make you a new one."

"Just stop the pain," whimpered the fox, wiping some tears away.

Despite his misery, he realised he had a tasty little morsel in his mouth, and his jaw began to quiver. "Keep open!" yelled Doctor De Soto.

"Wide open!" yelled his wife.

"I'm giving you gas now," said Doctor De Soto. "You won't feel a thing when I yank that tooth."

Soon the fox was in dreamland. "M-m-m, yummy," he mumbled. "How I love them raw...with just a pinch of salt, and a...dry...white wine."

They could guess what he was dreaming about. Mrs De Soto handed her husband a pole to keep the fox's mouth open.

Doctor De Soto fastened his extractor to the bad tooth. Then he and his wife began turning the winch. Finally, with a sucking sound, the tooth popped out and hung swaying in the air.

"I'm bleeding!" the fox yelped when he came to.

Doctor De Soto ran up the ladder and stuffed some gauze in the hole. "The worst is over," he said. "I'll have your new tooth ready tomorrow. Be here at eleven sharp."

The fox, still woozy, said goodbye and left. On his way home, he wondered if it would be shabby of him to eat the De Sotos when the job was done.

After office hours, Mrs De Soto moulded a tooth of pure gold and polished it. "Raw with salt, indeed," muttered Doctor De Soto. "How foolish to trust a fox!"

"He didn't know what he was saying," said Mrs De Soto. "Why should he harm us? We're helping him."

"Because he's a fox!" said Doctor

De Soto. "They're wicked, wicked creatures."

That night the De Sotos lay awake worrying. "Should we let him in tomorrow?" Mrs De Soto wondered.

"Once I start a job," said the dentist firmly, "I finish it. My father was the same way."

"But we must do something to protect ourselves," said his wife. They talked and talked until they formed a plan. "I think it will work," said Doctor De Soto. A minute later he was snoring.

The next morning, promptly at eleven, a very cheerful fox turned up. He was feeling not a particle of pain.

When Doctor De Soto got into his mouth, he snapped it shut for a moment, then opened wide and laughed. "Just a joke!" he chortled.

"Be serious," said the dentist sharply. "We have work to do." His wife was lugging the heavy tooth up the ladder.

"Oh, I love it!" exclaimed the fox. "It's just beautiful."

Doctor De Soto set the gold tooth in its socket and hooked it up to the teeth on both sides.

The fox caressed the new tooth with his tongue. "My, it feels good," he thought. "I really shouldn't eat them. On the other hand, how can I resist?"

"We're not finished," said Doctor De Soto, holding up a large jug. "I have here a remarkable preparation developed only recently

by my wife and me. With just one application, you can be rid of toothaches forever. How would you like to be the first one to receive this unique treatment?"

"I certainly would!" the fox declared. "I'd be honoured." He hated any kind of personal pain.

"You will never have to see us again," said Doctor De Soto.

"*No one* will see you again," said the fox to himself. He had definitely made up his mind to eat them – with the help of his brand-new tooth.

Doctor De Soto stepped into the fox's mouth with a bucket of secret formula and proceeded to paint each tooth. He hummed as he worked. Mrs De Soto stood by on the ladder, pointing out spots he had missed. The fox looked very happy.

When the dentist was done, he stepped out. "Now close your jaws tight," he said, "and keep them closed for a full minute." The fox did as he was told. Then he tried to open his mouth – but his teeth were stuck together!

"Ah, excuse me, I should have mentioned," said Doctor De Soto, "you won't be able to open your mouth for a day or two. The secret formula must first permeate the dentine. But don't worry. No pain ever again!"

The fox was stunned. He stared at Doctor De Soto, then at his wife. They smiled, and waited. All he could do was say, "Frank oo berry mush" through his clenched teeth, and get up and leave. He tried to do so with dignity.

Then he stumbled down the stairs in a daze.

Doctor De Soto and his assistant had outfoxed the fox. They kissed each other and took the rest of the day off.

# Hans Christian Andersen, *retold by James Riordan*

# THUMBELINA

*Illustrated by Wayne Anderson*

ONCE UPON A TIME there was an old widow who wished to have a child of her own. So she went to the wise woman of the village saying, "How I long for a little child. Can you help me?"

"Maybe I can, and maybe I cannot," replied the sage. "Take this magic barleycorn and plant it in a flowerpot. Then you shall see what you shall see."

"Thank you," said the widow, handing her a silver coin before hurrying home with the seed.

No sooner had she planted it than a tulip began to grow and bloom before her very eyes.

"What a pretty flower," she cried, kissing the petals. At once the tulip burst open with a pop. And in the very centre of the flower sat a teeny tiny girl, neat and fair, and no bigger than the woman's thumb. So she called her Thumbelina.

The widow made a bed from a varnished walnut shell, a mattress out of violet leaves: and sheets from the petals of a rose. Here Thumbelina slept at night. In the daytime she played upon the table top. Sometimes she would

210

row a little boat from one side of the lake to the other. Her boat was, in truth, a tulip leaf; her oars, two stiff white horse's hairs; the lake, a bowl of water ringed with daisies.

One night, however, while she lay sleeping in her cosy bed, a toad entered the room through a broken windowpane. It was big, wet and ugly, and it hopped upon the table where Thumbelina slept beneath her rose-petal sheet. When it saw the little child it croaked, "Here is the very wife for my son!"

Thereupon, it seized the walnut bed and hopped with it through the broken window and down into the garden.

Now, at the bottom of the garden flowed a stream; it was here, amidst the mud and the slime, that the toad lived with her son. And that son was more loathsome than his mother.

"Croak, croak, cro-o-ak," was all he said when he saw the little maid.

"Hush, you'll wake her," said the mother. "We won't be able to catch her if she runs away, she's as light as dandelion fluff. I'll put her on a water-lily leaf and that way she'll be safe while we make your home ready for the wedding."

Out in the stream grew a host of water lilies, their broad green leaves floating on the water. The mother toad set Thumbelina down on the leaf farthest from the bank. When the poor girl awoke the next day she found herself stranded and began to cry. There was no way she could reach the safety of the bank.

The little fishes in the water now popped up their heads to peer at the tiny maid. When they saw how sad she was, they decided to help her escape. Crowding about the leaf's green stalk, they nibbled on the stem until the leaf broke free. Slowly it drifted down the stream, bearing Thumbelina to safety.

On and on sailed the leaf, taking Thumbelina on a journey she knew not where.

For a time a dainty butterfly hovered overhead, then finally settled on the leaf. Thumbelina was so glad to have company that she took the ribbon from her waist and tied one end to the butterfly and one to the leaf. Now her boat fairly raced across the water, on and on and on.

But Thumbelina's happiness was not to last. Presently, a large mayfly swooped down, seized her in its claws and flew up into a nearby tree. How frightened was poor Thumbelina as she soared through the air.

The mayfly set Thumbelina down upon the largest leaf, brought her honey from the flower pollen and sang her praises to the skies, even though she was nothing like a mayfly. By and by, all the mayflies that dwelt within the tree came to stare at the tiny girl. Two lady mayflies waggled their feelers in

disgust, muttering scornfully, "But she has neither *wings* nor *feelers*. How ugly she is."

The mayfly who had captured Thumbelina began to have his doubts;

dark passage and put it over the bird's still form. "Farewell, pretty bird," she said. She pressed her head against the swallow's breast and was startled by a faint sound. The bird's heart was beating! She pressed the straw closer about its breast and fetched her own blanket to cover its head.

Next night she stole down the passageway again and was overjoyed to find the bird much better, although still weak.

"You must stay here in your warm bed until you are strong," said Thumbelina. "I will care for you."

The bird stayed underground the winter through, Thumbelina never breathing a word to the mole or mouse.

When spring arrived, it was time for the swallow to bid farewell. The tiny girl made a hole for it through the tunnel roof. How bright it was when the sun shone in.

"Come with me," said the swallow. "Sit upon my back and I'll take you far away to safety in the green wood."

But Thumbelina thought the fieldmouse would be lonely without her, so she shook her head sighing, "I cannot."

"Farewell then, little Thumbelina," said the swallow as it soared into the spring sunshine. Sadly she watched him go.

Thumbelina was cast down. The corn would soon be so tall that the mouse's house would be hidden from the sun.

"You must spend your time preparing for your wedding," said the fieldmouse, for the mole had finally proposed. "You should sew your wedding dress, and make the linen for your household."

The mole hired four strong spiders to help spin the thread and all through the summer Thumbelina spun and wove and sewed.

Every evening the mole came by to visit his wife-to-be, but all he said was, "Drat the summer. Hurry on winter." (For the sun baked the soil hard and made it difficult to dig. And once summer had passed and autumn came they would be wed.)

With every passing day Thumbelina began to dislike the mole more and more; he was so dull and vain.

Autumn came and Thumbelina's wedding dress was ready. "Four weeks more and you'll be wed," said the fieldmouse.

Thumbelina wept. "I cannot marry the mole!" she cried.

"Nonsense!" said the mouse. "He'll make the perfect husband; his velvet coat is fit for a king; his house has many rooms and larders. You ought to think yourself lucky."

The wedding day arrived. Mole came to fetch his bride and take her to his deep-down house. She would never see the blue sky again, never feel the

sun's rays, nor smell the flowers she loved. One last time she went outside to say goodbye to the world. She lifted up her arms towards the sky and stepped into the light. The corn was cut, but amid the stubble grew a lonely poppy bloom. "Farewell," she murmured. "If you see the swallow, give him my regards." Suddenly she heard a familiar sound.

"Tweet, tweet, tweet."

Looking up she saw her friend. Thumbelina told him all; how she had to marry the mole and live forever in the deep dark earth. She wept as she spoke.

"Winter will soon be here," said the swallow, "and I must fly away. Come with me; sit tight upon my back and we'll fly to a land where the sun always shines and where flowers blossom all the year through. You saved my life when I lay frozen and near death. Now it is my turn to help you." Thumbelina climbed upon the swallow's back and up they soared, above forests and lakes and snowy mountains.

At last they reached the land where the sun's breath was warm. But still the swallow did not stop. On it flew until it came to a tree-fringed lake.

"Choose a flower growing down below," said the swallow, "and there I will leave you to make your home." Thumbelina clapped her tiny hands.

On the soft green grass below lay fallen pillars of stone, around which grew pale, pure lilies. The swallow set her down upon a leaf. Imagine the girl's surprise when she saw a young man sitting in the centre of the flower. He was just as tiny, just as neatly formed and dainty as herself; yet he was wearing a pair of wings. "How lovely he is," said Thumbelina to the swallow.

"In every flower there dwells a youth or maiden," said the bird. "Each one is the spirit of the flower."

The young man looked at Thumbelina and thought her the loveliest creature he had ever seen. Taking her hand, he asked her to be his bride. Now here was a better husband than the loathsome toad or the mole in the velvet coat. Thumbelina readily agreed.

Right at that moment there appeared from every flower a tiny boy or girl, each bearing a gift. But the best gift of all was a pair of wings to enable her to fly.

"You shall have a new name," said the flower spirit. "From now on we will call you Maya."

"Farewell then, Maya," sang the swallow as he took flight.

Soon he would start his journey north to Denmark. It was there he had a nest, above the window of a storyteller – Hans Christian Andersen by name – who wrote down the tale related here.

# Chris Van Allsburg
# THE POLAR EXPRESS

ON CHRISTMAS EVE, many years ago, I lay quietly in my bed. I did not rustle the sheets. I breathed slowly and silently. I was listening for a sound – a sound a friend had told me I'd never hear – the ringing bells of Santa's sleigh.

"There is no Santa," my friend had insisted, but I knew he was wrong.

Late that night I did hear sounds, though not of ringing bells. From outside came the sounds of hissing steam and squeaking metal. I looked through my window and saw a train standing perfectly still in front of my house.

It was wrapped in an apron of steam. Snowflakes fell lightly around it. A guard stood at the open door of one of the cars. He took a large pocket watch from his jacket, then looked up at my window. I put on my slippers and dressing-gown. I tiptoed downstairs and out of the door.

"All aboard," the guard cried out. I ran up to him.

"Well," he said, "are you coming?"

"Where?" I asked.

"Why, to the North Pole of course," was his answer. "This is the Polar Express." I took his outstretched hand and he pulled me aboard.

The train was filled with other children, all in their pyjamas and nightgowns. We sang Christmas carols and ate sweets with nougat centres as white as snow. We drank hot cocoa as thick and rich as melted chocolate bars. Outside, the lights of towns and villages flickered in the distance as the Polar Express raced northwards.

Soon there were no more lights to be seen. We travelled through cold, dark forests, where lean wolves roamed and white-tailed rabbits hid from our train as it thundered through the quiet wilderness.

We climbed mountains so high it seemed as if we would scrape the moon. But the Polar Express never slowed down. Faster and faster we ran along, rolling over peaks and through valleys like a car on a roller coaster.

The mountains turned into hills, the hills to snow-covered plains. We crossed a barren desert of ice – the Great Polar Ice Cap. Lights appeared in the distance. They looked like the lights of a strange ocean liner sailing on a frozen sea. "There," said the guard, "is the North Pole."

The North Pole. It was a huge city standing alone at the top of the world, filled with factories where every Christmas toy was made.

At first we saw no elves.

"They are gathering at the centre of the city," the guard told us. "That is where Santa will give the first gift of Christmas."

"Who receives the first gift?" we all asked.

The guard answered, "He will choose one of you."

"Look," shouted one of the children, "the elves." Outside we saw hundreds of elves. As our train drew closer to the centre of the North Pole, we slowed to a crawl, so crowded were the streets with Santa's helpers. When the Polar Express could go no farther, we stopped and the guard led us outside.

We pressed through the crowd to the edge of a large, open circle. In front

of us stood Santa's sleigh. The reindeer were excited. They pranced and paced, ringing the silver sleigh bells that hung from their harnesses. It was a magical sound, like nothing I'd ever heard. Across the circle, the elves moved apart and Santa Claus appeared. The elves cheered wildly.

He marched over to us and, pointing to me, said, "Let's have this fellow here." He jumped into his sleigh. The guard helped me up. I sat on Santa's knee and he asked, "Now, what would you like for Christmas?"

I knew that I could have any gift I could imagine. But the thing I wanted most for Christmas was not inside Santa's giant bag. What I wanted more than anything was one silver bell from Santa's sleigh. When I asked, Santa smiled. Then he gave me a hug and told an elf to cut a bell from a reindeer's harness. The elf tossed it up to Santa. He stood, holding the bell high above him, and called out, "The first gift of Christmas!"

A clock struck midnight as the elves roared their approval. Santa handed the bell to me, and I put it in my dressing-gown pocket. The guard helped me down from the sleigh. Santa shouted out the reindeer's names and cracked his whip. His team charged forward and climbed into the air. Santa circled once above us, then disappeared in the cold, dark polar sky.

As soon as we were back inside the Polar Express, the other children asked to see the bell. I reached into my pocket, but the only thing I felt was a hole. I had lost the silver bell from Santa Claus's sleigh. "Let's hurry outside and look for it," one of the children said. But the train gave a sudden lurch and started moving. We were on our way home.

It broke my heart to lose the bell. When the train reached my house, I sadly left the other children. I stood at my doorway and waved goodbye. The guard said something from the moving train, but I couldn't hear him. "What?" I yelled out.

He cupped his hands around his mouth. "MERRY CHRISTMAS," he shouted. The Polar Express let out a loud blast from its whistle and sped away.

On Christmas morning my little sister Sarah and I opened our presents. When it looked as if everything had been unwrapped, Sarah found one last small box behind the tree. It had my name on it. Inside was the silver bell! There was a note: "Found this on the seat of my sleigh. Mend that hole in your pocket." Signed, "Mr C."

I shook the bell. It made the most beautiful sound my sister and I had ever heard.

But my mother said, "Oh, that's too bad."

"Yes," said my father, "it's broken."

When I'd shaken the bell, my parents had not heard a sound.

At one time most of my friends could hear the bell, but as years passed, it fell silent for all of them. Even Sarah found one Christmas that she could no longer hear its sweet sound. Though I've grown old, the bell still rings for me as it does for all who truly believe.

> *"Mirror, mirror on the wall,*
> *Who is the fairest of us all?"*

And a soft, magical voice always answered,

> *"You are the fairest of them all."*

Then the proud queen was satisfied.

Snow-white lived in a different part of the castle. She had her nurse and her own cook. When she was old enough a governess came to instruct her, and an old gentleman to teach her music and dancing. Years passed, and she grew to be so kind, and gentle, and funny, and clever, that everybody loved her.

Only the king did not visit her as often as he should, because she reminded him too painfully of the dead queen, her mother, whom he still loved. As for her stepmother, she thought Snow-white a timid, poor-spirited child, not worth a second glance.

But one day, when the stepmother queen bent her beautiful head to the magic looking-glass, and asked as usual,

> *"Mirror, mirror on the wall,*
> *Who is the fairest of us all?"*

the mirror answered,

> *"Queen, you are full fair, 'tis true,*
> *But Snow-white fairer is than you."*

Then the queen was horribly shocked. Her beautiful face turned yellow with envy and rage, and from that moment she hated Snow-white with all her heart. She could get no different answer out of the mirror, and she knew that it spoke the truth.

The queen's wicked passions grew in her, until she had no peace, day or night. At last she sent for a certain huntsman who was discontented with the king's service. She said to him, "You must take that evil girl Snow-white into the forest and kill her, and bring me back her heart as a proof."

He looked at her and said, "What will you give me if I do it?"

So she handed him a purse full of gold.

Next day, when Snow-white went riding, the huntsman lay in wait for her, and he grabbed her pony by the bridle, and led her deep into the forest by secret paths no one could follow. Then he pulled out his knife. But the trembling maiden threw herself at his feet, weeping and pleading for mercy. And she was so lovely, and cried so piteously, that in the end he could not bear to hurt her; besides, he knew that wild beasts would devour her quickly enough, once night fell. He killed a young boar instead and cut out its heart, which he gave secretly to the queen as a token.

The king sent all his soldiers into the forest to look for Snow-white, but she was nowhere to be found. So everyone went into mourning for her, and many bitter tears were shed. Even the wicked queen dressed herself in black velvet, while she was exulting in her heart.

Now when the huntsman rode away, leaving Snow-white alone in the forest, she stared about her in terror; even the rustling of the trees made her

heart beat pit-a-pat. So she started to run. And the wild beasts of the forest ran too, but for company, not to harm her; they pitied her as she fled, bruising her poor feet and scratching herself on the brambles that grew everywhere under the trees.

She ran on and on until she was utterly exhausted. She had reached a clearing in the forest; it was already evening, and one star shone in the patch of sky above the trees. There in front of her stood a little house, with a neat garden all round. She went up the path and knocked on the door. Nobody answered ... Still nobody ... But she was so tired that she could not help it, she had to go in to rest.

The door opened into a nice clean kitchen. There was a table spread with a cloth and laid for supper: seven little plates of bread and cheese she counted, and seven little cups of wine. She was so hungry and thirsty that she took just a mouthful of bread and cheese from each plate, so as not to finish a helping. From each cup she took a sip of wine.

In the next room she found seven little beds lined against the wall, each with a spotless white pillow and quilt. She was so tired that she lay down on one of them, and praying to God that He would look after her, she fell asleep.

Now this little house belonged to a family of dwarfs, who toiled all day in the gold mines, deep within the mountains.

When it was quite dark, they came home, and they noticed at once that somebody had called while they were out. So they struck flint and lit their seven candles, so that the room was a blaze of light.

First they saw that their suppers had been tasted, and next they found Snow-white, fast asleep in the little white bed. They crowded round her, lifting up their candles with cries of astonishment. "O goodness! O gracious!" they exclaimed. "What beautiful child is this?" and they were full of joy and excitement, though they were careful not to wake her.

Snow-white was very frightened next morning, when she went into the kitchen and saw seven little men sitting round the table. But they were polite

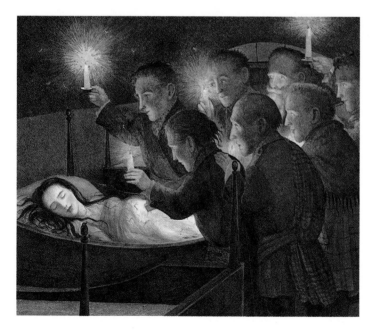

and friendly, and when she had told them her story, they said, "If you will keep house for us, cook and clean and wash and sew and knit, you may stay with us and we will look after you always."

"With all my heart," said Snow-white, and so the bargain was made. All day the seven dwarfs were away digging for gold in the mountain. When they came home, they found their supper ready, their clothes clean and mended, and the house neat as a new pin. So the weeks passed. But the good dwarfs never forgot to warn Snow-white, as they left the house each morning. "Beware of your stepmother, the wicked queen!" they said. "She will soon find you out. Take care, do not let anybody in!"

Now, the queen was sure that Snow-white was dead. But one day she drew back the veil from the magic looking-glass.

> *"Mirror, mirror on the wall,*
> *Who is the fairest of us all?"*

she asked with a smile. To her astonishment, the soft voice replied,

> *"O Queen, thou art of beauty rare,*
> *But Snow-white, living in the glen*
> *With the seven little men,*
> *Is a thousand times more fair."*

The queen turned white with fury, and her eyes glinted like a serpent's. She never doubted the mirror; she knew at once that the huntsman had deceived her, but he had gone where she could not get at him. So she disguised herself as an ugly old woman, and set off secretly to the house of the seven dwarfs.

The queen could not find her way through the forest; besides, the wild beasts would certainly have eaten her. So, instead, she had to walk a long and weary way, over seven mountains, until at last she came to the cottage. She limped up the path crying, "Collars and laces, belts and buttons! Pretty trifles for wives and maidens!"

Snow-white called from the window, "Good-day, Granny. What have you to sell?"

Then the old woman held up the silken laces which so pleased Snow-white that she said to herself, What harm can there be in this good old woman? So she unbarred the door, and the pedlar woman glided in.

"What a beautiful figure you have, my dear, to be sure!" she exclaimed. This was true, though she only pretended to admire it. "You shall have the laces as a present, only let me thread them for you."

And with quick fingers she threaded the coloured silks into Snow-white's

Still, she looked longingly at the fruit, all ripe and delicious in the woman's basket.

"Never mind, you are wise to be careful, and I shall take my fruit somewhere else. Bless you, pretty face! I shall leave you an apple, all the same," and she pretended to select the finest, and showed it to Snow-white, who shook her head at the window.

"Indeed, I cannot take it. I promised them I would not!"

"Are you afraid of poison? But I shall cut it, and eat half myself."

For the apple was made so that all the poison was in the red side. "The white for me, and you shall have the red!" cried the old woman, and took a bite from the white half and handed the rosy piece to Snow-white, who then could not resist biting into it. As soon as she tasted it, she shrieked and fell as if she had been stabbed to the heart. Then the wicked queen leered at her through the window, and cackled like a witch, "Well, well, my dear! I think you have done with being the fairest!"

As soon as she got home, the queen hastened to unveil her looking-glass.

*"Mirror, mirror, on the wall,
    Who is the fairest of us all?"*
Then at last came the reply,
    *"You are fairest now of all."*

So her jealous heart had peace – as much as a jealous heart can have.

The good little dwarfs came home at sunset. Once more they found their beloved Snow-white lying as dead upon the ground, but this time nothing they did could bring her back to life. They unlaced her, combed out her hair, washed her with water and wine – it was no use. Then they were full of grief, and prayed and lamented three bitter days, clustered round her bed in tears. After that, they would have buried her, except that they could not bear to put her into the ground; for her cheeks were still pink, as if she was sleeping and not dead.

So they made a glass coffin, and laid her in it, and wrote on it in letters of gold, "I am Snow-white, a king's daughter." Then they carried out the coffin, and arranged a place for it on the mountainside, and took it in turns so that one of them always watched over it. Three birds also came there to mourn for Snow-white – an owl, a raven, and a dove.

Snow-white lay in her glass coffin on the mountainside, and the days passed, the weeks and months passed, but she never changed – she was still as white as snow, as red as blood, and as black as ebony.

One day, it chanced that a prince rode that way who had been hunting in the forest. And when he looked in the coffin and saw Snow-white, he fell straightway in love with her. He gazed at her long and long, and at last he said to the dwarfs, "Let me have the coffin, and I will give you whatever you ask."

The dwarfs told him that they could not part with it for all the money in the world. But he begged more and more. "Dear dwarfs," he said, "I cannot live without this maiden. I beseech you to give her to me. I swear I shall honour you always, and look after you as if you were my brothers."

So at last they pitied him, and allowed him to take the coffin, and the prince told his servants to carry it away on their shoulders. But as they were taking it down the mountain, one of them stumbled, and the crumb of poison flew out of Snow-white's throat. She stirred, opened her eyes, and astonished at finding herself in a glass box, raised the lid and sat up, alive and well. Then the prince and the dwarfs were overcome with joy at the miracle, and the prince, falling at once to his knees, begged the beautiful girl to be his bride.

He took her to his father's castle, and the seven dwarfs he made his counsellors. A splendid feast was arranged, and wedding invitations were sent out all through the country. The stepmother queen received one; she did not know who the bride was. She put on her grandest clothes, and stood in front of her magic looking-glass for the last time, and said,

*"Mirror, mirror on the wall,*
*Who is the fairest of us all?"*
But the soft voice answered,
*"O Queen, although you are of beauty rare,*
*The young bride is a thousand times more fair."*

The queen then raged and swore, and bit her nails and vowed she would not go to the wedding. However, she did go, because there was no peace for her until she saw the bride. But she took with her a poisonous rose that she meant to leave on the young bride's pillow.

When she saw that it was Snow-white who was married, so happy and so beloved, the evil queen turned quite mad with jealousy, so that in her passion she clutched this deadly rose. Then she died miserably of her own poison.

But Snow-white and her prince, and the seven venerable counsellors, lived happily ever after.

Darkness fell, but they shot up flares and went on playing. By three o'clock in the morning Tom had won by 85 to 10. As the last flare went up above the garden he looked down from the ramp at the defeated Captain and his hired sportsmen and he said, "Maybe that will teach you not to fool around with a boy who knows how to fool around."

Captain Najork broke down and wept, but Aunt Fidget Wonkham-Strong had him put to bed and brought him peppermint tea, and then he felt better.

Tom took his boat and pedalled to the next town down the river. There he advertised in the newspaper for a new aunt. When he found one that he liked, he told her, "No greasy bloaters, no mutton and no cabbage-and-potato sog. No Nautical Almanac. And I do lots of fooling around. Those are my conditions."

The new aunt's name was Bundlejoy Cosysweet. She had a floppy hat with flowers on it. She had long, long hair.

"That sounds fine to me," she said. "We'll have a go."

Aunt Fidget Wonkham-Strong married Captain Najork even though he had lost the sneedball game, and they were very happy together. She made the hired sportsmen learn off pages of the Nautical Almanac every night after dinner.

# Susan Varley
# BADGER'S PARTING GIFTS

BADGER WAS DEPENDABLE, reliable, and always ready to lend a helping paw. He was also very old, and he knew almost everything. Badger was so old that he knew he must soon die.

Badger wasn't afraid of death. Dying meant only that he would leave his body behind and, as his body didn't work as well as it had in days gone by, Badger wasn't too concerned about that. His only worry was how his friends would feel when he was gone. Hoping to prepare them, Badger had told them that someday soon he would be going down the Long Tunnel, and he hoped they wouldn't be too sad when it happened.

One day, as Badger was watching Mole and Frog race down the hillside, he felt especially old and tired. He wished more than anything that he could run with them, but he knew his old legs wouldn't let him. He watched Mole and Frog for a long time, enjoying the sight of his friends having a good time.

It was late when he arrived home. He wished the moon good night and closed the curtains on the cold world outside. He made his way slowly down to the warm fire that was waiting for him deep underground.

He had his supper and then sat down at his desk to write a letter. When he had finished, he settled down in his rocking chair near the fire. He gently rocked himself to and fro and soon was fast asleep having a strange yet wonderful dream like none he'd ever had before.

Much to Badger's surprise, he was running. Ahead of him was a very long tunnel. His legs felt strong and sure as he ran towards it. He no longer needed his walking stick, so he left it lying on the floor of the tunnel. Badger moved swiftly, running faster and faster through the long passageway, until his paws no longer touched the earth. He felt himself turning head over paws, falling and tumbling, but nothing hurt. He felt free. It was as if he had fallen out of his body.

The following day Badger's friends gathered anxiously outside Badger's door. They were worried because he hadn't come out to say good morning as he always did.

Fox broke the sad news that Badger was dead and read Badger's note to them. It said simply, "Gone down the Long Tunnel. Bye bye, Badger."

All the animals had loved Badger, and everyone was very sad. Mole especially felt lost, alone and desperately unhappy.

In bed that night Mole could think only of Badger. Tears rolled down his velvety nose, soaking the blankets he clung to for comfort.

Outside, it began to snow. Winter had begun, and soon a thick layer of

snow hid the animals' homes, where they would stay snug and warm during the cold months.

The snow covered the countryside, but it didn't conceal the sadness that Badger's friends felt.

Badger had always been there when anyone needed him. The animals all wondered what they would do now that he was gone. Badger had told them not to be unhappy, but it was hard not to be.

As spring drew near, the animals often visited each other and talked about the days when Badger was alive.

Mole was good at using scissors, and he told about the time Badger had taught him how to cut out a chain of moles from a piece of folded paper. Paper moles had littered the ground that day. Mole remembered the joy he'd felt when he had finally succeeded in making a complete chain of moles with all the paws joined.

Frog was an excellent skater. He recalled how

Badger had helped him take his first slippery steps on the ice. Badger had gently guided him across the ice until he had gained enough confidence to glide out on his own.

Fox remembered how, when he was a young cub, he could never knot his tie properly until Badger showed him how.

"Starting with the wide end of the tie, it's right over left, once around to the back, up, then down through the crossover and, holding the back of the tie, push the knot up to the neck."

Fox could now tie every knot ever invented and some he'd made up himself. And of course his own necktie was always perfectly knotted.

Badger had given Mrs Rabbit his special recipe for gingerbread and had shown her how to bake gingerbread rabbits. Mrs Rabbit was well known throughout the countryside for her excellent cooking. As she talked

"Well, in that case," said the mouse, "I suppose you're supplying me with *my* livelihood when you leave the cover off the cheese dish in the larder, hee, hee!"

"You little thief!" shouted Mrs Pepperpot, shaking her tiny fist at the mouse. "You push it off yourself, you and your wretched family. But I'll set a trap for you this very evening!"

"Did I hear a mouse?" asked another voice from the door. It was the cat. "Where is it? I'm just ready for my dinner."

"No, no!" shrieked Mrs Pepperpot, waving her arms at the cat, while the mouse was trying to hide behind her skirt. "You leave the mouse alone, you great brute, you. He hasn't done you any harm, has he?"

"Woof! Woof! Who's a brute round here?" The head of a strange dog was peering round the door. When he caught sight of the cat he darted after her, knocking Mrs Pepperpot over as he ran round the table.

The cat managed to get out of the door with the dog close behind her when, luckily, at that moment Mrs Pepperpot grew to her normal size! She lost no time in throwing a stick at the dog while Pussy jumped on to the shed roof. The dog went on barking till Mrs Pepperpot gave him a bone. Then he trotted off down the hill.

"Dear me, what a to-do!" thought Mrs Pepperpot. "But it makes you wonder; every little creature is hunted by a bigger creature who in turn is hunted by a bigger one. Where does it all end?"

"Right here!" said a deep voice behind her.

Mrs Pepperpot nearly jumped out of her skin, but when she turned round it was her husband standing there.

"Oh," she said, "I thought you were an ogre come to gobble me up!"

"Well!" said Mr Pepperpot. "Is that all the thanks I get for coming home early to help with the spring cleaning?"

"You darling man!" said Mrs Pepperpot, giving him a great big kiss.

because of his many wounds. Tramping the roads towards the city he met an old woman who asked him what he hoped to find. "I hardly know myself," he laughed. "Perhaps I'll discover where the princesses dance away the night. Why, then I might even get to be king."

The old woman studied him closely. "That's not very hard," she said. "Just don't drink the wine they bring you in the evening, and then pretend to be fast asleep – and here's something else." She handed him a rolled-up cloth. "This is a cloak," she said. "When you put it on you'll be invisible, and so you can follow the girls wherever they choose to go."

The soldier had been joking, but the cloak and the good advice made him take the matter seriously. So he gathered up his courage and went before the king. He was greeted warmly, as the others had been; his rags were exchanged for princely clothes, and he was given the same adjoining room. As he was getting ready for bed, the eldest princess brought him a goblet of wine. But the soldier was cunning; he had tied a sponge under his chin, and let all the wine run into this, so that he didn't taste a drop. Then he lay down, and after a little while he began to snore as though he were soundly asleep.

When the princesses heard him they laughed. "There's another who doesn't value his life!" said the eldest. They began to open cupboards and boxes, pulling out gowns and jewels. Then they skipped about in their beautiful clothes, prinking before the mirrors. Only the youngest was distracted. "Do you know," she said, "I have a feeling tonight that our luck is out. Something is going wrong."

"Don't be silly," chided her eldest sister. "You're always worrying. You've seen enough princes come and go to know that there's nothing to fear. Why, this clod would have slept through even without the potion." Still, they looked once more at the soldier, but his eyes were shut tight and his breathing heavy and slow, and they felt safe.

Then the eldest princess went to her bed and tapped on it three times. It sank into the ground, and one by one the princesses disappeared through the opening, the eldest in the lead. Quickly, the soldier threw on his cloak and followed after the last and youngest down a flight of stairs. Halfway down, he stepped on the edge of her dress, and she stopped in fright. "What's that?" she cried. "Who's pulling at my dress?"

"Don't be a fool," snapped the eldest sister. "You must have caught the hem on a nail."

When they reached the bottom of the stairs, they emerged into a marvellous avenue of trees with silver leaves that sparkled as they moved. "I'd better take some proof," the soldier thought to himself, and reached up and broke off a branch.

The tree let out a terrible roar. "What's that?" cried the youngest princess. "I tell you something is wrong."

"Oh, for heaven's sake," sighed the eldest, "they're just firing a salute at the palace."

Next they came to a magnificent avenue of trees with leaves of gold, and finally to a third whose trees had leaves of glittering diamonds. The soldier broke a branch from each kind of tree, and both times there was such a roar that the youngest jumped and shook with fear even when the sound was gone. But the eldest princess still insisted that all the noises came from gun salutes.

On they walked until they came to a great river. Twelve boats were drawn up to the shore, and in each boat sat a handsome young prince. Each of the princesses went to a different boat and climbed on board, the soldier following the youngest. "I don't know why," said the prince, a little out of breath, "but the boat seems so much heavier tonight. It takes all my strength to row."

"Perhaps it is the heat," said the princess. "I feel quite strange myself."

On the other side of the river there was a brightly lit palace, and from it lively music could be heard. As soon as they were across, the young couples hurried into the palace, and through the night every prince danced every dance with his own princess. The soldier amused himself by dancing too. And whenever a princess put down her goblet of wine he drained it dry, so that when she picked it up again it was empty. These games made the youngest princess feel more nervous than ever, but the eldest pooh-poohed her fears.

They danced until three in the morning, when their shoes were all worn through and they had to stop. The princes rowed them back across the river, and this time the soldier sat in the front boat with the eldest girl. Then, on the bank, the couples said goodbye to each other, and the princesses promised to return the following night.

The invisible soldier raced on ahead, up the stairs, and by the time the sisters came in, slow with exhaustion, he was snoring so loudly that they all began to laugh. "We needn't worry about *him*," they said, and after putting away their fine clothes and setting their worn-out shoes under their beds, they lay down and collapsed into sleep.

The soldier decided not to say anything to the king just yet, but to learn a little more about these strange goings-on. He followed the princesses again on the second and third nights, and everything was the same as before. The third time, the soldier took away a goblet as evidence. When the time came for him to appear before the king he took with him the goblet, and the silver, gold and diamond boughs.

The twelve princesses hid behind the door to hear what he would say. "Well," said the king, "have you discovered how my daughters manage to dance through their shoes every night?"

"As a matter of fact," said the soldier, "I have." And he told the king about the twelve princes and the underground palace, and brought out the branches and the goblet to prove his tale. When the princesses were sent for, they saw there was no use in lying and so they admitted everything. Then the king asked the soldier which princess he would like for his wife. "I'm not so young any more," said the soldier. "I had better have your eldest girl."

The wedding was held that same day, and the king declared that when he died the soldier would inherit his kingdom. As for the twelve princes, the spell they were under was lengthened for exactly as many nights as they had helped the twelve princesses to dance away their shoes.

# *John Agard*
# HAPPY BIRTHDAY, DILROY!

*Illustrated by John Richardson*

MY name is Dilroy,
I'm a little black boy
And I'm eight today.

My birthday cards say
It's great to be eight
And they sure right
Coz I got a pair of skates
I want for a long long time.

My birthday cards say
Happy Birthday, Dilroy!
But, Mummy, tell me why
They don't put a little boy
That looks a bit like me.
Why the boy on the card so white?

# PART THREE

# *Joan Aiken*

# THERE'S SOME SKY IN THIS PIE

## from A Necklace of Raindrops

### *Illustrated by Jan Pieńkowski*

THERE WAS AN OLD MAN and an old woman, and they lived in a very cold country. One winter day the old man said to the old woman,

"My dear, it is so cold, I should like it very much if you would make a good, hot apple pie."

And the old woman said, "Yes, my dear, I will make an apple pie."

So she took sugar, and she took spices, and she took apples, and she put them in a pie-dish. Then she took flour, and she took fat, and she took water, and she began to make pastry to cover the pie. First she rubbed the fat into the flour, then she made it into a lump with a little water.

Then she took a roller and began to roll out the pastry.

While she was doing this, the old man said, "Look out of the window, my dear, see, it is beginning to snow."

And the old woman looked out of the window at the snow, coming down so fast out of the white sky.

Then she went on rolling the pastry. But what do you think happened? A little corner of the sky that she had been looking at got caught in the pastry. And that little bit of sky was pulled under the roller, just the way a shirt is pulled into the wringer. So when the old woman rolled her pastry flat and put it on the pie-dish, there was a piece of sky in it! But the old woman did not know this. She put the pie in the oven, and soon it began to smell very good.

"Is it dinner time yet?" said the old man.

"Soon," said the old woman. She put spoons and forks and plates on the table.

"Is it dinner time now?" said the old man.

"Yes," said the old woman, and she opened the oven door.

But what do you think? That pie was so light, because of the bit of sky in it, that it floated out of the oven, right across the room.

"Stop it, stop it!" cried the old woman. She made a grab, and he made a grab, but the pie floated out of the door, and they ran after it into the garden.

"Jump on it!" cried the old man. So he jumped on it, and she jumped on it.

But the pie was so light that it carried them up into the air, through the snow-flakes falling out of the white sky.

Their little black-and-white cat Whisky was in the apple tree, looking at the snow.

"Stop us, stop us!" they called to Whisky. So he jumped on to the pie. But he was too light to stop it, and still it went floating on through the falling snow. They went higher and higher. The birds called to them:

"Old woman, old man, little puss, so high,
Sailing along on your apple pie,
Why are you floating across the sky?"

And the old woman answered, "Because we can't stop, that's the reason why."

They went on, and they came to a plane that had run out of fuel. So there it was, stuck, in the middle of the sky. And the airman was inside, and he was very cold. He called out,

"Old woman, old man, little puss, so high,
Sailing along on your apple pie,

Why are you floating across the sky?"

And the old woman answered, "Because we can't stop, that's the reason why."

"May I come with you?" called the airman.

"Yes, of course you may."

So he jumped on the pie and went floating along with them.

They went a little farther and they saw a duck who had forgotten how to fly. So there it was in the middle of a cloud. And the duck called,

"Old woman, old man, little puss, and airman, so high,
Sailing along on your apple pie,
Why are you floating across the sky?"

And the old woman answered, "Because we can't stop, that's the reason why."

"May I come with you?"

"Yes, of course you may."

So the duck jumped on the pie and went floating along with them.

They went a little farther and they passed a tall mountain. On the tip-top of the mountain was a mountain goat, who had forgotten the way down. So he called to them,

"Old woman, old man, little puss, and
airman, and duck, so high,
Sailing along on your apple pie,
Why are you floating across the sky?"
And the old woman answered, "Because
we can't stop, that's the reason why."
"May I come with you?"
"Yes, of course you may."
So the goat jumped on the pie too.

Then they went a little farther and they
came to a big city with high, high buildings. And on top of one of the buildings
was a sad, cross, homesick elephant,
looking sadly and crossly at the snow. She
called to them,
"Old woman, old man, little puss, and
airman, and duck, and goat, so high,
Sailing along on your apple pie,
Why are you floating across the sky?"
And the old woman answered, "Because
we can't stop, that's the reason why."
"Your pie smells so warm and spicy, it
makes me think of my homeland," said the
elephant. "May I come with you?"
"Yes, of course you may."
So the elephant jumped on to the pie
and they went floating on. But the
elephant was so heavy that she made the
pie tip to one side.

Now as they floated on, by and by they
left the cold and the snow behind, and
came to where it was warm. Down below
was the blue, blue sea, and in the blue sea
were many little islands with white sand
and green trees.

By this time the pie was beginning to
cool off, and as it cooled it went down and
down.

"Let us land on one of these lovely
islands," said the old man. "They have
white sand and green trees, and ever so
many flowers."
"Yes, let us!" said the old woman, and
Whisky the cat, and the duck, and the
mountain goat, and the airman, and the
elephant.

But the people on the island saw them
coming and put up a big sign that said
NO PARKING FOR PIES.

So they went a little farther and they
came to another island. But the people
on that island also put up a big sign that
said
NO PARKING FOR PIES.

"Oh dear," said the old woman, "will
no one let us land?"

By this time the pie was so cool that it
sank down on the sea.

"Now we are all right," said the old
man. "Our own pie makes a very fine
island."

"There are no trees!" said the old
woman. "There are no flowers! And what
shall we eat, and what shall we drink?"

But the sun was so warm that fine apple
trees soon grew up, with green leaves, and
pink flowers, and red apples. And the
mountain goat gave them milk, and the
duck gave them eggs, and Whisky the cat
caught fish in the sea. And the elephant
picked apples for them off the trees with
her trunk.

So they lived happily on the island and
never went home again.

And all this happened because the old
woman baked a bit of sky in her pie!

# *Trish Cooke*
# MAMMY, SUGAR FALLING DOWN

*Illustrated by Alicia Garcia de Lynam*

## Best Friends

*Elizabeth has just arrived in England and her only
friends are the fruit, vegetables and sauces from her old home
in the West Indies that live in the kitchen cupboard.*

ELIZABETH HAD DECIDED to accept English weather as it came. She had never seen days that could go through all four seasons before. She was used to sun and more sun and sometimes a little rain. It was on one of those "Don't know how the weather's going to turn out" days when Elizabeth got up to the sound of the alarm clock. Her mother had set it for the special day ahead: Elizabeth's first day at school.

Mr Hot Pepper and the others marvelled at Elizabeth's school uniform when she came downstairs. "Looking good! Looking good!" Mr Hot Pepper cheered, but Elizabeth felt too cold and lonely to smile with him. She felt too sad at leaving her friends behind.

Elizabeth's teacher was called Miss Gregg. When Miss Gregg brought Elizabeth into the classroom everybody was giggling. Elizabeth could not see them giggling, but she could feel their stares. Miss Gregg told Elizabeth to sit next to Ian Fuller, who made a funny face to the others and the whole class laughed out loud.

"Hush now," Miss Gregg had said. 'This is Elizabeth. Elizabeth is not only new to this school, she is also new to this country, so I want you all to be on best behaviour so she can see how well behaved English children can be." Elizabeth did not notice all the children sit up straight, she was too busy looking at the bright coloured walls covered in pictures of different shaped trees.

"Would you like to tell us what the classrooms are like in Dominica?" Miss

Gregg asked Elizabeth. Elizabeth drew an invisible pattern on the desk top with her finger. She began to sing a tune.

"Now, now Elizabeth, it will not do to be rude," Miss Gregg said. Elizabeth was not being rude. That was exactly what the classrooms were like – long oblongs with open windows, the way she had drawn it on her desk top. And she sang because that was how she had learnt her alphabet:

"ABCDEFG ♪ HIJKLMN ♫ ' OP QRSTU ♫ VWXYZ."

"What about the weather. I'm sure you would like to tell us about the weather," Miss Gregg said.

Elizabeth tried to say "Hot" but her mouth was dry and no sound came out.

"What's the weather like?" Miss Gregg repeated quietly. Elizabeth wanted to cry but she did not want the others to see so she ran out of the classroom and cried in the cloakroom.

"Are you crying?" A pair of eyes was looking over the top of the coats. Elizabeth looked up at the thick brown curls sitting on the top of Ian Fuller's head.

"Miss Gregg sent me to look for you," he said.

"I not crying," Elizabeth lied. "I jus' col'."

"I suppose you're sad because…" Ian began.

"I not sad, I don't care!" Elizabeth yelled.

"Oh," said Ian. "I expect you don't have any friends…yet?"

"I have friends," Elizabeth said. "At home…"

"I live on the same street as you and I've never seen 'em," Ian boasted.

"That's because…" Elizabeth began, but she knew it was no use explaining that she had meant her friends in the kitchen cupboard. Ian wouldn't understand.

"I'll be your friend, if you want," said Ian, "I don't have any friends either." Elizabeth looked back at the classroom remembering the rest of them laughing with Ian.

"They laugh at me, too," said Ian, "because of these." He pointed to each of his eyes in turn and Elizabeth noticed that one was brown and the other blue.

"Oh," said Elizabeth. "I don't want to be your friend either then." Ian Fuller made a rude sign with his fingers and Elizabeth copied.

"Elizabeth John Baptiste!" said Miss Gregg, catching Elizabeth in the act.

"I didn't do noffin," Elizabeth pleaded.

"Now, come and sit down in the classroom."

Elizabeth went to sit down next to Ian Fuller, who slumped across his desk and stared out of the window. She did not really mind his eyes, in fact they were quite special. She'd never seen anybody with anything quite so special before. Miss Gregg did not ask Elizabeth any more questions but every so often she smiled at her to show she had not forgotten that she was there. When the bell rang everybody ran outside. Elizabeth did not know where to go.

"You coming?" Ian called from the doorway. Elizabeth followed him pretending she did not want to go, but she did. She liked her new friend.

Once in the playground Ian sat on the wall. "Can you play Jacks?" he asked, emptying a small bag he had taken from his pocket.

"Jacks?" said Elizabeth, curious to know what her friend was going to do.

"Yeh, it's a game," Ian said, spreading out the jacks on the wall. He threw one up in the air and picked up the others before he caught it.

"Pick Up," Elizabeth laughed, remembering back home. When she played the same game in Dominica they called it Pick Up. Elizabeth looked at her friend and liked what she saw. He reminded her of "home". She decided Ian Fuller would be her best friend.

# Hugh Lofting

# THE STORY OF DOCTOR DOLITTLE

## Animal Language

*Doctor Dolittle's human patients no longer visit him because they do not like all the animals he keeps.*

IT HAPPENED ONE DAY that the Doctor was sitting in his kitchen talking with the cat's-meat man, who had come to see him with a stomach ache.

"Why don't you give up being a people's doctor, and be an animal doctor?" asked the cat's-meat man.

The parrot, Polynesia, was sitting in the window looking out at the rain and singing a sailor song to herself. She stopped singing and started to listen.

"You see, Doctor," the cat's-meat man went on, "you know all about animals - much more than what these here vets do. That book you wrote about cats - why, it's wonderful! I can't read or write myself, or maybe *I'd* write some books. But my wife, Theodosia, she's a scholar, she is. And she read your book to me. Well, it's wonderful - that's all can be said - wonderful. You might have been a cat yourself. You know

the way they think. And listen: you can make a lot of money doctoring animals. Do you know that? You see, I'd send all the old women who had sick cats or dogs to you. And if they didn't get ill fast enough, I could put something in the meat I sell 'em to make 'em bad, see?"

"Oh, no," said the Doctor quickly. "You mustn't do that. That wouldn't be right."

"Oh, I didn't mean real bad," answered the cat's-meat man. "Just a little something to make them droopy-like was what I had reference to. But as you say, maybe it ain't quite fair on the animals. But they'll get ill anyway because the old women always give 'em too much to eat. And look, all the farmers round about who had lame horses and weak lambs – they'd come. Be an animal doctor."

When the cat's-meat man had gone the

parrot flew off the window on to the Doctor's table and said, "That man's got sense. That's what you ought to do. Be an animal doctor. Give the silly people up if they haven't brains enough to see you're the best doctor in the world. Take care of animals instead. *They'll* soon find it out. Be an animal doctor."

"Oh, there are plenty of animal doctors," said John Dolittle, putting the flower pots outside on the window-sill to get the rain.

"Yes, there *are* plenty," said Polynesia. "But none of them are any good at all. Now listen, Doctor, and I'll tell you something. Did you know that animals can talk?"

"I knew that parrots can talk," said the Doctor.

"Oh, we parrots can talk in two languages – people's language and bird language," said Polynesia proudly. "If I say 'Polly wants a cracker,' you understand me. But hear this: *Ka-ka oi-ee, fe-fee?*"

"Good gracious!" cried the Doctor. "What does that mean?"

"That means, 'Is the porridge hot yet?' in bird language."

"My! You don't say so!" said the Doctor. "You never talked that way to me before."

"What would have been the good?" said Polynesia, dusting some biscuit crumbs

## Allan Ahlberg

# TEN IN A BED

*Illustrated by André Amstutz*

## Too Many Bears

ONE EVENING A LITTLE GIRL named Dinah Price kissed her mum and dad goodnight, climbed the stairs, went into her room – and found three bears in her bed. These bears were a father bear, a mother bear and a baby bear. They were lying side by side, with the baby bear in the middle. They appeared to be sleeping.

Dinah Price knew a bit about bears. When she was an even littler girl, her mum used to tell her a story about some bears and the trouble they had had with another little girl named Goldilocks. So Dinah went up to the bed with the bears in it and said, "Who's this sleeping in *my* bed?"

Straight away the bears opened their eyes and shouted, "Us!" And they laughed – all three of them. They were only pretending to be asleep.

Dinah Price stood at the foot of the bed and looked at the bears. The evening sunlight was shining into the room. Through the open window came the sound of a lawn-mower. The next-door neighbour was cutting his grass.

The bears lay in the bed and looked at Dinah Price. From time to time they gave each other a little nudge and smiled. They did not seem embarrassed to be in someone else's bed. They showed no sign of leaving.

"What are you doing here?" said Dinah.

"Resting," said the father bear.

"But how did you get in?"

"That would be telling. Maybe we climbed up the drainpipe."

"Or down the chimney," said the mother bear.

"Like Santa Claus!" the baby bear said.

"There isn't a chimney," said Dinah. "We've got central heating."

At that moment through the open window came the chimes of an ice-cream van. The baby bear's little eyes lit up. "Can we go home now?"

"No," said the mother bear. "We've only just got here." Then, in a whisper to Dinah, she added, "Take no notice. What he really wants is an ice-cream."

"What are you whispering about?" said the baby bear. And he said, "Can I have an ice-cream?"

"Wait and see," said the mother bear.

Dinah Price thought for a minute. She would not have minded an ice-cream herself. She said, "But shouldn't you be going home anyway? It's bedtime!"

jelly and sleeping in her bed."

"She's got a nerve," said the mother bear.

"Then the bears promised to leave if only Goldilocks would tell them a story; so she did. She told them a story and they listened and said thank-you-very-much. After that they went home – because a promise is a promise – they went home and – "

"Wait a minute," the baby bear said. "What was the story *she* told?"

"I don't remember. Anyway, that's another story!"

"I bet I know what it was," said the mother bear. She began to smile. "I bet it was like this: Goldilocks said, 'Once upon a time there were three bears.' Then the little, small, wee bear said he had heard it already – '

"I have heard it already *already*!" said the baby bear.

And the father bear said, "My head is spinning. How many bears have we got now?"

"Then the three bears went out for a walk," said the mother bear, "and came to Goldilocks's house and went inside and ate her pineapple jelly."

"Only the little, small, wee bear ate the jelly," said the baby bear.

"No – they all ate it this time," said the mother bear. "In fact, come to think of it, the middle-sized bear ate most of it. Well, they ate the jelly and went upstairs for a lie-down, and Goldilocks came back and found them there and – "

"Told them to clear off out of it!" said

Dinah, who was getting impatient.

"No, she didn't," said the baby bear.

"Yes, she did. She said, 'You bears get out of here or I will fetch my daddy, who is a hunter.'"

"A hunter?" The baby bear looked puzzled. "What's a hunter?"

"Don't answer that," whispered the mother bear. "We haven't told him about the hunters yet. He's too young."

"What are you whispering about?" said the baby bear. And he said, "What's a hunter?"

"A man," the mother said. "A man who cuts the trees down."

"That's a wood-cutter!"

The mother bear turned to Dinah. "Go on with the story."

"Right," said Dinah. "So anyway, Goldilocks told the three bears about her daddy and his gun, and that was enough for them."

"What's a gun?" said the baby bear.

"Don't answer *that*," the mother bear said.

"That was enough for them," said Dinah. "They wasted no time, but jumped out of the bed, out of the window and ran off through the woods to their own house, their own pineapple jelly – and *their own beds*! The End."

At this point Dinah slammed the book shut, startling the father bear, who had been dozing off. The mother bear sat up in the bed. "That wasn't a bad story." She yawned and stretched. "Except for the last bit."

Dinah Price stood up and put the book on her bedside table. It was darker in the room now. A smell of cut grass was coming through the open window. The noise of the mower had stopped. In a tree outside the window, birds were twittering. Downstairs the phone began to ring.

"Was Goldilocks's father really a 'you-know-what'?" the mother bear said.

"What's a you-know-what?" said the baby bear.

"Yes, he was." Dinah could feel her feet getting cold inside her slippers. "He was a terror." And she said, "Are you going home now?"

"Certainly," said the mother bear.

And the father bear said, "We can take a hint."

The three bears clambered out of the bed. The father bear and the mother bear tidied the bedclothes and plumped up the pillow.

"Do you have far to go?" said Dinah.

"That would be telling," said the mother bear. "It could be miles and miles!"

"Or just down the road," the father bear said.

Then Dinah spotted the baby bear. He was trying to sneak off with her woolly duck. Luckily, the mother bear spotted him too. She made him give it back.

After that the three bears climbed out on to the window ledge, said goodbye to Dinah Price, went down the drainpipe and across the grass, waved goodbye to Dinah – who was watching them go – and disappeared into the rhododendron bushes at the far end of the garden.

The last words Dinah heard was the baby bear halfway down the drainpipe saying, "Can we have pineapple jelly when we get home?" And his mother's reply: "Wait and see."

Dinah Price shut the window and pulled the curtains across. She said to herself, "I will tell my friend about this tomorrow." After that she got into the bed – still warm from the bears – and slept till morning.

# Roald Dahl
# THE BFG

*Illustrated by Quentin Blake*

## Sophie Meets the BFG

THE GIANT PICKED UP the trembling Sophie with one hand and carried her across the cave and put her on the table.

Now he really is going to eat me, Sophie thought.

The Giant sat down and stared hard at Sophie. He had truly enormous ears. Each one was as big as the wheel of a truck and he seemed to be able to move them inwards and outwards from his head as he wished.

"I is hungry!" the Giant boomed. He grinned, showing massive square teeth. The teeth were very white and very square and they sat in his mouth like huge slices of white bread.

"P . . . please don't eat me," Sophie stammered.

The Giant let out a bellow of laughter. "Just because I is a giant, you think I is a man-gobbling cannybull!" he shouted. "You is about right! Giants is all cannybully and murderful! And they *does* gobble up human beans! We is in Giant Country now! Giants is everywhere around! Out there us has the famous Bonecrunching Giant! Bonecrunching Giant crunches up two wopsey whiffling human beans for supper every night! Noise is earbursting! Noise of crunching bones goes crackety-crack for miles around!"

"Owch!" Sophie said.

"Bonecrunching Giant only gobbles human beans from Turkey," the Giant said. "Every night Bonecruncher is galloping off to Turkey to gobble Turks."

Sophie's sense of patriotism was suddenly so bruised by this remark that she became quite angry. "Why Turks?" she blurted out. "What's wrong with the English?"

"Bonecrunching Giant says Turks is tasting oh ever so much juicier and more scrumdiddlyumptious! Bonecruncher says Turkish human beans has a glamourly flavour. He says Turks from Turkey is tasting of turkey."

"I suppose they would," Sophie said.

"Of course they would!" the Giant shouted. "Every human bean is diddly and different. Some is scrumdiddlyumptious and some is uckyslush. Greeks is all full of uckyslush. No giant is eating Greeks, ever."

"Why not?" Sophie asked.

"Greeks from Greece is all tasting greasy," the Giant said.

"I imagine that's possible too," Sophie

Cuchulain began to feel uneasy. Perhaps he was wrong to come in search of Finn Mac Cool. Glancing nervously towards the cradle, he saw the child was sucking its thumb again.

"He'll be crying for some cake any minute now," says Oona. "It's his feeding time."

Just then, Finn began to howl, "CAAA-AAKKE!"

"Put that in your mouth," says she. And she handed Finn a cake from the top shelf.

"How can a baby eat that?" said Cuchulain scornfully.

But in the twinkling of an eye, Finn had eaten every crumb, then roared out again, "CAAA-AAKKE!"

When the baby was well into his third cake, Cuchulain got up to go.

"I'm off now, Mrs Mac Cool," he says. "If that baby's anything like its dad, Finn'll be more than a match for me. 'Tis a bonny baby you have, ma'am."

"If you're so fond of babies, come and have a closer look at this one," says she.

And she took Cuchulain by the arm to guide him to the cradle, removing the blanket from Finn as she did so. Thereupon Finn kicked his legs in the air and yelled at the top of his voice.

"By golly, what a pair of legs he has on him!" gasped Cuchulain.

"You ought to have seen his father at that age," says Oona. "Why, he was out in the bogs wrestling with bulls at one year old."

"Is that a fact?" sighed Cuchulain, eager to get away from the house before Finn returned.

"The baby's teeth are coming through well, though," continues Oona. "Have a feel of them."

Thinking to please the woman before making his escape, Cuchulain put his fingers into the baby's mouth to feel its teeth.

And can you guess what happened?

When he pulled his fingers out, there were only four left: his middle finger had been bitten off.

You could have heard the yell from there to Venezuela!

Now that his strength was gone, the once mighty Cuchulain began to grow smaller and smaller, until he was no bigger than the cake he had bitten into. High above him Oona and Finn Mac Cool laughed and mocked the little man. The tiny figure tottered out of the house and down the mountain, fleeing for his life. And he was never seen again in Ireland.

As for Finn, he was ever grateful for the brains of his dear wife Oona.

# L. Frank Baum
# THE WIZARD OF OZ

*Illustrated by W. W. Denslow*

## The Cowardly Lion

*A tornado transports Dorothy from her farm in Kansas to Munchkinland.*
*Determined to find a way home, she is off to to the Emerald City to seek the advice*
*of the Wizard, with her companions the Scarecrow and the Tin Woodman.*
*On the way, they meet the Cowardly Lion.*

"WHAT MAKES YOU A COWARD?" asked Dorothy, looking at the great beast in wonder, for he was as big as a small horse.

"It's a mystery," replied the Lion. "I suppose I was born that way. All the other animals in the forest naturally expect me to be brave, for the Lion is everywhere thought to be the King of Beasts. I learned that if I roared very loudly every living thing was frightened and got out of my way. Whenever I've met a man I've been awfully scared; but I just roared at him, and he has always run away as fast as he could go. If the elephants and the tigers and the bears had ever tried to fight me, I should have run myself – I'm such a coward; but just as soon as they hear me roar they all try to get away from me, and of course I let them go."

"But that isn't right. The King of Beasts shouldn't be a coward," said the Scarecrow.

"I know it," returned the Lion, wiping a tear from his eye with the tip of his tail; "it is my great sorrow, and makes my life very unhappy. But whenever there is danger my heart begins to beat fast."

"Perhaps you have heart disease," said the Tin Woodman.

"It may be," said the Lion.

"If you have," continued the Tin Woodman, "you ought to be glad, for it proves you have a heart. For my part, I have no heart; so I cannot have heart disease."

"Perhaps," said the Lion, thoughtfully, "if I had no heart I should not be a coward."

"Have you brains?" asked the Scarecrow.

"I suppose so. I've never looked to see," replied the Lion.

"I am going to the great Oz to ask him to give me some," remarked the Scarecrow, "for my head is stuffed with straw."

"And I am going to ask him to give me a heart," said the Woodman.

"And I am going to ask him to send Toto and me back to Kansas," added Dorothy.

"Do you think Oz could give me courage?" asked the Cowardly Lion.

"Just as easily as he could give me brains," said the Scarecrow.

"Or give me a heart," said the Tin Woodman.

"Or send me back to Kansas," said Dorothy.

"Then, if you don't mind, I'll go with you," said the Lion, "for my life is simply unbearable without a bit of courage."

"You will be very welcome," answered Dorothy, "for you will help to keep away the other wild beasts. It seems to me they must be more cowardly than you are if they allow you to scare them so easily."

"They really are," said the Lion; "but that doesn't make me any braver, and as long as I know myself to be a coward I shall be unhappy."

So once more the little company set off upon the journey, the Lion walking with stately strides at Dorothy's side.

During the rest of that day there was no other adventure to mar the peace of their journey. Once, indeed, the Tin Woodman stepped upon a beetle that was crawling along the road, and killed the poor little thing. This made the Tin Woodman very unhappy, for he was always careful not to hurt any living creature; and as he walked along he wept several tears of sorrow and regret. These tears ran slowly down his face and over the hinges of his jaw, and there they rusted. When Dorothy presently asked him a question the Tin Woodman could not open his mouth, for his jaws were tightly rusted together. He became greatly frightened at this and made many motions to Dorothy to relieve him, but she could not understand. The Lion was also puzzled to know what was wrong. But the Scarecrow seized the oil-can from Dorothy's basket and oiled the Woodman's jaws, so that after a few moments he could talk as well as before.

"This will serve me a lesson," said he, "to look where I step. For if I should kill

# Hilaire Belloc
# MATILDA

## Who told Lies, and was Burned to Death

### Illustrated by Posy Simmonds

MATILDA told such Dreadful Lies,
It made one Gasp and Stretch one's Eyes;
Her Aunt, who from her earliest Youth,
Had kept a Strict Regard for Truth,

Attempted to Believe Matilda:
The effort very nearly killed her,
And would have done, had not She
Discovered this Infirmity.

For once, towards the Close of Day,
Matilda, growing tired of play,
And finding she was left alone...
Went tiptoe to the Telephone
And summoned the Immediate Aid
Of London's Noble Fire Brigade.

Within an hour the Gallant Band
Were pouring in on every hand,
From Putney, Hackney Downs and Bow,
With Courage high and Hearts a-glow
They galloped, roaring through the Town...
"Matilda's House is Burning Down!"

Inspired by British Cheers and Loud
Proceeding from the Frenzied Crowd,
They ran their ladders through a score
Of windows on the Ball Room Floor;
And took Peculiar Pains to Souse
The Pictures up and down the House,

Until Matilda's Aunt succeeded
In showing them they were not needed
And even then she had to pay
To get the Men to go away!

It happened that a few Weeks later
Her Aunt was off to the Theatre
To see that Interesting Play
*The Second Mrs Tanqueray.*
She had refused to take her Niece
To hear this Entertaining Piece:
A Deprivation Just and Wise
To Punish her for telling Lies.

That Night a Fire *did* break out –
You should have heard Matilda Shout!
You should have heard her Scream and Bawl,
And throw the window up and call
To People passing in the Street –
(The rapidly increasing Heat
Encouraging her to obtain
Their confidence)
– but all in vain!

For every time She shouted "Fire!"
They only answered "Little Liar!"

And therefore when her Aunt returned,
Matilda, and the House, were Burned.

# J. M. Barrie

# PETER PAN

### Illustrated by Susie Jenkin-Pearce

## The Flight

*Wendy, John and Michel Darling have left their
London nursery and are flying through the night sky with Peter Pan,
who is taking them to the Neverland.*

"SECOND TO THE RIGHT, and straight on till morning."

That, Peter had told Wendy, was the way to the Neverland; but even birds, carrying maps and consulting them at windy corners, could not have sighted it with these instructions. Peter, you see, just said anything that came into his head.

At first his companions trusted him implicitly, and so great were the delights of flying that they wasted time circling round church spires or any other tall objects on the way that took their fancy.

John and Michael raced, Michael getting a start.

They recalled with contempt that not so long ago they had thought themselves fine fellows for being able to fly round a room.

Not so long ago. But how long ago? They were flying over the sea before this thought began to disturb Wendy seriously. John thought it was their second sea and their third night.

Sometimes it was dark and sometimes light, and now they were very cold and again too warm. Did they really feel hungry at times, or were they merely pretending, because Peter had such a jolly new way of feeding them? His way was to pursue birds who had food in their mouths suitable for humans and snatch it from them; then the birds would follow and snatch it back; and they would all go chasing each other gaily for miles, parting at last with mutual expressions of good-will. But Wendy noticed with gentle concern that Peter did not seem to know that this was rather an odd way of getting your bread and butter, nor even that there are other ways.

Certainly they did not pretend to be sleepy, they were sleepy; and that was a danger, for the moment they popped off, down they fell. The awful thing was that Peter thought this funny.

"There he goes again!" he would cry gleefully, as Michael suddenly dropped like a stone.

"Save him, save him!" cried Wendy, looking with horror at the cruel sea far below. Eventually Peter would dive through the air, and catch Michael just before he could strike the sea, and it was lovely the way he did it; but he always waited till the last moment, and you felt it was his cleverness that interested him and not the saving of human life. Also he was fond of variety, and the sport that engrossed him one moment would suddenly cease to engage him, so there was always the possibility that the next time you fell he would let you go.

He could sleep in the air without falling, by merely lying on his back and floating, but this was, partly at least, because he was so light that if you got behind him and blew he went faster.

"Do be more polite to him," Wendy whispered to John, when they were

playing "Follow my Leader".

"Then tell him to stop showing off," said John.

When playing Follow my Leader, Peter would fly close to the water and touch each shark's tail in passing, just as in the street you may run your finger along an iron railing. They could not follow him in this with much success, so perhaps it was rather like showing off, especially as he kept looking behind to see how many tails they missed.

"You must be nice to him," Wendy impressed on her brothers. "What could we do if he were to leave us?"

"We could go back," Michael said.

"How could we ever find our way back without him?"

"Well, then, we could go on," said John.

"That is the awful thing, John. We should have to go on, for we don't know how to stop."

This was true; Peter had forgotten to show them how to stop.

John said that if the worst came to the worst, all they had to do was to go straight on, for the world was round, and so in time they must come back to their own window.

"And who is to get food for us, John?"

"I nipped a bit out of that eagle's mouth pretty neatly, Wendy."

"After the twentieth try," Wendy reminded him. "And even though we became good at picking up food, see how we bump against clouds and things if he is not near to give us a hand."

Indeed they were constantly bumping. They could now fly strongly, though they still kicked far too much; but if they saw a cloud in front of them, the more they tried to avoid it, the more certainly did they bump into it. If Nana had been with them she would have had a bandage round Michael's forehead by this time.

Peter was not with them for the moment, and they felt rather lonely up there by themselves. He could go so much faster than they that he would suddenly shoot out of sight, to have some adventure in which they had no share. He would come down laughing over something fearfully funny he had been saying to a star, but he had already forgotten what it was, or he would come up with mermaid scales still sticking to him, and yet not be able to say for certain what had been happening. It was really rather irritating to children who had never seen a mermaid.

"And if he forgets them so quickly," Wendy argued, "how can we expect that he will go on remembering us?"

Indeed, sometimes when he returned he did not remember them, at least not well. Wendy was sure of it. She saw recognition come into his eyes as he was about to pass them the time of day and go on; once even she had to tell him her name.

"I'm Wendy," she said agitatedly.

He was very sorry. "I say, Wendy," he whispered to her, "always if you see me forgetting you, just keep on saying 'I'm Wendy,' and then I'll remember."

Of course this was rather unsatisfactory.

However, to make amends he showed them how to lie out flat on a strong wind that was going their way, and this was such a pleasant change that they tried it several times and found they could sleep thus with security. Indeed they would have slept longer, but Peter tired quickly of sleeping, and soon he would cry in his captain voice, "We get off here." So with occasional tiffs, but on the whole rollicking, they drew near the Neverland; for after many moons they did reach it, and, what is more, they had been going pretty straight all the time, not perhaps so much owing to the guidance of Peter or Tink as because the island was out looking for them. It is only thus that anyone may sight

those magic shores.

"There it is," said Peter calmly.

"Where, where?"

"Where all the arrows are pointing."

Indeed a million golden arrows were pointing out the island to the children, all directed by their friend the sun, who wanted them to be sure of their way before leaving them for the night.

Wendy and John and Michael stood on tiptoe in the air to get their first sight of the island. Strange to say, they all recognised it at once, and until fear fell upon them they hailed it, not as something long dreamt of and seen at last, but as a familiar friend to whom they were returning home for the holidays.

# Dick King-Smith

# FIND THE WHITE HORSE

*Illustrated by Larry Wilkes*

## Run For It

*Squintum the Siamese cat lives in a Dogs' Home. Lubber, a friendly mongrel, arrives and as the days pass, the cat becomes more and more worried. Unless he is claimed within two weeks, Squintum's new friend will die.*

SQUINTUM SAT WAITING and watching, his long thin tail curled neatly round him, as the kennelmaid opened Lubber's door. Lubber, of course, was asleep. Five minutes more, thought Squintum, and you will sleep for ever.

"Come on, old chap!" said the kennelmaid brightly. "We're going for a little walk," and as the big dog got to his feet, yawning, she fastened a lead on to his collar.

"What a shame!" she said, stroking the hairy head. "Can't think why someone hasn't claimed you. Or why someone didn't want you for a pet. Must have been because you're such a lazy old thing, I think. Every time anybody came to choose a dog, you were asleep. They probably thought you were ill. Ah well! Come along then, Lubber. At least you won't feel anything."

She led Lubber out and along the corridor. Squintum followed. It was three minutes to eleven.

In the surgery, the vet was loading a syringe. He turned as the door opened and the kennelmaid and the dog came in. Unobserved, Squintum slipped through behind them.

The vet looked consideringly at Lubber.

"He's a big one," he said, laying down the syringe. "Don't try to lift him up on to the table by yourself, you'll slip a disc. I'll give you a hand. Does he need muzzling?"

"No," said the kennelmaid. "He wouldn't bite anyone. It'd be too much effort. He's ever such a lazy old thing."

Together they lifted Lubber up on to the table, where he stood patiently, wagging his tail, slowly, so as not to tire himself, and gave them a smily look from under his bushy eyebrows.

The vet picked up a pair of scissors.

"Just going to take a little of this hair off your foreleg, old fellow," he said, and he snipped away, making a small, close-cropped patch. Then he felt for a vein.

"Right," said the vet, "that'll do," and

334

to the kennelmaid he said, "Just grip the leg tight, here," and he picked up the syringe. With his other hand he patted Lubber, who wagged a trifle faster.

"Now," said the vet, "this won't hurt."

Through the surgery window came the sound of a distant church clock, striking the first stroke of eleven.

Siamese have particularly harsh voices, unpleasant to many people's ears, and just as the vet was about to slip the needle into the vein, Squintum let out a sudden ear-splitting yowl.

To the two startled humans the noise, of course, meant nothing. It was just a nuisance and a distraction, making the vet put down his syringe and the kennelmaid release her hold on the dog's leg.

But to Lubber, wondering why he was being made to stand on a table and feeling he would be much more comfortable lying down and perhaps taking a nap, it was clear what the Siamese was saying.

"Run for it!" squalled Squintum at the top of his awful voice. "Follow me! Or else they'll kill you!"

335

Lubber. "The people at the Dogs' Home?"

"They will," said Squintum, "and not only with you. I think I'd better steer clear of the place for a while."

"But don't you belong to someone?" asked Lubber. "I do."

Squintum chose not to answer the dog's question. Instead he said, "Just now you mentioned your people at home. Whereabouts is your home?"

Lubber hung his head.

"I don't know," he said.

The Siamese cat leaped nimbly up on to the balustrade that surrounded the covered bandstand. From this vantage point, he could see all around the park. He settled himself comfortably.

"Tell me, Lubber," he said. "How exactly did you come to be lost?"

Lubber sighed.

"I expect you think I'm a bit thick in the head," he said.

"Oh, what an idea!" said Squintum. "Why do you say such a thing?"

"Well, you must think it funny that I don't know where my home is. But you see, Squintum, it's nowhere near here. In fact, it must be hundreds of miles from this town."

"You've walked hundreds of miles?"

"No. I rode."

"In a car?"

"No. In a furniture van."

"Start at the beginning," said Squintum.

"Well," said Lubber, "I belong to two old ladies, sisters they are, and we live in a thatched cottage in a little village under a big hill. Ever so nice to me, they are –

were – and I was as happy as could be. Mind you, their legs weren't too strong, even though they each had three of them."

"Three legs each!" said Squintum.

Lubber's eyes twinkled under his bushy brows.

"Yes," he said. "Two ordinary ones and a wooden one. They both walked with a stick, you see. I was pulling *your* leg. Anyway, we never had to walk very far, which was a mercy. I'm not too fond of exercise. What's more, I like to take a nap every now and then."

He yawned.

"All that running's tired me out," he said. "Can't I tell you the rest later?"

"No," said Squintum sharply. "Go on."

"One day," said Lubber, "the family in the house next door to our cottage were moving, you see, and this big furniture van came and parked outside. My old ladies had gone down to the shop at the other end of the village – I kept out of the way, it's a good quarter of a mile – and then it came on to rain and I couldn't get into the cottage. So I climbed into this furniture van. The removal men were inside the house – they'd finished loading everything and I expect they were having a cup of tea – so I thought I'd just shelter for a bit. Now one of the things in the van was a very comfy-looking sofa, and I suddenly felt like having forty winks. I dare say you can guess the rest."

"They shut the doors and drove off," said Squintum.

"That's right. Next thing I knew we were moving. I couldn't see out and I didn't know where we were going. I just hoped it wouldn't be too far, and then perhaps I could walk home."

"That would have been very tiring, surely?" said Squintum.

"I suppose so," said Lubber. "But as it was, we went on and on for ages before at last they stopped and opened the doors and I jumped out and ran off. Like I said, I must be hundreds of miles from home. I wandered round the town for a bit, sleeping rough, you know, eating out of dustbins, that sort of thing, until a man in uniform caught me…"

"…the Dog Warden," said Squintum.

"…and put me in that place where you live."

"And where you nearly died."

"Grrrrr!" said Lubber, shaking himself. "Whatever am I to do, Squintum?"

The Siamese stood up on the balustrade of the bandstand and looked all around the park for possible danger. Seeing none, he stretched himself luxuriously, unsheathing his claws and dragging each forefoot in turn along the wooden rail with a rasping sound.

"Talk about needles in haystacks!" he said. "A thatched cottage in a little village under a big hill. Gordon Bennett! There must be thousands of such cottages."

"Ah, but wait!" said Lubber. "I've just remembered. There's a White Horse on the hill. We can see it from our garden."

"There must be thousands of white horses," said Squintum. "Anyway, the horse might have been moved to another place or sold or anything."

"No, no! Not a live horse. A great picture of one, cut into the turf of the hillside."

Squintum's tail-tip twitched.

"That's interesting," he said. "They don't have such things in these northern parts. Must be chalk country. Looks as if we should head south."

Lubber, who had lain down, exhausted by so much talking, sprang to his feet.

"'We'?" he said. "D'you mean…?"

"Thought I might accompany you," said Squintum. "I can't say I'm very happy here, and I'm still young, and I've a good few lives left. Mind if I come along?"

"Mind?" barked Lubber. "I should say not! Why, with you to help me, I might stand a better chance of finding my way home. And my old ladies would love you!"

What a nice sort of animal you are, he thought.

"But," Lubber went on, "I don't know why you should do this for me. I don't know why you saved my life this morning. Have you done that before, for other dogs?"

"No," said Squintum.

"Why me?" said Lubber.

I don't really know, thought the Siamese. I just rather like you.

"Ask me no questions and I'll tell you no lies," he said. "And now get some sleep. I'll keep watch. As soon as darkness falls, we must be off."

## *Beverley Nichols*
# THE STREAM THAT STOOD STILL

*Illustrated by Richard Kennedy*

## Lord Salmon

*The stream is no ordinary stream, and beneath its
silvery surface is a world of enchantment and excitement. Wearing her
magic water mask, Jill dives down to its pale green depths in search of
her brother, Jack, who has been turned into a fish by the
wicked witch Miss Smith.*

JILL BLINKED, and stared around her. So this was Lord Salmon's cave – this was the real heart and centre of the life of the stream!

It was tall and spacious, and at first she could not understand how it was so well lit, for the light of day filtered only feebly through the entrance. Then, looking upwards, she noticed that the water did not quite reach the ceiling, and that the light seemed to come from a rocky shelf, that jutted out a few inches above the surface of the water. "Can they possibly have electricity in here?" she asked herself. And then to her astonishment, she saw that the light came from a long row of glow-worms, sitting close together on the shelf, and blinking down at the scene below with tiny, brilliant tails, that shone through the water like torches.

"His Lordship will be here in a moment," whispered P. C. Gudgeon. "Mind you treat him with the greatest respect. And whatever you do, don't mention the subject of cans."

"I certainly won't," whispered Jill.

"And another thing. Keep off cucumber. You've only got to say 'cucumber' to his Lordship, and he sees red."

Jill nodded gravely. "I promise."

They stayed still and waited. Jill was so fascinated by all that she saw that she forgot to be afraid. All around the cave, on rocky shelves, were rows of books, beautifully bound in closely woven seaweed, with their titles picked out in little coloured shells. Among them Jill noticed such strange works as the following:

*Sharks in Shrimps' Clothing.*
*Songs by a Sardine.*

*My Life Upstairs* by Laura Goldfish.

There was also one book, much larger than the others, entitled:

*Famous Leaps* by Lord Salmon.

In the centre of the cave was a huge rock shaped like a desk, and on the desk was a pen, a pencil and a pad. P. C. Gudgeon nudged her. "You see that pad?" he whispered. "That's a blotter."

"But how can it be a blotter?" asked Jill. "If you put blotting paper in water it would soak it all up."

"*This* doesn't," retorted Mr Gudgeon. "This is made of linoleum. And it won't soak *anything* up. That's why it's called a blotter." He nodded in such a superior way that Jill had not the heart to contradict him. Besides, at this moment, there was a stir at the back of the cave, and P. C. Gudgeon, drawing his fins sharply in to his sides, shouted:

"Silence for his Lordship!"

A second later, two very beautiful little fishes appeared, so brilliantly coloured that they looked as if they were wearing jewelled waistcoats. These Jill recognised as Rainbow-Trouts... and later on she was to learn that the Rainbow-Trouts thought themselves very superior to the ordinary trouts – indeed, Mrs Rainbow-Trout had the reputation of being the biggest snob in the whole stream.

And then, after the Rainbow-Trouts, he came himself, the great Lord Salmon. "What a *beautiful* person!" thought Jill, as he glided slowly towards his desk. "What an *impressive* person too – no wonder they chose him as Lord of the Stream!" And he did look very grand and dignified, for he was nearly four feet long, and his skin was a rich mixture of green and blue and violet and silver.

But at first it seemed that his Lordship was none too pleased to see her. He regarded her with a cold, judicial eye that boded no good.

"So this," he said, in a deep, growling voice, "is the Human?"

"Yes, m'lud," agreed P. C. Gudgeon nervously.

"She has been searched?"

"Oh yes, m'lud."

"No rods, hooks, lines... no nets?"

"None, m'lud."

His Lordship's voice went even deeper. "No... no *cans*?"

"Not a sign of a can, m'lud."

His Lordship sighed heavily. "That, at least, is a point in her favour." He, and his family, had particularly painful memories of cans, which was only natural, for to be canned, if you are a salmon, is about the end of everything.

"The Human may proceed," he proclaimed.

So once again Jill told her story.

As she went on, her heart sank lower and lower, and her hopes grew dimmer and dimmer, for it was quite obvious that his Lordship had little sympathy with her. When she came to the part about the witch he interrupted her sharply:

"How do you *know* she was a witch?"

"Your Lordship... she changed my brother into a fish."

"Is that so very terrible, to be a fish?"

"Well…" stammered Jill, "…if you were born a human…"

"I repeat," he demanded, "do you think it is so terrible to be a fish?"

Jill trembled. She felt that the answer she gave was very important. For a moment she thought hard. Then, in a gentle voice she said: "I do not think it terrible to *be* a fish. But I think it terrible for a human to be *changed* into a fish, just as you, my lord, would think it terrible for a fish to be changed into a human."

She waited breathlessly to see the effect of her answer. Then she sighed with relief. Lord Salmon nodded. "That was well spoken," he muttered. But once again he glared at her. "In this court," he said, "our memories of the human race are not too happy. All we ask is that we should be allowed to go our own way, to live our lives in peace. But always there is that danger from above! You do not come down here to meet us face to face. But you send your hooks, your cruel baits, your wicked nets…"

"Not me!" cried Jill. "Not me!"

"Not you perhaps," he agreed, "but your kind. At this very moment, I have a daughter, my only daughter, who is missing."

All eyes in court were riveted on his Lordship as he made this statement.

"When a fish is missing, there is usually only one explanation. And *that*…" He did not finish the sentence. He merely cast his eyes up to the ceiling. Jill knew, all too well, what he meant.

There was silence, broken only by the ripple of the water against the rocks.

And then, from outside, there came a shrill scream.

"Help! Help!"

It was a tiny voice, but it went straight to Jill's heart.

Lord Salmon gave an agonised cry.

"It's her!" cried P. C. Gudgeon. "It's his daughter!"

"Save her! Save her!" Lord Salmon shot like a rocket through the arch, and in a swirl of bubbles the whole Court followed, the Rainbow-Trouts, P. C. Gudgeon and all the spectators. It was a scene of wild confusion, but as Jill emerged from the cave, into the current of the main stream, she saw one thing all too clearly, the figure of a tiny fish, writhing backwards and forwards, with a terrible hook in its mouth, and a long cord that tugged and tugged towards the surface. Leaping up and down, in a tragic, hopeless effort to save her, was Lord Salmon, with a swarm of sticklebacks in his wake.

Never had Jill thought so clearly or so quickly; her brain worked like lightning. "This is the witch's doing!" she told herself. "No one has ever fished for salmon in the Magic Stream. At the other end of that line she is standing, doing her evil work! She knows that if she wins, I am finished – the fishes will turn against me, and against all humans… and all chance of saving Jack, without their help, will have gone for ever. Well… it's me against the witch, and we'll see who wins!"

With a single powerful stroke she shot

up to the aid of the fish. "Leave it to me!" she gasped to Lord Salmon, as she stretched out her hands. And to the little fish she murmured: "Don't struggle...I am your friend!"

There was a moment's awful suspense. Panting, the tiny figure lay in her fingers. The cord was slack but she could see it tightening again. With one deft movement of her fingers she opened its mouth and gently drew out the hook, just as the cord was tugged fiercely away from her. With a feeble flick of its tail the tiny creature dived to safety. The cord, with its cruel hook, flashed away, empty. Jill had won!

She stared upwards, through the few inches of water that separated her from the world. There, scowling at her, like a face in a cracked mirror, she saw the evil features of Miss Smith, staring at the surface of the stream with baffled rage.

A few hours later, Jill was given the Freedom of the Stream.

Nothing was too good for her.

Lord Salmon, his heart almost bursting with gratitude, had issued orders that she was to be lodged in the finest cave that could be found, and a platoon of sticklebacks had bustled in and out, backwards and forwards, hanging the rocks with gaily-coloured weeds, and decorating the floor with bright pebbles. Mr and Mrs Frog, who were just as much at home above as below, had bitten off a big dock-leaf, collected a dozen excited glow-

worms, steered them in through the arch, and placed them proudly on a shelf above the water-level, so that the cave was almost as bright by night as by day.

"Anything... *anything* that I can do to make your stay with us a happy one, I will do," said Lord Salmon.

"There is only one thing I want," she replied gravely, "and that is to find my brother."

"I understand. We will search high and low. I will send out messengers who will swim up the stream into the mountains and down the stream till they reach the sea."

"If only we had some clue!" sighed Jill.

"Yes. It will not be easy, for we do not really know exactly what sort of fish we are looking for. He might even be one of the little minnows."

"Oh dear – do you think he might be as small as *that*?"

"We have no means of telling. But the messengers will bring us a clue...have no fear!"

# William Allingham
# THE FAIRIES

Up the airy mountain,
Down the rushy glen,
We daren't go a-hunting
For fear of little men;
Wee folk, good folk,
Trooping all together;
Green jacket, red cap,
And white owl's feather!

Down along the rocky shore
Some make their home,
They live on crispy pancakes
Of yellow tide-foam;
Some in the reeds
Of the black mountain-lake,
With frogs for their watch-dogs,
All night awake.

High on the hill-top
The old King sits;
He is now so old and grey
He's nigh lost his wits.
With a bridge of white mist
Columbkill he crosses,
On his stately journeys
From Slieveleague to Rosses;
Or going up with music
On cold, starry nights,
To sup with the Queen
Of the gay Northern Lights.

They stole little Bridget
For seven years long;
When she came down again
Her friends were all gone.
They took her lightly back,
Between the night and morrow,
They thought that she was fast asleep
But she was dead with sorrow.
They have kept her ever since
Deep within the lake,
On a bed of flag-leaves,
Watching till she wake.

By the craggy hill-side,
Through the mosses bare,
They have planted thorn-trees
For pleasure here and there.
Is any man so daring
As dig them up in spite,
He shall find their sharpest thorns
In his bed at night.

Up the airy mountain,
Down the rushy glen,
We daren't go a-hunting
For fear of little men;
Wee folk, good folk,
Trooping all together;
Green jacket, red cap,
And white owl's feather!

# Lewis Carroll
# ALICE'S ADVENTURES IN WONDERLAND

*Illustrated by Peter Weevers*

## A Mad Tea-Party

THERE WAS A TABLE set out under a tree in front of the house, and the March Hare and the Hatter were having tea at it: a Dormouse was sitting between them, fast asleep, and the other two were using it as a cushion, resting their elbows on it, and talking over its head. "Very uncomfortable for the Dormouse," thought Alice; "only, as it's asleep, I suppose it doesn't mind."

The table was a large one, but the three were all crowded together at one corner of it. "No room! No room!" they cried out when they saw Alice coming. "There's *plenty* of room!" said Alice indignantly, and she sat down in a large arm-chair at one end of the table.

"Have some wine," the March Hare said in an encouraging tone.

Alice looked all round the table, but there was nothing on it but tea. "I don't see any wine," she remarked.

"There isn't any," said the March Hare.

"Then it wasn't very civil of you to offer it," said Alice angrily.

"It wasn't very civil of you to sit down without being invited," said the March Hare.

"I didn't know it was *your* table," said Alice; "it's laid for a great many more than three."

"Your hair wants cutting," said the Hatter. He had been looking at Alice for some time with great curiosity, and this was his first speech.

"You should learn not to make personal remarks," Alice said with some severity: "it's very rude."

The Hatter opened his eyes very wide on hearing this; but all he *said* was, "Why is a raven like a writing-desk?"

"Come, we shall have some fun now!" thought Alice. "I'm glad they've begun asking riddles – I believe I can guess that," she added aloud.

"Do you mean that you think you can find out the answer to it?" said the March Hare.

"Exactly so," said Alice.

"Then you should say what you mean," the March Hare went on.

"I do," Alice hastily replied; "at least – at least I mean what I say – that's the same thing, you know."

"Not the same thing a bit!" said the Hatter. "Why, you might just as well say that 'I see what I eat' is the same thing as

pinched it on both sides at once.

The Dormouse slowly opened its eyes. "I wasn't asleep," it said in a hoarse, feeble voice, "I heard every word you fellows were saying."

"Tell us a story!" said the March Hare.

"Yes, please do!" pleaded Alice.

"And be quick about it," added the Hatter, "or you'll be asleep again before it's done."

"Once upon a time there were three little sisters," the Dormouse began in a great hurry; "and their names were Elsie, Lacie, and Tillie; and they lived at the bottom of a well – "

"What did they live on?" said Alice, who always took a great interest in questions of eating and drinking.

"They lived on treacle," said the Dormouse, after thinking a minute or two.

"They couldn't have done that, you know," Alice gently remarked. "They'd have been ill."

"So they were," said the Dormouse; "*very* ill."

Alice tried a little to fancy to herself what such an extraordinary way of living would be like, but it puzzled her too much: so she went on: "But why did they live at the bottom of a well?"

"Take some more tea," the March Hare said to Alice, very earnestly.

"I've had nothing yet," Alice replied in an offended tone, "so I can't take more."

"You mean you can't take *less*," said the Hatter; "it's very easy to take *more* than nothing."

"Nobody asked *your* opinion," said Alice.

"Who's making personal remarks now?" the Hatter asked triumphantly.

Alice did not quite know what to say to this: so she helped herself to some tea and bread-and-butter, and then turned to the Dormouse, and repeated her question. "Why did they live at the bottom of a well?"

The Dormouse again took a minute or two to think about it, and then said, "It was a treacle-well."

"There's no such thing!" Alice was beginning very angrily, but the Hatter and the March Hare went "Sh! Sh!" and the Dormouse sulkily remarked, "If you can't be civil, you'd better finish the story for yourself."

"No, please go on!" Alice said very humbly. "I won't interrupt you again. I dare say there may be *one*."

"One, indeed!" said the Dormouse indignantly. However, it consented to go on. "And so these three little sisters – they were learning to draw, you know – "

"What did they draw?" said Alice, quite forgetting her promise.

"Treacle," said the Dormouse, without considering at all, this time.

"I want a clean cup," interrupted the Hatter: "let's all move one place on."

He moved on as he spoke, and the Dormouse followed him: the March Hare moved into the Dormouse's place, and Alice rather unwillingly took the place of the March Hare. The Hatter was the only one who got any advantage from the change; and Alice was a good deal worse off than before, as the March Hare had just upset the milk jug into his plate.

Alice did not wish to offend the Dormouse again, so she began very cautiously: "But I don't understand. Where did they draw the treacle from?"

"You can draw water out of a water-well," said the Hatter; "so I should think you could draw treacle out of a treacle-well – eh, stupid?"

"But they were *in* the well," Alice said to the Dormouse, not choosing to notice this last remark.

"Of course they were," said the Dormouse: "well in."

This answer so confused poor Alice, that she let the Dormouse go on for some time without interrupting it.

"They were learning to draw," the Dormouse went on, yawning and rubbing its eyes, for it was getting very sleepy; "and they drew all manner of things – everything that begins with an M –"

"Why with an M?" said Alice.

"Why not?" said the March Hare.

Alice was silent.

The Dormouse had closed its eyes by this time, and was going off into a doze; but, on being pinched by the Hatter, it woke up again with a little shriek, and went on: " – that begins with an M, such as mouse-traps, and the moon, and memory, and muchness – you know you say things are 'much of a muchness' – did you ever see such a thing as a drawing of a muchness?"

"Really, now you ask me," said Alice, very much confused, "I don't think –"

"Then you shouldn't talk," said the Hatter.

This piece of rudeness was more than Alice could bear: she got up in great disgust, and walked off; the Dormouse fell asleep instantly, and neither of the others took the least notice of her going, though she looked back once or twice, half hoping that they would call after her: the last time she saw them, they were trying to put the

Dormouse into the teapot.

"At any rate I'll never go *there* again!" said Alice, as she picked her way through the wood. "It's the stupidest tea-party I ever was at in all my life!"

Just as she said this, she noticed that one of the trees had a door leading right into it. "That's very curious!" she thought. "But everything's curious today. I think I may as well go in at once." And in she went.

Once more she found herself in the long hall, and close to the little glass table. "Now, I'll manage better this time," she said to herself, and began by taking the little golden key, and unlocking the door that led into the garden. Then she set to work nibbling at the mushroom (she had kept a piece of it in her pocket) till she was about a foot high: then she walked down the little passage: and *then* – she found herself at last in the beautiful garden, among the bright flower-beds and the cool fountains.

# Lewis Carroll
# JABBERWOCKY

'TWAS brillig, and the slithy toves
 Did gyre and gimble in the wabe;
All mimsy were the borogoves,
 And the mome raths outgrabe.

"Beware the Jabberwock, my son!
 The jaws that bite, the claws that catch!
Beware the Jubjub bird, and shun
 The frumious Bandersnatch!"

He took his vorpal sword in hand:
 Long time the manxome foe he sought –
So rested he by the Tumtum tree,
 And stood awhile in thought.

And, as in uffish thought he stood,
 The Jabberwock, with eyes of flame,
Came whiffling through the tulgey wood,
 And burbled as it came!

One, two! One, two! And through and through
 The vorpal blade went snicker-snack!
He left it dead, and with its head
 He went galumphing back.

"And hast thou slain the Jabberwock!
 Come to my arms, my beamish boy!
O frabjous day! Callooh! Callay!"
 He chortled in his joy.

'Twas brillig, and the slithy toves
 Did gyre and gimble in the wabe;
All mimsy were the borogoves,
 And the mome raths outgrabe.

*Retold by Julius Lester*

# BRER RABBIT AND THE TAR BABY

*from* The Tales of Uncle Remus

*Illustrated by Jerry Pinkney*

EARLY ONE MORNING, even before Sister Moon had put on her negligee, Brer Fox was up and moving around. He had a glint in his eye, so you know he was up to no good.

He mixed up a big batch of tar and made it into the shape of a baby. By the time he finished, Brer Sun was yawning himself awake and peeping one eye over the topside of the earth.

Brer Fox took his Tar Baby down to the road, the very road Brer Rabbit walked along every morning. He sat the Tar Baby in the road, put a hat on it, and then hid in a ditch.

He had scarcely gotten comfortable (as

comfortable as one can get in a ditch), before Brer Rabbit came strutting along like he owned the world and was collecting rent from everybody in it.

Seeing the Tar Baby, Brer Rabbit tipped his hat. "Good morning! Nice day, ain't it? Of course, any day I wake up and find I'm still alive is a nice day far as I'm

concerned." He laughed at his joke, which he thought was pretty good. (Ain't too bad if I say so myself.)

Tar Baby don't say a word. Brer Fox stuck his head up out of the ditch, grinning.

"You deaf?" Brer Rabbit asked the Tar

Baby. "If you are, I can talk louder." He yelled, *"How you this morning? Nice day, ain't it?"*

Tar Baby still don't say nothing.

Brer Rabbit was getting kinna annoyed. "I don't know what's wrong with this young generation. Didn't your parents teach you no manners?"

Tar Baby don't say nothing.

"Well, I reckon I'll teach you some!" He hauls off and hits the Tar Baby. BIP! And his fist was stuck to the side of the Tar Baby's face.

"You let me go!" Brer Rabbit yelled. "Let me go or I'll really pop you one." He twisted and turned, but he couldn't get loose. "All right! I warned you!" And he smacked the Tar Baby on the other side of its head. BIP! His other fist was stuck.

Brer Rabbit was sho' 'nuf mad now. "You turn me loose or I'll make you wish you'd never been born." THUNK! He kicked the Tar Baby and his foot was caught. He was cussing and carrying on something terrible and kicked the Tar Baby with the other foot and THUNK! That foot was caught. "You let me go or I'll butt you with my head." He butted the

Tar Baby under the chin and THUNK! His head was stuck.

Brer Fox sauntered out of the ditch just as cool as the sweat on the side of a glass of ice tea. He looked at Brer Rabbit stuck to the Tar Baby and laughed until he was almost sick.

"Well, I got you now," Brer Fox said when he was able to catch his breath. "You floppy-eared, pom-pom-tailed good-for-nothing! I guess you know who's having rabbit for dinner this night!"

Brer Rabbit would've turned around and looked at him if he could've unstuck his head. Didn't matter. He heard the drool in Brer Fox's voice and knew he was in a world of trouble.

"You ain't gon' be going around through the community raising commotion any more, Brer Rabbit. And it's your own fault too. Didn't nobody tell you to be so friendly with the Tar Baby. You stuck yourself on that Tar Baby without so much as an invitation. There you are and there you'll be until I get my fire started and my barbecue sauce ready."

Brer Rabbit always got enough lip for anybody and everybody. He even told God

# C. S. Lewis
# THE LION, THE WITCH AND THE WARDROBE

*Illustrated by Pauline Baynes*

## Through the Wardrobe

*Peter, Susan, Edmund and Lucy have been
evacuated to a strange house in Wales. It is raining and so
the children decide to explore.*

IT WAS THE SORT OF HOUSE that you never seem to come to the end of, and it was full of unexpected places. The first few doors they tried led only into spare bedrooms, as everyone had expected that they would; but soon they came to a very long room full of pictures and there they found a suit of armour; and after that was a room all hung with green, with a harp in one corner; and then came three steps down and five steps up, and then a kind of little upstairs hall and a door that led out on to a balcony, and then a whole series of rooms that led into each other and were lined with books – most of them very old books and some bigger than a Bible in a church. And shortly after that they looked into a room that was quite empty except for one big wardrobe; the sort that has a looking-glass in the door. There was nothing else in the room at all except a dead blue-bottle on the window-sill.

"Nothing there!" said Peter, and they all trooped out again – all except Lucy. She stayed behind because she thought it would be worth while trying the door of the wardrobe, even though she felt almost sure that it would be locked. To her surprise it opened quite easily, and two moth-balls dropped out.

Looking into the inside, she saw several coats hanging up – mostly long fur coats. There was nothing Lucy liked so much as the smell and feel of fur. She immediately stepped into the wardrobe and got in among the coats and rubbed her face against them, leaving the door open, of course, because she knew that it is very foolish to shut oneself into any wardrobe. Soon she went further in and found that there was a second row of coats hanging up behind the first one. It was almost quite dark in there and she kept her arms stretched out in front of her so as not to bump her face into the back of the wardrobe. She took a step further in – then two or three steps – always expecting to feel woodwork against the tips of her fingers. But she could not feel it.

"This must be a simply enormous wardrobe!" thought Lucy, going still further in and pushing the soft folds of the coats aside to make room for her. Then she noticed that there was something crunching under her feet. "I wonder is that more moth-balls?" she thought, stooping down to feel it with her hand. But instead of feeling the hard, smooth wood of the floor

bury her nose in her apron which unfortunately only buried half of it, because it was a long nose and a short apron.

"This liquid," said the Professor, all of a tremble with excitement, "will bring to life any picture to which it is applied. Look at this."

He poured some of the sparkling liquid into a glass jar, drew some up in the syringe and squirted it over a picture of some apples on the cover of a book. Nothing happened, except that the picture got wet.

"Very good, Sir, I'm sure," said Mrs Flittersnoop in a muffled sort of voice from inside the apron. "And now I must be getting back to my cakes." She was out of the room and halfway to the kitchen before the Professor could stop her and drag her back.

"Wait, wait, wait, wait," he shouted excitedly. "It takes time. Look, look!" he pointed with a quivering finger at the picture.

"Oo-er," said his housekeeper. "It's going all lumpy like."

It certainly was. The apples began to swell up, the picture went all nobbly. Green smoke rose from the paper. The smell would have got worse only it couldn't. Then suddenly four lovely rosy apples rolled out of the picture on to the table, as real and solid as you please.

"Oh my!" exclaimed Mrs Flittersnoop.

"Try one," said the Professor, and together they munched the apples. And except for a rather papery flavour and a funny feeling they gave you as if you were

eating an apple in a dream that wasn't there at all but only seemed to be, the apples were certainly a success.

"It is rather a pity," said the Professor, spraying a picture of a box of chocolates to life, "that it costs more to make the liquid for doing this than it would cost to buy the things."

"You don't say!" said Mrs Flittersnoop, taking a handful of the chocolates and not bothering about her cakes any more, which had burned themselves into cinders in the meantime, only neither of them could smell them because of the other smell, and thinking the Professor could just spray a few cakes out of a book if he wanted them.

"Yes," said the Professor, hunting about among his books and papers, "and there are certain limitations to the power of the liquid. The things it brings to life go back as they were when the liquid dries off."

"Oo-er," said Mrs Flittersnoop, thinking of the apples and chocolates she had eaten. But the Professor was pulling out a book with a picture of a cat in it.

"Let me try this," he said, "I don't know yet whether it will work with animals or people."

He filled the syringe again while Mrs

Flittersnoop hid behind the door in case the cat was a scratchy sort of one, which it was quite likely to be, because most of the Professor's books were about wildish kinds of animals.

"Phiz-z-z-z-," went the spray. They waited, the paper bulged, the picture smoked, the smell didn't get worse, just as before. Then – "Meow!" – out jumped the cat.

But oh good gracious and heavens above, the next minute with a terrific whoosh of a zoom the whole room was full of an elephant!

"Amazing!" gasped the Professor, struggling out of the waste-paper basket where the elephant had knocked him. But Mrs Flittersnoop slammed the door and rushed screaming all the way to her sister Aggie's in Lower Pagwell without even stopping to wipe the flour off her nose.

The cat jumped out of the window and followed her, still meowing because the picture of it had showed it meowing and it didn't seem to be able to stop. But most definitely awkward of all, the elephant squeezed its big self through the french windows and followed her too.

"Heavens!" gasped the Professor, getting so worked up that his socks came down.

And he dashed after the elephant, dropping his glasses all over the place and holding his handkerchief hoping to be able to catch it and dry the wonderful liquid off it and make it go back into a picture, but not hoping so very much.

But while the Professor was chasing the elephant who was running after the cat who seemed to want to catch up with Mrs Flittersnoop, who definitely did want to get to her sister Aggie's, the most absolute things were going on in the Professor's room. Voices could have been heard if there had been anyone about to hear them. Rumblings and rustlings were occurring. Chatterings went up. People started talking round the place like goodness knows what.

When the elephant had come out of the picture so suddenly he'd upset the jar of wonderful liquid all over the Professor's photograph album. Good gracious, what a thing to do! Liquid that could make things come to life and all! And upset on a photograph album of all places!

When the Professor, who had given up the chase at Pagwell Gardens, came staggering back all out of breath the first thing he noticed was himself opening the door to himself.

"Good afternoon," said the Professor, not recognising himself.

"Don't take it for a moment, the sun's in my eyes," said the other one of him.

The Professor was just wondering what the answer to that was when two more of himself, one at sixteen and one at twenty-two, came out of the study, followed by three of Mrs Flittersnoop in different hats of her sister Aggie's, two of Colonel

liquid off photos, then will go back into album."

Round the house they dashed, brandishing blotters right and left. The little Professors were caught and blotted up quite easily, but Colonel Dedshott got away from himself three times, and the Mrs Flittersnoop in fancy dress kept dodging the Professor round the banisters.

Slap slap, bump bang, scuffle biff. "Don't take it yet, I've got the sun in my eyes. Hold it perfectly still…" "How will my uniform come out?" "Ploof woo woo muffn…" Round and round the house, up and down the stairs. The real Professor and Colonel caught each other eight times. The half policeman was hopping about like a canary shouting his half piece half at the top of his voice. Some of the Professors had got hold of blotting-paper and were joining in the chase. Then a window blew open and the draught from the open front door blew them all out of it and down the road, for they were beginning to get a bit light now that the effects of the liquid were wearing off.

"After them!" panted the Colonel, drawing his sword and falling over it.

Out they dashed and down the road. Clouds of Professors and Mrs Flittersnoops were all over the place. A real policeman stopped

and gaped at the half policeman, who shouted "Pass along p – " for the last time and then went zzzzzzzzp back into the photograph he had come from, with the Professor aged twenty.

"Hurray, hurray!" roared the Colonel, throwing his hat in the air and not bothering to catch it, when it landed on the real Professor's head. "Victory! The enemy is routed."

And so they were, for the sun had come out and quickly dried the wonderful liquid off the unreasonable crowd of extra sort of people and soon the road was strewn with photographs which the Colonel and the Professor carefully burned, making an awful smoke all over the place, but never mind.

Next day a note came up from Mrs Flittersnoop, written on the back of a picture of an elephant, to say that if the Professor would promise not to do it again she would come back.

"Well, well, well," he said. "All the liquid has been used up and I've forgotten the recipe so I shan't be able to do it again, thank goodness. But it was most instructive."

So back came Mrs Flittersnoop, and the Professor wrote a book about his wonderful liquid but nobody believed it.

## Roger McGough
# P. C. PLOD AT THE PILLAR BOX

It's snowing out
streets are thiefproof
A wind that blows
straight up yer nose
no messin
A night
not fit to be seen with a dog
out in

On the corner
P. C. Plod (brave as a mountain lion)
passes the time of night
with a pillar box
"What's 7 times 8 minus 56?"
he asked mathematically
The pillar box was silent for a moment
and then said
nothing
"Right first time,"
said the snowcapped cop
and slouched off towards Bethlehem
Avenue

# Clive King
# STIG OF THE DUMP

*Illustrated by Dick van der Maat and Edward Ardizzone*

## Barney's Fall

FAR BELOW was the bottom of the pit. The dump. Barney could see strange bits of wreckage among the moss and elder bushes and nettles. Was that the steering wheel of a ship? The tail of an aeroplane? At least there was a real bicycle. Barney felt sure he could make it go if only he could get at it. They didn't let him have a bicycle.

Barney wished he was at the bottom of the pit.

And the ground gave way.

Barney felt his head going down and his feet going up. There was a rattle of falling earth beneath him. Then he was falling, still clutching the clump of grass that was falling with him.

This is what it's like when the ground gives way, thought Barney. Then he seemed to turn a complete somersault in the air, bumped into a ledge of chalk half-way down, crashed through some creepers and ivy and branches, and landed on a bank of moss.

His thoughts did those funny things they do when you bump your head and you suddenly find yourself thinking about what you had for dinner last Tuesday, all mixed up with seven times six. Barney lay with his eyes shut, waiting for his thoughts to stop being mixed up. Then he opened them.

He was lying in a kind of shelter. Looking up he could see a roof, or part of a roof, made of elder branches, a very rotten old carpet, and rusty old sheets of iron. There was a big hole, through which he must have fallen. He could see the white walls of the cliff, the trees and creepers at the top, and the sky with clouds passing over it.

Barney decided he wasn't dead. He didn't even seem to be very much hurt. He turned his head and looked around him. It was dark in this den after looking at the white chalk, and he couldn't see what sort of a place it was. It seemed to be partly a cave dug into the chalk, partly a shelter built out over the mouth of the cave.

There was a cool, damp smell. Woodlice and earwigs dropped from the roof where he had broken through it.

But what had happened to his legs? He couldn't sit up when he tried to. His legs wouldn't move. Perhaps I've broken them, Barney thought. What shall I do then? He looked at his legs to see if they were all right, and found they were all tangled up with creeper from the face of the cliff. Who tied me up? thought Barney. He kicked his legs to try to get them free, but it was no use, there were yards of creeper trailing down from the cliff. I suppose I got tangled up when I fell, he thought.

# Judy Blume
# SUPERFUDGE

*Illustrated by Susan Hellard*

## Small Ones Are Sweeter

*Peter has a lot to contend with: moving to*
*Princeton; Fudge, his incorrigible younger brother;*
*and Tootsie, his new baby sister.*

OUR HOUSE, that is, Millie and George's house, is so old that the bathtub stands off the floor, on legs. And the hot and cold water don't come out of the same tap, so when you're washing your hands, you either freeze them or burn them. Mom says you're supposed to put the plug in and mix the water in the basin. But that's a lot of trouble. At least we don't have chamber pots. The toilets actually flush.

Outside, the house is painted yellow and the shutters are white. The windows and doorways are slightly crooked. Dad says that's part of the charm of the house. I know better than to tell him what I think. Inside, the floors are wooden and they creak when you walk across them.

Downstairs, there is a living-room with a piano, a dining-room with a table so big you have to shout to make yourself heard, a kitchen with pots and pans hanging all over the place, and a library, where the walls are lined with books, arranged according to colour. There's a brown leather section, a green leather section, a red leather section and a tan leather section. Upstairs there are four bedrooms, all in row. And everywhere you look there are fire-places. There's one in every bedroom, there's one in the living-room, another in the dining-room and still another in the library. There aren't any in the bathrooms or the kitchen.

My mother and father call the house "fantastic", "fabulous", "unbelievable". I hear them talking to their friends on the phone, and those are the dumb words they use to describe this place.

Our neighbourhood is a lot like our house. Old. Every house on the block is a lot like this one, with a small front yard and a big back one. In our backyard we have George's rose garden and Millie's herb and vegetable garden. The first day we were there, Dad bought a stack of books with titles like *Know Your Roses, Know Your Herbs, Organic Vegetables and You,* and my favourite, *The Agony of Beetles in Your Garden.*

"You didn't have to worry about beetles in New York, did you, Dad?" I said at dinner.

"That's enough Peter," Dad said to me.

"That's enough, Pee-tah," Fudge repeated.

"Cut that out!" I told him.

"Cut that out!" he said back to me.

Fudge's new game is repeating everything I say. He's really driving me crazy this time.

"Pass the salt, please," I said to Mom.

"Pass the salt, please," he said, laughing.

I pushed back my chair. "I can't take it any more. I mean it. Do something, will you?" I begged my parents.

But he was already at it. "I can't take it any more ... Do something, will you ..." And he laughed so hard he choked.

"That's right," Mom said. "I really don't."

"Why not?" Fudge asked.

"It's nothing I can explain." Mom went back to weeding the garden. Fudge followed her.

"Is your family always like that?" Alex asked.

"You haven't seen anything yet!" I told him.

On our way to Mrs Muldour's house, I thought I remembered reading that worms regenerate when you cut them in half. But I wasn't sure. So I asked Alex if he'd ever tried that.

"Sure," Alex said, "plenty of times."

"And what happens?"

"Nothing. You get two little worms."

"Right...and if Mrs Muldour pays you five cents a worm..."

A slow smile spread across Alex's face. "I see what you mean," he said. "How come I never thought of that?"

I didn't answer.

We dumped our worms on the sidewalk and cut all but one in half. That one was big enough to cut into thirds. So now, instead of sixteen worms, we had thirty-three.

Mrs Muldour lived in an old house that was painted grey, with blue shutters. Alex rang her bell. A big, round woman with hair the colour of her house and glasses halfway down her nose came to the door. She wore sneakers and blue jeans and a red and white shirt.

"Well, hello Alex...long time no see."

"Hi, Mrs Muldour," Alex said. "I've got a new partner now."

She looked at me over the top of her glasses.

"I'm Peter Hatcher. We just moved in down the street." She kept looking at me, so I kept talking. "In the Wentmans' house ...Millie and George Wentman...they're friends of my mother and father...We're just here for the year...to see how we like being away from the city..."

"Are you finished?" she asked.

"Yes."

"Good. Then let's get down to business."

"We've got thirty-three for you today, Mrs Muldour," Alex said. "Real beauties."

"Thirty-three..." She held up the jar and studied them. "They look awfully small."

"Small ones are sweeter," I said.

She gave me a strange look this time.

So I quickly added, "They'll get bigger later in the summer."

"Really? I should think they'd be at their best now."

"Oh no," I told her. "They'll be getting fatter and longer by August, and by September they'll be in their prime."

"Is that a fact?" she asked.

"Uh huh," I said, praying that she wouldn't guess I didn't know what I was talking about.

"Well, live and learn," Mrs Muldour said. She went inside and came back with her wallet. "You know," she told us, "I could go down to the filling station and buy a container of worms, but I think freshly dug ones are so much better." She opened her wallet. "Let's see … five cents times thirty-three worms … that's one dollar and fifty cents." She handed the money to Alex.

"Excuse me, Mrs Muldour," Alex said, "but it's one, sixty-five."

Mrs Muldour laughed. "Can't fool you, can I, Alex?"

"No, Mrs Muldour, not when it comes to maths. Would you like more worms next week?"

"Of course. As many as you can bring me. You can't have too many worms, you know."

Alex gave me a look, and we thanked Mrs Muldour and walked away. Once we were out of earshot, Alex said, "Small ones are sweeter…" and he gave me an elbow in the ribs.

"Worm soup tonight," I told him. And we exploded, laughing.

After supper Mom got Tootsie into her sling, and the five of us went off to Baskin-Robbins. When we got there, Fudge walked up to the girl behind the counter and said, "Worm ice cream."

"Beg pardon?" the girl said.

"Worm ice cream," he repeated.

"We don't have…"

"For flavour of the month," Fudge told her. "Worm ice cream."

"Are you saying…" she began.

"Yes, he is," I said. "Worm … that's w-o-r-m…"

"I can spell," the girl said, annoyed. "But I really don't think that people would go for that flavour."

"Some people would… Right, Pee-tah?" Fudge asked.

"Sure," I said. "Some people right in this town might think it's terrific."

"Look, kids … we're very busy tonight, so cut out the wise guy stuff and tell me what you want… Okay?"

"I'll have a chocolate-chip-mint sundae with the works," I told her.

"And I'll have a fudge ripple cone," Fudge said. "Just like my name."

"Oh, your name is Cone?" she asked.

"No."

"Ripple?"

"No."

"I suppose you're going to tell me it's Fudge… Right?"

"That's right," Fudge said, putting his chin on the counter.

"Cute kid," she mumbled to herself. "Real cute."

# PART FOUR

# Mary Norton
# THE BORROWERS

*Illustrated by Diana Stanley*

## Arrietty Goes Borrowing

*Under the grandfather clock is the hidden entrance to the home of the*
*Borrowers – Pod, Homily and Arrietty – a tiny family who live by "borrowing" from the humans*
*"upstairs". To Pod's horror, he is seen by a human boy while on a borrowing expedition,*
*although he keeps this a secret from his daughter, Arrietty. Reluctantly,*
*he agrees to teach her how to borrow.*

For the next three weeks Arrietty was especially "good": she helped her mother tidy the store-rooms; she swept and watered the passages and trod them down; she sorted and graded the beads (which they used as buttons) into the screw tops of aspirin bottles; she cut old kid gloves into squares for Pod's shoemaking; she filed fish-bone needles to a bee-sting sharpness; she hung up the washing to dry by the grating so that it blew in the soft air; and at last the day came – that dreadful, wonderful, never-to-be-forgotten day – when Homily, scrubbing the kitchen table, straightened her back and called "Pod!"

He came in from his workroom, last in hand.

"Look at this brush!" cried Homily. It was a fibre brush with a plaited, fibre back.

"Aye," said Pod, "worn down."

"Gets me knuckles now," said Homily, "every time I scrub."

Pod looked worried. Since he had been "seen", they had stuck to kitchen borrowing, the bare essentials of fuel and food. There was an old mouse-hole under the kitchen stove upstairs which, at night when the fire was out or very low, Pod could use as a chute to save carrying. Since the window-curtain incident they had pushed a matchbox chest of drawers below the mouse-hole, and had stood a wooden chest on the chest of drawers; and Pod, with much help and shoving from Homily, had learned to squeeze up the chute instead of down. In this way he need not venture into the great hall and passages, he could just nip out, from under the vast black stove in the kitchen, for a clove or a carrot or a tasty piece of ham. But it was not a satisfactory arrangement: even when the fire was out, often there was hot ash and cinders under the stove and once, as he emerged, a great brush came at him wielded by Mrs Driver; and he slithered back, on top of Homily, singed, shaken, and coughing dust. Another time, for some reason, the fire had been in full blaze and Pod had arrived suddenly beneath a glowing inferno, dropping white-hot coals. But usually, at night, the fire was out, and Pod could pick his way through the cinders into the kitchen proper.

"Mrs Driver's out," Homily went on. "It's her day off. And She" – they always spoke of Aunt

"As for that," exclaimed Homily, "a boy's even better. You can hear a boy a mile off. Well," she went on after a moment, "please yourself. But it's not like you to talk of risks …"

Pod sighed. "All right," he said and turned away to fetch his borrowing-bag.

"Take the child," called Homily after him.

Pod turned. "Now, Homily," he began in an alarmed voice.

"Why not?" asked Homily sharply. "It's just the day. You aren't going no farther than the front door. If you're nervous you can leave her by the clock, ready to nip underneath and down the hole. Let her just *see* at any rate. Arrietty!"

As Arrietty came running in Pod tried again. "Now listen, Homily – " he protested.

Homily ignored him. "Arrietty," she said brightly, "would you like to go along with your father and borrow me some brush fibre from the door-mat in the hall?"

Arrietty gave a little skip. "Oh," she cried, "could I?"

"Well, take your apron off," said Homily, "and change your boots. You want light shoes for borrowing – better wear the red kid." And then as Arrietty spun away Homily turned to Pod: "She'll be all right," she said, "you'll see."

As she followed her father down the passage Arrietty's heart began to beat faster. Now the moment had come at last she found it almost too much to bear. She felt light and trembly, and hollow with excitement.

They had three borrowing-bags between the two of them ("In case," Pod had explained, "we pick up something. A bad borrower loses many a chance for lack of an extra bag"), and Pod laid these down to open the first gate, which was latched by a safety-pin. It was a big pin, too strongly sprung for little hands to

Sophy as "She" – "is safe enough in bed."

"It's not them that worries me," said Pod.

"Why," exclaimed Homily sharply, "the boy's not still here?"

"I don't know," said Pod; "there's always a risk," he added.

"And there always will be," retorted Homily, "like when you was in the coal-cellar and the coal-cart came."

"But the other two," said Pod, "Mrs Driver and Her, I always know where they are, like."

from the top of the step. "That's all right," he said after a moment's stare, "but never climb down anything that isn't fixed like. Supposing one of them came along and moved the shoe-scraper – where would you be then? How would you get up again?"

"It's heavy to move," said Arrietty.

"Maybe," said Pod, "but it's movable. See what I mean? There's rules, my lass, and you got to learn."

"This path," Arrietty said, "goes round the house. And the bank does too."

"Well," said Pod, "what of it?"

Arrietty rubbed one red kid shoe on a rounded stone.

"It's my grating," she explained. "I was thinking that my grating must be just round the corner. My grating looks out on to this bank."

"Your grating!" exclaimed Pod. "Since when has it been your grating?"

"I was thinking," Arrietty went on. "Suppose I just went round the corner and called through the grating to mother?"

"No," said Pod, "we're not going to have none of that. Not going round corners."

"Then," went on Arrietty, "she'd see I was all right like."

"Well," said Pod, and then he half smiled, "go quickly then and call. I'll watch for you here. Not loud mind!"

Arrietty ran. The stones in the path were firmly bedded and her light, soft shoes hardly seemed to touch them. How glorious it was to run – you could never run under the floor: you walked, you stooped, you crawled – but you never ran. Arrietty nearly ran past the grating. She saw it just in time after she turned the corner. Yes, there it was quite close to the ground, embedded deeply in the old wall of the house; there was moss below it in a spreading, greenish stain.

Arrietty ran up to it. "Mother!" she called, her nose against the iron grille. "Mother!" She waited quietly and, after a moment, she called again.

At the third call Homily came. Her hair was coming down and she carried, as though it were heavy, the screw lid of a pickle jar, filled with soapy water. "Oh," she said in an annoyed voice, "you didn't half give me a turn! What do you think you're up to? Where's your father?"

Arrietty jerked her head sideways. "Just there – by the front door!" She was so full of happiness that, out of Homily's sight, her toes danced on the green moss. Here she was on the other side of the grating – here she was at last, on the outside – looking in!

"Yes," said Homily, "they open that door like that – the first day of spring. Well," she went on briskly, "you run back to your father. And tell him, if the morning-room door happens to be open that I wouldn't say no to a bit of red blotting-paper. Mind out of my way now – while I throw the water!"

"That's what grows the moss," thought Arrietty as she sped back to her father, "all the water we empty through the grating..."

Pod looked relieved when he saw her but frowned at the message. "How's she expect me to climb that desk without me pin? Blotting-paper's a curtain-and-chair job and she should know it. Come on now! Up with you!"

"Let me stay down," pleaded Arrietty, "just a bit longer. Just till you finish. They're all out. Except Her. Mother said so."

"She'd say anything," grumbled Pod, "when she wants something quick. How does she know She won't take it into Her head to get out of that bed of Hers and come downstairs with a stick? How does she know Mrs Driver ain't stayed at home today – with a headache? How does she know that boy ain't still here?"

"What boy?" asked Arrietty.

Pod looked embarrassed. "What boy?" he repeated vaguely and then went on: "Or maybe Crampfurl – "

"Crampfurl isn't a boy," said Arrietty.

"No he isn't," said Pod, "not in a manner of speaking. No," he went on as though thinking this out, "no, you wouldn't call Crampfurl a boy. Not, as you might say, a boy – exactly. Well," he said, beginning to move away, "stay down a bit if you like. But stay close!"

Arrietty watched him move away from the step and then she looked about her. Oh, glory! Oh, joy! Oh, freedom! The sunlight, the grasses, the soft, moving air and halfway up the bank, where it curved round the corner, a flowering cherry-tree! Below it on the path lay a stain of pinkish petals and, at the tree's foot, pale as butter, a nest of primroses.

Arrietty threw a cautious glance towards the front doorstep and then, light and dancey, in her soft red shoes, she ran towards the petals. They were curved like shells and rocked as she touched them. She gathered several up and laid them one inside the other...up and up ...like a card castle. And then she spilled them. Pod came again to the top of the step and looked along the path. "Don't you go far," he said after a moment. Seeing his lips move, she smiled back at him: she was too far already to hear the words.

# Colin Dann

# BATTLE FOR THE PARK

## Dash Tests her Speed

*Illustrated by Frances Broomfield*

*The animals of Farthing Wood were different from other creatures.*
*They had sworn to help each other and it is this spirit of co-operation which*
*finally brought them to the safety of White Deer Park – a nature reserve. However,*
*even here, there are dangers. As their numbers increase, the animals notice that*
*their friends seem to be disappearing. Who is responsible?*

THE HARE HADN'T TRAVELLED FAR into the Park when she noticed a small group of men in her path. Something about the attitude of these humans alarmed her. She veered and doubled back, then set off again on a different route. Normally she would have avoided them altogether but this time she felt compelled to return, approaching the men from behind. She was curious to discover why they were strung out at intervals in a line as though intent on barring the progress of any creature in the vicinity. She was very cautious. She hid herself behind a clump of purple honesty. She sniffed the air. She could detect the smell of other animals, although she could see none. She could hear animal noises – muffled but distinctly nervous and frightened cries. Where were these creatures? She looked about her. A motor vehicle belonging to the men stood at some distance, parked on a flat piece of ground. Dash's huge ears picked up the sounds from that quarter. She flicked her

ears anxiously. The animals were inside the van! What was happening? She dared not move but she could see the van was open at the back. Inside there was an assortment of containers – boxes, crates and the like, with wire-mesh sides. From where she sat, quivering with agitation, these containers looked to Dash to be harmless examples of the kind of objects that humans always seemed to carry around with them. She didn't understand what they were. But she did understand the animal cries – cries of fear and helplessness. Then she noticed a little ripple of movement inside one of the boxes – just a flash, but unmistakable. Then in another…and another …and she knew then beyond any doubt that there were animals trapped inside them. Trapped by these very humans who were now poised ready to catch others as they ran across their path.

Dash backed away and turned to make her escape. But before she could do so she saw

another creature captured. And she also saw the cunning of the humans at work. She hadn't noticed – just as none of the captured animals had noticed – that in front of the line of men was a net, camouflaged and coloured to confuse unsuspecting wildlife, and half obscured by shrubs and bushes. Now other humans hidden elsewhere began to shout and make a noise. An animal was driven from cover – this time a rabbit. Frightened and panicking, it blundered unwittingly into the folds of the net, entangling itself instantly. Before it could get free one of the men pounced and held it fast. Another came with a sack, into which the animal was stowed before being transferred to one of the containers inside the van. Dash saw a second rabbit taken and then a smaller animal, which could have been a squirrel but whose capture was so swift it was impossible for her to be sure of its identity.

She had seen enough. She was horrified by the scene. How many poor beasts had lost their liberty this way? And were there bands of humans all over the Park doing the same thing? The loss of Plucky could at last, perhaps, be explained. Groups of men had been around the Reserve for a long time. The group she had witnessed was operating in the daytime, but there could equally well be others working by night, when those animals with nocturnal habits could be rounded up: animals like badgers, hedgehogs, stoats, weasels…and foxes. Dash pelted full speed across the Park to the Farthing Wood animals' corner. She had to warn them to beware and now she feared to discover what other losses had taken place in her absence. Her mind was in a whirl. Animals had always been safe from human interference in White Deer Park. What was going on? How could this be happening under the nose of the Warden? *Their* Warden, the animals'

Warden, whom all creatures trusted? How could these events occur without his knowledge? Was he somehow involved in them?

Dash burst into Fox and Badger's little wood. It was broad daylight so none of the foxes was about. Badger snored comfortably in his set, having dined richly on earthworms and beetle grubs. Dash heard the reverberations with frustration. Was there no one around she could tell her news to? She thought about Plucky – removed from the Park, then taken to a strange place…and for what? She dared not think about that. She shuddered. Who knew what had happened to him by now? Oh, it was unbearable to think she would never see him and frolic with him again. She needed to unburden herself. She began to call, in the first place for Vixen.

After a while Vixen appeared at her earth's entrance, blinking sleepily. "What – what is it? Who called me?"

"I did," Dash said. "Vixen, I have to – "

"It's you!" Vixen cried. "We'd given you up. Where have you been? We thought you were lost, like the others."

Dash gasped. Were there more gone? "The – others?"

"Plucky and Weasel."

"Is my father – "

"He's safe. So far. Now tell me, Dash, what you've found out."

The young hare panted out all she knew. She explained hurriedly about her stay on the open downland and what she had almost stumbled into on her return. "It's the men, Vixen! The men are taking the animals!"

Vixen was shocked. She didn't understand how such a situation could have arisen in a protected nature reserve. "I'll speak to Fox," she whispered.

Fox's sleep was interrupted. He emerged promptly from the den and gave himself a good shake. "Right," he said. "Tell me everything, Dash. Vixen's confused."

Dash went over her story again, describing as clearly as she could what she had seen.

"The animals are being *trapped*?" Fox barked. "But this can't be so. This is a wildlife sanctuary." He racked his brains. "There's a reason for this, there's got to be." He turned to Vixen. "Do you think the animals are being removed for their own safety?"

"How can anywhere be safer than here?" she questioned. "Outside the Reserve is all hostile country."

"The thought has occurred to me," said Fox in a low voice, "that there could be some danger from the rats. Supposing they are infecting other animals in some way, the Warden would need to take steps on our behalf."

"He'd be more likely to get rid of the rats," was Vixen's opinion. She sounded very sure on the point.

"I dare say you're right," Fox allowed. "Then what can it be?"

Dash knew nothing about rats. She begged the foxes to explain to her.

"Brown rats are infiltrating the Park," Fox informed her. "In dribs and drabs so far, but their numbers are increasing. We've been trying to keep them in check."

Dash suddenly recalled Vixen's mention of Weasel. "Has poor Weasel disappeared?"

"Yes, he's gone," said Fox. He looked hard at Dash, as if all at once the implication had hit him. Weasel captured by humans! He couldn't go along with this – he, Fox, the leader of the Farthing Wood community! "Tell me where you saw the group of men," he snapped urgently.

Dash jumped. She was startled. "It was – it was – as I came past the deer pasture," she explained. "The men were standing in a line by the rough grass. There were no deer about. Perhaps they've gone too?"

"No. I don't think so," Fox said. "They

# Noel Streatfeild
# BALLET SHOES

*Illustrated by Susie Jenkin-Pearce*

## Posy Learns to Dance

*Adopted as babies by Great Uncle Matthew, Pauline, Petrova
and Posy Fossil are determined to make a name for themselves
– and to help their uncle and their cousin Sylvia.*

THE FOSSILS BECAME some of the busiest children in London. They got up at half past seven and had breakfast at eight. After breakfast they did exercises with Theo for half an hour. At nine they began lessons. Posy did two hours' reading, writing, and kindergarten work with Sylvia, and Pauline and Petrova did three hours with Doctor Jakes and Doctor Smith. They were very interesting lessons, but terribly hard work; for if Doctor Smith was teaching Pauline, Doctor Jakes taught Petrova, and the other way on, and as both doctors had spent their lives coaching people for terribly stiff examinations – though of course they taught quite easy things to the children – they never got the idea out of their minds that a stiff examination was a thing everybody had to pass some day. There was a little break of ten minutes in the middle of the morning when milk and biscuits were brought in; but after a day or two they were never eaten or drunk. Both doctors had lovely ideas about the sort of things to have in the middle of lessons – a meal they called a beaver. They took turns to get it ready. Sometimes it was chocolate with cream on it, and sometimes Doctor Jakes' ginger drink, and once it was ice-cream soda; and the things to eat were never the same: queer biscuits, little ones from Japan with delicate

flowers painted on them in sugar, cakes from Vienna, and specialities of different kinds from all over England. They had their beavers sitting round the fire in either of the doctors' rooms, and they had discussions which were nothing to do with lessons. At twelve o'clock they went for a walk with Nana or Sylvia. They liked it best when Sylvia took them. She had better ideas about walks; she thought the Park the place to go to, and thought it a good idea to take hoops and things to play with. Nana liked a nice clean walk up as far as the Victoria and Albert and back. On wet days Sylvia thought it a good plan to stay in and make toffee or be read out loud to. Nana thought nicely brought-up children ought to be out of the house between twelve and one, even on a wet day, and she took them to see the dolls' houses in the Victoria and Albert. The children liked the dolls' houses; but there are a lot of wet days in the winter, and they saw them a good deal. Pauline and Petrova had lunch with Sylvia, Posy had hers with Nana. After lunch they all had to take a book on their beds for half an hour. In the afternoons there was another walk, this one always with Nana. It lasted an hour, and as they had usually walked to the Victoria and Albert in the morning, they did not have to go there again, but took turns to choose where they went.

# Rudyard Kipling
# THE JUNGLE BOOK
### Illustrated by Stuart Tresilian
## Mowgli Makes a Promise

*This is the story of how the boy Mowgli was brought up
in the jungle. When Mowgli was a baby, he was saved from the tiger, Shere Khan,
by a pair of wolves, who took him to their Pack Council. The price of acceptance
was the good word of Baloo, the sleepy old brown bear, and a bull killed
by Bagheera, the black panther.*

NOW YOU MUST BE CONTENT to skip ten or eleven whole years, and only guess at all the wonderful life that Mowgli led among the wolves, because if it were written out it would fill ever so many books. He grew up with the cubs, though they, of course, were grown wolves almost before he was a child, and Father Wolf taught him his business, and the meaning of things in the Jungle, till every rustle in the grass, every breath of the warm night air, every note of the owls above his head, every scratch of a bat's claws as it roosted for a while in a tree, and every splash of every little fish jumping in a pool, meant just as much to him as the work of his office means to a business man. When he was not learning, he sat out in the sun and slept, and ate and went to sleep again; when he felt dirty or hot he swam in the forest pools; and when he wanted honey (Baloo told him that honey and nuts were just as pleasant to eat as raw meat) he climbed up for it, and that Bagheera showed him how to do. Bagheera would lie out on a branch and call, "Come along, Little Brother," and at first Mowgli would cling like the sloth, but afterward he would fling himself through the branches almost as boldly as the grey ape. He took his place at the Council Rock, too, when the Pack met, and there he discovered that if he stared hard at any wolf, the wolf would be forced to drop his eyes, and so he used to stare for fun. At other times he would pick the long thorns out of the pads of his friends, for wolves suffer terribly from thorns and burs in their coats. He would go down the hillside into the cultivated lands by night, and look very curiously at the villagers in their huts, but he had a mistrust of men because Bagheera showed him a square box with a drop-gate so cunningly hidden in the Jungle that he nearly walked into it, and told him that it was a trap. He loved better than anything else to go with Bagheera into the dark warm heart of the forest, to sleep all through the drowsy day, and at night to see how Bagheera did his killing. Bagheera killed right and left as he felt hungry, and so did Mowgli – with one exception. As soon as he was old enough to understand things, Bagheera told him that he must never touch cattle because he had been

bought into the Pack at the price of a bull's life. "All the Jungle is thine," said Bagheera, "and thou canst kill everything that thou art strong enough to kill; but for the sake of the bull that bought thee thou must never kill or eat any cattle, young or old. That is the Law of the Jungle." Mowgli obeyed faithfully.

And he grew and grew strong as a boy must grow who does not know that he is learning any lessons, and who has nothing in the world to think of except things to eat.

Mother Wolf told him once or twice that Shere Khan was not a creature to be trusted, and that some day he must kill Shere Khan; but though a young wolf would have remembered that advice every hour, Mowgli forgot it because he was only a boy – though he would have called himself a wolf if he had been able to speak in any human tongue.

Shere Khan was always crossing his path in the Jungle, for as Akela grew older and feebler the lame tiger had come to be great friends with the younger wolves of the Pack, who followed him for scraps, a thing that Akela would never have allowed if he had dared to push his authority to the proper bounds. Then Shere Khan would flatter them and wonder that such fine young hunters were content to be led by a dying wolf and a man's cub. "They tell me," Shere Khan would say, "that at Council ye dare not look him between the eyes"; and the young wolves would growl and bristle.

Bagheera, who had eyes and ears everywhere, knew something of this, and once or twice he told Mowgli in so many words that Shere Khan would kill him some day; and Mowgli would laugh and answer: "I have the Pack and I have thee; and Baloo, though he is so lazy, might strike a blow or two for my sake. Why should I be afraid?"

It was one very warm day that a new notion came to Bagheera – born of something that he had heard. Perhaps Ikki the Porcupine had told him; but he said to Mowgli when they were deep in the Jungle, as the boy lay with his head on Bagheera's beautiful black skin: "Little Brother, how often have I told thee that Shere Khan is thy enemy?"

"As many times as there are nuts on that palm," said Mowgli, who, naturally, could not count. "What of it? I am sleepy, Bagheera, and Shere Khan is all long tail and loud talk – like Mao, the Peacock."

"But this is no time for sleeping. Baloo knows it; I know it; the Pack know it; and even the foolish, foolish deer know. Tabaqui (the Jackal) has told thee, too."

"Ho! ho!" said Mowgli. "Tabaqui came to me not long ago with some rude talk that I was a naked man's cub and not fit to dig pig-nuts; but I caught Tabaqui by the tail and swung him twice against a palm-tree to teach him better manners."

"That was foolishness; for though Tabaqui is a mischief-maker, he would have told thee of something that concerned thee closely. Open those eyes, Little Brother. Shere Khan dare not kill thee in the Jungle; but remember, Akela is very old, and soon the day comes when he cannot kill his buck, and then he will be leader no more. Many of the wolves that looked thee over when thou wast brought to the Council first are old too, and the young wolves believe, as Shere Khan has taught them, that a man-cub has no place with the Pack. In a little time thou wilt be a man."

"And what is a man that he should not run with his brothers?" said Mowgli. "I was born in the Jungle. I have obeyed the Law of the Jungle, and there is no wolf of ours from whose paws I have not pulled a thorn. Surely they are my brothers!"

Bagheera stretched himself at full length, and half shut his eyes. "Little Brother," said he, "feel under my jaw."

Mowgli put up his strong brown hand, and just under Bagheera's silky chin, where the giant rolling muscles were all hid by the glossy hair, he came upon a little bald spot.

"There is no one in the Jungle that knows that I, Bagheera, carry that mark – the mark of the collar; and yet, Little Brother, I was born among men, and it was among men that my mother died - in the cages of the King's Palace at Oodeypore. It was because of this that I paid the price for thee at the Council when thou wast a little naked cub. Yes, I too was born among men. I had never seen the Jungle. They fed me behind bars from an iron pan till one night I felt that I was Bagheera – the Panther – and no man's plaything, and I broke the silly lock with one blow of my paw and came away; and because I had learned the ways of men, I became more terrible in the Jungle than Shere Khan. Is it not so?"

"Yes," said Mowgli; "all the Jungle fear Bagheera – all except Mowgli."

"Oh, *thou* art a man's cub," said the Black Panther, very tenderly; "and even as I returned to my Jungle, so thou must go back to men at last – to the men who are thy brothers – if thou art not killed in the Council."

"But why – but why should any wish to kill me?" said Mowgli.

"Look at me," said Bagheera; and Mowgli looked at him steadily between the eyes. The big panther turned his head away in half a minute.

"*That* is why," he said, shifting his paw on the leaves. "Not even I can look thee between the eyes, and I was born among men, and I love thee, Little Brother. The others they hate thee because their eyes cannot meet thine – because thou art wise – because thou hast pulled out thorns from their feet – because thou art a man."

from the kill, and in all my time not one has been trapped or maimed. Now I have missed my kill. Ye know how that plot was made. Ye know how ye brought me up to an untried buck to make my weakness known. It was cleverly done. Your right is to kill me here on the Council Rock now. Therefore, I ask, who comes to make an end of the Lone Wolf? For it is my right, by the Law of the Jungle, that ye come one by one."

against us?" clamoured Shere Khan. "No; give him to me. He is a man, and none of us can look him between the eyes."

Akela lifted his head again, and said: "He has eaten our food. He has slept with us. He has driven game for us. He has broken no

There was a long hush, for no single wolf cared to fight Akela to the death. Then Shere Khan roared: "Bah! what have we to do with this toothless fool! He is doomed to die! It is the man-cub who has lived too long. Free People, he was my meat from the first. Give him to me. I am weary of this man-wolf folly. He has troubled the Jungle for ten seasons. Give me the man-cub, or I will hunt here always, and not give you one bone. He is a man, a man's child, and from the marrow of my bones I hate him!"

Then more than half the Pack yelled: "A man! a man! What has a man to do with us? Let him go to his own place."

"And turn all the people of the villages

word of the Law of the Jungle."

"Also, I paid for him with a bull when he was accepted. The worth of a bull is little, but Bagheera's honour is something that he will perhaps fight for," said Bagheera, in his gentlest voice.

"A bull paid ten years ago!" the Pack snarled. "What do we care for bones ten years old?"

"Or for a pledge?" said Bagheera, his white teeth bared under his lip. "Well are ye called the Free People!"

"No man's cub can run with the people of the Jungle," howled Shere Khan. "Give him to me!"

"He is our brother in all but blood," Akela

went on; "and ye would kill him here! In truth, I have lived too long. Some of ye are eaters of cattle, and of others I have heard that, under Shere Khan's teaching, ye go by dark night and snatch children from the villager's doorstep. Therefore I know ye to be cowards, and it is to cowards I speak. It is certain that I must die, and my life is of no worth, or I would offer that in the man-cub's place. But for the sake of the Honour of the Pack — a little matter that by being without a leader ye have forgotten — I promise that if ye let the man-cub go to his own place, I will not, when my time comes to die, bare one tooth against ye. I will die without fighting. That will at least save the Pack three lives. More I cannot do; but if ye will, I can save ye the shame that comes of killing a brother against whom there is no fault — a brother spoken for and bought into the Pack according to the Law of the Jungle."

"He is a man — a man — a man!" snarled the Pack; and most of the wolves began to gather round Shere Khan, whose tail was beginning to switch.

"Now the business is in thy hands," said Bagheera to Mowgli. "*We* can do no more except fight."

Mowgli stood upright — the fire-pot in his hands. Then he stretched out his arms, and yawned in the face of the Council; but he was furious with rage and sorrow, for, wolf-like, the wolves had never told him how they hated him. "Listen, you!" he cried. "There is no need for this dog's jabber. Ye have told me so often tonight that I am a man (and indeed I would have been a wolf with you to my life's end), that I feel your words are true. So I do not call ye my brothers any more, but *sag* [dogs], as a man should. What ye will do, and what ye will not do, is not yours to say. That matter is with *me*; and that we may see the matter more plainly, I, the man, have brought here a little of the Red Flower, which ye, dogs, fear."

He flung the fire-pot on the ground, and some of the red coals lit a tuft of dried moss that flared up, as all the Council drew back in terror before the leaping flames.

Mowgli thrust his dead branch into the fire till the twigs lit and crackled, and whirled it above his head among the cowering wolves.

"Thou art the master," said Bagheera, in an undertone. "Save Akela from the death. He was ever thy friend."

Akela, the grim old wolf who had never asked for mercy in his life, gave one piteous look at Mowgli as the boy stood all naked, his long black hair tossing over his shoulders in the light of the blazing branch that made the shadows jump and quiver.

"Good!" said Mowgli, staring round slowly. "I see that ye are dogs. I go from you to my own people — if they be my own people. The Jungle is shut to me, and I just forget your talk, and your companionship; but I will be more merciful than ye are. Because I was all but your brother in blood, I promise that when I am a man among men I will not betray ye to men as ye have betrayed me." He kicked the fire with his foot, and the sparks flew up. "There shall be no war between any of us and the Pack. But here is a debt to pay before I go." He strode forward to where Shere Khan sat blinking stupidly at the flames, and caught him by the tuft on his chin. Bagheera followed in case of accidents. "Up, dog!" Mowgli cried. "Up, when a man speaks, or I will set that coat ablaze!"

Shere Khan's ears lay flat back on his head, and he shut his eyes, for the blazing branch was very near.

"This cattle-killer said he would kill me in the Council because he had not killed me when I was a cub. Thus and thus, then, do we beat dogs when we are men. Stir a whisker, Lungri, and I ram the Red Flower down thy gullet!" He beat Shere Khan over the head with the branch, and the tiger whimpered and whined in an agony of fear.

"Pah! Singed jungle-cat – go now! But remember when next I come to the Council Rock, as a man should come, it will be with Shere Khan's hide on my head. For the rest, Akela goes free to live as he pleases. Ye will *not* kill him, because that is not my will. Nor do I think that ye will sit here any longer, lolling out your tongues as though ye were some-bodies, instead of dogs whom I drive out – thus! Go!" The fire was burning furiously at the end of the branch, and Mowgli struck right and left round the circle, and the wolves ran howling with the sparks burning their fur. At last there were only Akela, Bagheera, and perhaps ten wolves that had taken Mowgli's part. Then something began to hurt Mowgli inside him, as he had never been hurt in his life before, and he caught his breath and sobbed, and the tears ran down his face.

"What is it? What is it?" he said. "I do not wish to leave the Jungle, and I do not know what this is. Am I dying, Bagheera?"

"No, Little Brother. Those are only tears such as men use," said Bagheera. "Now I know thou art a man, and a man's cub no longer. The Jungle is shut indeed to thee henceforward. Let them fall, Mowgli. They are only tears." So Mowgli sat and cried as though his heart would break; and he had never cried in all his life before.

"Now," he said, "I will go to men. But first I must say farewell to my mother"; and he went to the cave where she lived with Father Wolf, and he cried on her coat, while the four cubs howled miserably.

"Ye will not forget me?" said Mowgli.

"Never while we can follow a trail," said the cubs. "Come to the foot of the hill when thou art a man, and we will talk to thee; and we will come into the croplands to play with thee by night."

"Come soon!" said Father Wolf. "Oh, wise little frog, come again soon; for we be old, thy mother and I."

"Come soon," said Mother Wolf, "little naked son of mine; for, listen, child of man, I loved thee more than ever I loved my cubs."

"I will surely come," said Mowgli; "and when I come it will be to lay out Shere Khan's hide upon the Council Rock. Do not forget me! Tell them in the Jungle never to forget me!"

The dawn was beginning to break when Mowgli went down the hillside alone, to meet those mysterious things that are called men.

# *Ted Hughes*
# MOON-WIND

THERE is no wind on the moon at all
  Yet things get blown about.
In utter utter stillness
  Your candle shivers out.

In utter utter stillness
  A giant marquee
Booms and flounders past you
  Like a swan at sea.

In utter utter stillness
  While you stand in the street
A squall of hens and cabbages
  Knocks you off your feet.

In utter utter stillness
  While you stand agog
A tearing twisting sheet of pond
  Clouts you with a frog.

A camp of caravans suddenly
  Squawks and takes off.
A ferris wheel bounds along the skyline
  Like a somersaulting giraffe.

Roots and foundations, nails and screws,
  Nothing can hold fast,
Nothing can resist the moon's
  Dead-still blast.

# J. P. Martin
# UNCLE

### Illustrated by Quentin Blake

## Watercress Tower and the Little Lion

*Uncle is an elephant. He is immensely rich*
*and generally dresses in a purple dressing gown. He often rides about*
*in a traction engine, which he prefers to a car; and his house, which looks*
*like a hundred skyscrapers all joined together, is called Homeward.*
*His great enemy is Beaver Hateman.*

UNCLE WAS ABOUT TO HAVE his music lesson. He has a great fondness for music, but is rather a poor player. He is trying to learn the bass viol, and there's a little man called Gordono who comes to teach him. His real name is Thomaso Elsicar Gordono. He's an Italian, and everyone calls him the Maestro. The worst of it is he has such a dreadful temper. He gets into a passion over his music, and tries to throw himself out of the window because he can't bear to hear things played badly. He is always accompanied by a small lion, called the Little Lion. No one knows his real name.

That afternoon, the Maestro came as usual, and walking with him was his pet. Although he's grown-up, the lion is hardly larger than an Airedale dog, but he's fearfully tough and compact. He also has one curious power. He can make himself *heavy* beyond all reason. He does it in a moment. Try to get him out of a room. You might think it would be easy enough, but the moment you try to move him you find your mistake. He doesn't resist you. He simply makes himself heavy, and though you'd hardly believe it, he must weigh about a

ton! He seems to like music for he listens attentively to the Maestro.

That afternoon the Maestro played a brilliant waltz of his own composition on the piano, and then started to teach Uncle. Uncle is a bit heavy with the bow, and made one or two false notes. The moment he did so, the Maestro threw himself on the ground in a passion, grinding his teeth.

He got up and rushed to the window but realised then that he was on the ground floor. He looked rather sheepish, but contented himself with screaming a little. After a while he cooled down and the lesson proceeded.

When it was over, he said to Uncle:

"Have you ever been to Watercress Tower, where the Little Lion and I live?"

"No," replied Uncle.

"There you are! There you are!" said the Maestro. "Yet you can go over and over again to visit Butterskin Mute's wretched little farm! It's not fair!"

The Little Lion was squatting on a strong thick-legged stool. As the Maestro said these words, he made himself heavy, and the stool immediately collapsed.

"Now," said Uncle, "look what you've done! Spoilt a good stool!"

He knew the hopelessness of dragging or kicking the Little Lion out, so he said no more, but turned to the Maestro.

"It's true I've never been to Watercress Tower, but I'll come this afternoon, and – wait a bit – that's Butterskin Mute coming over the drawbridge. I'll bring Mute with me, and the Old Monkey."

"Righto!" said the Maestro with a smile. He was in high spirits all at once. One good thing about the Maestro is that his rages never last long, or else he would simply wear himself out. He was delighted at the thought of taking Uncle to see his dwelling place. The Little Lion stopped being heavy. He got on to his hind legs and briskly rubbed his eyes, as if preparing them for a good sight.

They set out almost at once. Mute was

quite willing to go, for watercress is the one thing he cannot grow, and he had often wondered where Uncle obtained his splendid supplies. He emptied his sack of choice young cabbages on the table, and said that he would like to go immensely.

"You'll want bathing costumes," said the Maestro. "I always bring one in my bag and change on the way."

So they all took bathing costumes. The Maestro said that there was a good place at the foot of the tower where they could change.

"Shall we have to take any provisions?" said Uncle.

"Oh no," replied the Maestro carelessly, "there's always a bit going up there."

So they set out. They went to the end of the hall and took a tube labelled Biscuit Tower. When they got to the Biscuit Tower they found a junction, and another tube labelled Watercress Tower. They were glad to find that it was driven by Noddy Ninety. They went through a lot of tunnels.

At last they reached the base of Watercress Tower. It was a very wet place, and they could easily see the need for bathing suits. Right up the side of the tower was a gigantic salmon ladder. I don't know whether you have seen a salmon ladder in a stream, but they are like steps with water running over them. They all changed into their bathing costumes (except the Little Lion, who travels in his own coat all the time), and started up the ladder.

It was an exhausting business after the first two hundred feet, and Uncle stopped a minute and said to the Maestro:

"Do you come up and down this every time you want to go out?"

"Every time," replied the Maestro firmly. "There is an electric lift in the tower, but I can't stick the things. They make me feel wobbly inside and the Little Lion hates them so much that when he gets on, he makes himself heavy, and then the lift won't work."

"Well, I suppose there's nothing for it but to go on," said Uncle gloomily. "I suppose now you're going to tell me the usual tale about it being only twenty storeys higher up!"

The Maestro was so enraged at this speech that he threw himself right off the salmon ladder. However, he missed the rocks, and, after swimming about for a bit, grew cooler and began to climb after them.

"I vote we sit down," said Uncle, panting. "There's a pool here where we can sit down while the Maestro catches us up!"

It felt very nice there with the water rushing past. The walls of all the towers looked pretty too, for they had ferns growing on them.

They all felt rested when the Maestro arrived. He seemed to be in the best of tempers

again, and had quite forgotten his annoyance. At last they reached the top. They arrived at a place where water came cascading out of a huge open door, and when they got inside they found themselves in a large room, with a stream running along the floor. They went through this and found themselves in another room about two feet deep in water, with stainless steel tables, chairs, bookcases, etc.

"I sometimes study here on a hot day," said the Maestro.

At the end of this room were two doors, with electric bells, and cards pinned beneath them.

One card said:

*Mr T. E. Gordono*

and the other:

*Mr L. Lion*

From underneath the doors came the stream of water.

The Maestro now drew out a latchkey and opened the door on the right. It opened on to a waterfall, or rather a flight of steps with water running down them. They waded up these steps, which looked very lovely with the foaming water pouring down them, and with lilies and ferns growing in the cracks of the stones. Then they found themselves on the shore of a gigantic lake on the top of a tower so huge that it seemed like a mountain. Most of the lake appeared to be overgrown with watercress.

On each side of the waterfall stood a little hut. On the door of one hut was

T. E. GORDONO

and on the other

L. LION

The lake looked fine, for there were cranes and herons flying around and enormous lemon-coloured fish swam lazily by.

The Maestro led them into his hut.

There was very little inside, except a grand piano, a violin and a camp bed. It was hard to see into the Little Lion's hut, for he dived in very quickly to have a rub down, and shut the door after him, but Uncle has very sharp eyes, and he noticed what looked very like a bottle of medicine on the table inside.

The Little Lion soon came out and joined them.

"Well," said Uncle, "you've got a snug place up here."

"Oh, it's all right," replied the Maestro. "But the rent's excessive!"

"The rent!" said Uncle severely. "I don't remember getting any rent from you."

"I don't pay *you*," said the Maestro.

"Indeed, and whom do you pay?"

"I always pay a man called Beaver Hateman. When I was looking for rooms in this neighbourhood, he met me, and said that he owned the tower, and that the lion and I could have rooms cheap."

When Uncle heard this, he trumpeted with rage. "Beaver Hateman!" he shouted. "Am I never to get out of sight and hearing of that chap? Here I am on the top of a lonely tower, preparing for a little intellectual conversation, and his hideous trail is here!

"Listen," he continued, "the man who charges you rent for these rooms is not only defrauding you, but his very presence is a menace. May I ask you what he charges?"

"He wanted fifty pounds, but I beat him down to twopence."

"Well, let me tell you that even at twopence per week you've been done. I only charge a halfpenny per week for large roomy flats, with electric light, and all conveniences."

When the Maestro heard this, he immediately rushed to the edge of the tower, but the Little Lion followed him, and, seeing that it would be a fatal drop, fixed his teeth in his trousers, made himself heavy and sat down.

The Maestro gave one pull, then, seeing the hopelessness of making a struggle, came quietly back to Uncle.

"I suppose you pay him regularly?" said Uncle.

"Yes, I pay him every quarter; that's two and twopence per quarter. I make him give me a receipt."

"I should like to see one of these receipts."

The Maestro reached up to a file, and took down a greasy piece of paper.

Uncle looked at it. It read:

> to Bever hateman, Esq.,
> rent of Rooms on watercress Tower
> 13 weaks @ 2d. 5/6d
> 
> 2/2
> 
> Received without thanks
> 
> *B Hatman*

"So he tried to make out that thirteen weeks at twopence came to five and sixpence. The SCOUNDREL!"

"Yes, he said he wasn't any good at figures."

Uncle turned over the receipt. It was written on the back of an old bill which read:

> To Thomas Minifer, Stationer.
> Supplying 50 black books, with
> "hating book" inscribed on back
> 
> 50 @ 5/-…£12 10s. 0d.

On the bottom was a note:

As this account has been presented in various ways during the past five years, we should like now to press for an immediate payment.

Uncle trumpeted again.

"This is vile!" he said. "He makes out his bill to you on the back of an unpaid bill of his own. I see he signed the receipt in red ink."

"No, he signed it in his own blood; he just stuck the pen deep in his arm and wrote."

"His own blood! Is there any end to the man's detestable ways!" Uncle snorted, then went on:

"But wait a bit, you've been supplying me with cress week by week, for which I paid you the very substantial sum of twopence per week."

"Yes, I used that to pay the rent."

"So the money I paid for cress went into Hateman's pocket! It's a wonder I haven't been poisoned. Well, in future, you pay me. D'you understand?"

"Certainly. I shall be glad to do so."

Uncle sat down fuming, but the Maestro brought him some very good cress sandwiches, and, after devouring a few platefuls of these, he felt better. The sun was setting and the great lake was all golden, except for the patches of bright-green cress.

A gentle breeze blew, and the Maestro went to the piano and began to play. You'd be surprised to hear how well the music sounded up there. The Little Lion seemed to be carried away by it, for he sat perfectly still, except for a flickering half-smile, and the rhythmic wagging of his tail. The Old Monkey and Butterskin Mute were enraptured.

Uncle began to feel calm and happy.

"After all," he said to himself, "I have not come here in vain. I have exposed and removed a grievous wrong; the afternoon has been by no means wasted."

Before he left, he bestowed on the Maestro the sum of five shillings to repay him for some of the wrongly charged rent, and he gave the Little Lion a voucher for the same amount to spend at the Old Man's on medicine. That little creature is mad on physic and drugs (which he certainly does not need), for he snatched the voucher from Uncle as though he were gaining a fortune.

Uncle soon bade them farewell. They went down by the first lift they saw. It stopped for a moment at the bottom of the salmon ladder, where they collected their clothes, then took them most of the way back to Homeward.

Uncle was curious to see how the Little Lion spent his money, so, after tea, he slipped up the elevator to the tower where the Old Man has his medicine store.

He crept up and peeped through the window.

Yes, there was the Little Lion. He had already purchased a bottle of Headache Mixture, and one of Headache Producer (for enemies), besides two bottles of Rheumatism Mixture, and a flask of Stomach Joy.★

Uncle smiled, and forbore to warn him, as he thought a sharp lesson might do the stubborn little creature good.

But the lion must have an inside of brass, for Uncle heard afterwards from the Maestro that he drank the whole flask of Stomach Joy and liked it, and seemed to be exceptionally bright and active next day.

★All the Old Man's medicines have the opposite effect from the one they claim. Therefore, Stomach Joy gives people the worst stomach ache of their life.

*Frances Hodgson Burnett*

# THE SECRET GARDEN

*Illustrated by Charles Robinson*

## A Visitor in the Night

*Mary's parents die in India and she is sent to live at her uncle's house in Yorkshire. There she finds a secret garden which has been locked up and forgotten ever since her pretty young aunt died, ten years before. Mary thinks she is the only child in the house, but one night…*

MARY HAD BEEN LYING AWAKE, turning from side to side for about an hour, when suddenly something made her sit up in bed and turn her head towards the door listening. She listened and she listened.

"It isn't the wind now," she said in a loud whisper. "That isn't the wind. It is different. It is that crying I heard before."

The door of her room was ajar and the sound came down the corridor, a far-off faint sound of fretful crying. She listened for a few minutes and each minute she became more and more sure. She felt as if she must find out what it was. It seemed even stranger than the secret garden and the buried key. Perhaps the fact that she was in a rebellious mood made her bold. She put her foot out of bed and stood on the floor.

"I am going to find out what it is," she said. "Everybody is in bed and I don't care about Mrs Medlock – I don't care!"

There was a candle by her bedside and she took it up and went softly out of the room. The corridor looked very long and dark, but she was too excited to mind that. She thought she remembered the corners she must turn to find the short corridor with the door covered with tapestry – the one Mrs Medlock had come through the day she lost herself. The sound had come up that passage. So she went on with her dim light, almost feeling her way, her heart beating so loud that she fancied she could hear it. The far-off, faint crying went on and led her. Sometimes it stopped for a moment or so and then began again. Was this the right corner to turn? She stopped and thought. Yes, it was. Down this passage and then to the left, and then up two broad steps, and then to the right again. Yes, there was the tapestry door.

She pushed it open very gently and closed it behind her, and she stood in the corridor and could hear the crying quite plainly, though it was not loud. It was on the other side of the wall at her left and a few yards farther on there was a door. She could see a glimmer of light coming from beneath it. The Someone was crying in that room, and it was

quite a young Someone.

So she walked to the door and pushed it open, and there she was standing in the room!

It was a big room with ancient, handsome furniture in it. There was a low fire glowing faintly on the hearth and a night-light burning by the side of a carved, four-poster bed hung with brocade, and on the bed was lying a boy, crying pitifully.

Mary wondered if she was in a real place or if she had fallen asleep again and was dreaming without knowing it.

The boy had a sharp, delicate face, the colour of ivory, and he seemed to have eyes too big for it. He had also a lot of hair which tumbled over his forehead in heavy locks and made his thin face seem smaller. He looked like a boy who had been ill, but he was crying more as if he were tired and cross than as if he were in pain.

Mary stood near the door with her candle in her hand, holding her breath. Then she crept across the room, and as she drew nearer the light attracted the boy's attention and he turned his head on his pillow and stared at her, his grey eyes opening so wide that they seemed immense.

"Who are you?" he said at last in a half-frightened whisper. "Are you a ghost?"

"No, I am not," Mary answered, her own whisper sounding half-frightened. "Are you one?"

He stared and stared and stared. Mary could not help noticing what strange eyes he had. They were agate-grey and they looked too big for his face because they had black lashes all round them.

"No," he replied, after waiting a moment or so. "I am Colin."

"Who is Colin?" she faltered.

"I am Colin Craven. Who are you?"

"I am Mary Lennox. Mr Craven is my uncle."

"He is my father," said the boy.

"Your father!" gasped Mary. "No one ever told me he had a boy! Why didn't they?"

"Come here," he said, still keeping his strange eyes fixed on her with an anxious expression.

She came close to the bed and he put out his hand and touched her.

"You are real, aren't you?" he said. "I have such real dreams very often. You might be one of them."

Mary had slipped on a woollen wrapper before she left her room and she put a piece of it between his fingers.

"Rub that and see how thick and warm it is," she said. "I will pinch you a little if you like, to show you how real I am. For a minute I thought you might be a dream, too."

"Where did you come from?" he asked.

"From my own room. The wind wuthered so I couldn't go to sleep and I heard someone crying and wanted to find out who it was. What were you crying for?"

"Because I couldn't go to sleep either, and my head ached. Tell me your name again."

"Mary Lennox. Did no one ever tell you I had come to live here?"

He was still fingering the fold of her wrapper, but he began to look a little more as if he believed in her reality.

"No," he answered. "They daren't."

"Why?" asked Mary.

"Because I should have been afraid you would see me. I won't let people see me and talk me over."

"Why?" Mary asked again, feeling more mystified every moment.

"Because I am like this always, ill and having to lie down. My father won't let people talk me over, either. The servants are not allowed to speak about me. If I live I may be a hunchback, but I shan't live. My father hates to think I may be like him."

"Oh, what a queer house this is!" Mary said. "What a queer house! Everything is a kind of secret. Rooms are locked up and gardens are locked up – and you! Have you been locked up?"

"No. I stay in this room because I don't want to be moved out of it. It tires me too much."

"Does your father come and see you?" Mary ventured.

"Sometimes. Generally when I am asleep. He doesn't want to see me."

"Why?" Mary could not help asking again.

A sort of angry shadow passed over the boy's face.

"My mother died when I was born and it makes him wretched to look at me. He thinks I don't know, but I've heard people talking. He almost hates me."

"He hates the garden, because she died," said Mary, half speaking to herself.

"What garden?" the boy asked.

"Oh! Just – just a garden she used to like," Mary stammered. "Have you been here always?"

"Nearly always. Sometimes I have been taken to places at the seaside, but I won't stay because people stare at me. I used to wear an iron thing to keep my back straight, but a grand doctor came from London to see me and said it was stupid. He told them to take it off and keep me out in the fresh air. I hate fresh air and I don't want to go out."

"I didn't when first I came here," said Mary. "Why do you keep looking at me like that?"

"Because of the dreams that are so real," he answered rather fretfully. "Sometimes when I open my eyes I don't believe I'm awake."

"We're both awake," said Mary. She glanced round the room with its high ceiling and shadowy corners and dim firelight. "It looks quite like a dream, and it's the middle of the night, and everybody in the house is asleep – everybody but us. We are wide awake."

"I don't want it to be a dream," the boy said restlessly.

Mary thought of something all at once.

"If you don't like people to see you," she began, "do you want me to go away?"

He still held the fold of her wrapper and he gave it a little pull.

"No," he said. "I should be sure you were a dream if you went. If you are real, sit down on that big footstool and talk. I want to hear about you."

Mary put down her candle on the table near the bed and sat down on the cushioned stool. She did not want to go away at all. She wanted to stay in the mysterious, hidden-away room and talk to the mysterious boy.

"What do you want me to tell you?" she said.

He wanted to know how long she had been at Misselthwaite; he wanted to know which corridor her room was on; he wanted to know what she had been doing; if she disliked the moor as he disliked it; where she had lived before she came to Yorkshire. She answered all these questions and many more, and he lay back on his pillow and listened. He made her tell him a great deal about India and about her voyage across the ocean. She found out that because he had been an invalid he had not learned things as other children had. One of his nurses had taught him to read when he was quite little and he was always reading and looking at pictures in splendid books.

Though his father rarely saw him when he was awake, he was given all sorts of wonderful things to amuse himself with. He never seemed to have been amused, however. He could have anything he asked for and was never made to do anything he did not like to do.

"Everyone is obliged to do what pleases me," he said indifferently. "It makes me ill to be angry. No one believes I shall live to grow up."

He said it as if he was so accustomed to the idea that it had ceased to matter to him at all. He seemed to like the sound of Mary's voice. As she went on talking he listened in a drowsy, interested way. Once or twice she wondered if he were not gradually falling into a doze. But at last he asked a question which opened up a new subject.

"How old are you?" he asked.

"I am ten," answered Mary, forgetting herself for the moment, "and so are you."

"How do you know that?" he demanded in a surprised voice.

"Because when you were born the garden door was locked and the key was buried. And it has been locked for ten years."

Colin half sat up, turning towards her, leaning on his elbows.

"What garden door was locked? Who did it? Where was the key buried?" he exclaimed, as if he were suddenly very much interested.

"It – it was the garden Mr Craven hates," said Mary nervously. "He locked the door. No one – no one knew where he buried the key."

"What sort of a garden is it?" Colin persisted eagerly.

"No one has been allowed to go into it for ten years," was Mary's careful answer.

But it was too late to be careful. He was too much like herself. He, too, had had nothing to think about, and the idea of a hidden garden attracted him as it had attracted her. He asked question after question. Where was it? Had she never looked for the door? Had she never asked the gardeners?

"They won't talk about it," said Mary. "I think they have been told not to answer questions."

"I would make them," said Colin.

"Could you?" Mary faltered, beginning to feel frightened. If he could make people answer questions, who knew what might happen?

"Everyone is obliged to please me. I told you that," he said. "If I were to live, this place would some time belong to me. They all know that. I would make them tell me."

Mary had not known that she herself had been spoiled, but she could see quite plainly that this mysterious boy had been. He thought that the whole world belonged to him. How peculiar he was and how coolly he spoke of not living.

"Do you think you won't live?" she asked, partly because she was curious and partly in hope of making him forget the garden.

"I don't suppose I shall," he answered as indifferently as he had spoken before. "Ever since I remember anything I have heard people say I shan't. At first they thought I was too little to understand, and now they think I don't hear. But I do. My doctor is my father's cousin. He is quite poor and if I die he will have all Misselthwaite when my father is dead. I should think he wouldn't want me to live."

"Do you want to live?" inquired Mary.

"No," he answered, in a cross, tired fashion. "But I don't want to die. When I feel ill I lie here and think about it until I cry and cry."

"I have heard you crying three times," Mary said, "but I did not know who it was. Were you crying about that?" She did so want him to forget the garden.

"They have to please me," he said. "I will make them take me there and I will let you go, too."

Mary's hands clutched each other. Everything would be spoiled – everything. Dickon would never come back. She would never again feel like a missel thrush with a safe hidden nest.

"Oh, don't – don't – don't – don't do that!" she cried out.

He stared as if he thought she had gone crazy!

"Why?" he exclaimed. "You said you wanted to see it."

"I do," she answered, almost with a sob in her throat, "but if you make them open the door and take you in like that it will never be a secret again."

He leaned still farther forward.

"A secret," he said. "What do you mean? Tell me."

Mary's words almost tumbled over one another.

"You see – you see," she panted, "if no one knows but ourselves – if there was a door, hidden somewhere under the ivy – if there was – and we could find it; and if we could slip through it together and shut it behind us, and no one knew anyone was inside and we called it our garden and pretended that – that we were missel thrushes and it was our nest, and if we played there almost every day and dug and planted seeds and made it all come alive – "

"Is it dead?" he interrupted her.

"It soon will be if no one cares for it," she went on. "The bulbs will live but the roses – "

He stopped her again as excited as she was herself.

"What are bulbs?" he put in quickly.

"They are daffodils and lilies and snow-drops. They are working in the earth now –

"I dare say," he answered. "Let us talk about something else. Talk about that garden. Don't you want to see it?"

"Yes," answered Mary in quite a low voice.

"I do," he went on persistently. "I don't think I ever really wanted to see anything before, but I want to see that garden. I want the key dug up. I want the door unlocked. I would let them take me there in my chair. That would be getting fresh air. I am going to make them open the door."

He had become quite excited and his strange eyes began to shine like stars and looked more immense than ever.

pushing up pale-green points because the spring is coming."

"Is the spring coming?" he said. "What is it like? You don't see it in rooms if you are ill."

"It is the sun shining on the rain and the rain falling on the sunshine, and things pushing up and working under the earth," said Mary. "If the garden was a secret and we could get into it we could watch the things grow bigger every day, and see how many roses are alive. Don't you see? Oh, don't you see how much nicer it would be if it was a secret?"

He dropped back on his pillow and lay there with an odd expression on his face.

"I never had a secret," he said, "except that one about not living to grow up. They don't know I know that, so it is a sort of secret. But I like this kind better."

"If you won't make them take you to the garden," pleaded Mary, "perhaps – I feel almost sure I can find out how to get in some time. And then – if the doctor wants you to go out in your chair, and if you can always do what you want to do, perhaps – perhaps we might find some boy who would push you, and we could go alone and it would always be a secret garden."

"I should – like – that," he said very slowly, his eyes looking dreamy. "I should like that. I should not mind fresh air in a secret garden."

Mary began to recover her breath and feel safer, because the idea of keeping the secret seemed to please him. She felt almost sure that if she kept on talking and could make him see the garden in his mind as she had seen it, he would like it so much that he could not bear to think that everybody might tramp into it when they chose.

"I'll tell you what I *think* it would be like, if you could go into it," she said. "It has been shut up so long things have grown into a tangle perhaps."

He lay quite still and listened while she went on talking about the roses which *might* have clambered from tree to tree and hung down – about the many birds which *might* have built their nests there because it was so safe. And then she told him about the robin and Ben Weatherstaff, and there was so much to tell about the robin and it was so easy and safe to talk about it that she ceased to feel afraid. The robin pleased him so much that he smiled until he looked almost beautiful, and at first Mary had thought that he was even plainer than herself, with his big eyes and heavy locks of hair.

"I did not know birds could be like that," he said. "But if you stay in a room you never see things. What a lot of things you know. I feel as if you had been inside that garden."

She did not know what to say, so she did not say anything. He evidently did not expect an answer and the next moment he gave her a surprise.

"I am going to let you look at something," he said. "Do you see that rose-coloured silk curtain hanging on the wall over the mantel-piece?"

Mary had not noticed it before, but she looked up and saw it. It was a curtain of soft silk hanging over what seemed to be some picture.

"Yes," she answered.

"There is a cord hanging from it," said Colin. "Go and pull it."

Mary got up, much mystified, and found the cord. When she pulled it the silk curtain ran back on rings and when it ran back it uncovered a picture. It was the picture of a girl with a laughing face. She had bright hair tied up with a blue ribbon and her gay, lovely eyes were exactly like Colin's unhappy ones, agate-grey and looking twice as big as they really were, because of the black lashes all round them.

"She is my mother," said Colin complainingly. "I don't see why she died. Sometimes I hate her for doing it."

"How queer!" said Mary.

"If she had lived I believe I should not have been ill always," he grumbled. "I dare say I should have lived, too. And my father would not have hated to look at me. I dare say I should have had a strong back. Draw the curtain again."

Mary did as she was told and returned to her footstool.

"She is much prettier than you," she said, "but her eyes are just like yours — at least they are the same shape and colour. Why is the curtain drawn over her?"

He moved uncomfortably.

"I made them do it," he said. "Sometimes I don't like to see her looking at me. She smiles too much when I am ill and miserable. Besides, she is mine, and I don't want everyone to see her."

There were a few moments of silence and then Mary spoke.

"What would Mrs Medlock do if she found out that I had been here?" she inquired.

"She would do as I told her to do," he answered. "And I should tell her that I wanted you to come here and talk to me every day. I am glad you came."

"So am I," said Mary. "I will come as often as I can, but" — she hesitated — "I shall have to look every day for the garden door."

"Yes, you must," said Colin, "and you can tell me about it afterwards."

He lay thinking a few minutes, as he had done before, and then he spoke again.

"I think you shall be a secret, too," he said. "I will not tell them until they find out. I can always send the nurse out of the room and say that I want to be by myself. Do you know Martha?"

"Yes, I know her very well," said Mary.

He nodded his head towards the outer corridor.

"She is the one who is asleep in the other room. The nurse went away yesterday to stay all night with her sister and she always makes Martha attend to me when she wants to go out. Martha shall tell you when to come here."

Then Mary understood Martha's troubled look when she had asked questions about the crying.

"Martha knew about you all the time?" she said.

"Yes; she often attends to me. The nurse likes to get away from me and then Martha comes."

"I have been here a long time," said Mary. "Shall I go away now? Your eyes look sleepy."

"I wish I could go to sleep before you leave me," he said rather shyly.

"Shut your eyes," said Mary, drawing her footstool closer, "and I will do what my Ayah used to do in India. I will pat your hand and stroke it and sing something quite low."

"I should like that perhaps," he said drowsily.

Somehow she was sorry for him and did not want him to lie awake, so she leaned against the bed and began to stroke and pat his hand and sing a very low little chanting song in Hindustani.

"That is nice," he said more drowsily still, and she went on chanting and stroking, but when she looked at him again his black lashes were lying close against his cheeks, for his eyes were shut and he was fast asleep. She got up softly, took her candle, and crept away without making a sound.

# Kenneth Grahame

# THE WIND IN THE WILLOWS

*Illustrated by Arthur Rackham*

## Mole Discovers the River

THE MOLE HAD BEEN WORKING very hard all the morning, spring-cleaning his little home. First with brooms, then with dusters; then on ladders and steps and chairs, with a brush and a pail of whitewash; till he had dust in his throat and eyes, and splashes of whitewash all over his black fur, and an aching back and weary arms. Spring was moving in the air above and in the earth below and around him, penetrating even his dark and lowly little house with its spirit of divine discontent and longing. It was small wonder, then, that he suddenly flung down his brush on the floor, said "Bother!" and "O blow!" and also "Hang spring-cleaning!" and bolted out of the house without even waiting to put on his coat. Something up above was calling him imperiously, and he made for the steep little tunnel which answered in his case to the gravelled carriage-drive owned by animals whose residences are nearer to the sun and air. So he scraped and scratched and scrabbled and scrooged, and then he scrooged again and scrabbled and scratched and scraped, working busily with his little paws and muttering to himself, "Up we go! Up we go!" till at last, pop! his snout came out into the sunlight, and he found himself rolling in the warm grass of a great meadow.

"This is fine!" he said to himself. "This is better than whitewashing!" The sunshine struck hot on his fur, soft breezes caressed his heated brow, and after the seclusion of the cellarage he had lived in so long the carol of happy birds fell on his dulled hearing almost like a shout. Jumping off all his four legs at once, in the joy of living, and the delight of spring without its cleaning, he pursued his way across the meadow till he reached the hedge on the further side.

"Hold up!" said an elderly rabbit at the gap. "Sixpence for the privilege of passing by the private road!" He was bowled over in an instant by the impatient and contemptuous Mole, who trotted along the side of the hedge chaffing the other rabbits as they peeped hurriedly from their holes to see what the row was about. "Onion-sauce! Onion-sauce!" he remarked jeeringly, and was gone before they could think of a thoroughly satisfactory reply. Then they all started grumbling at each other. "How *stupid* you are! Why didn't you tell him – " "Well, why didn't *you* say – " "You might have reminded him – " and so on, in the

usual way; but, of course, it was then much too late, as is always the case.

It all seemed too good to be true. Hither and thither through the meadows he rambled busily, along the hedgerows, across the copses, finding everywhere birds building, flowers budding, leaves thrusting – everything happy, and progressive, and occupied. And instead of having an uneasy conscience pricking him and whispering "Whitewash!" he somehow could only feel how jolly it was to be the only idle dog among all these busy citizens. After all, the best part of a holiday is perhaps not so much to be resting yourself, as to see all the other fellows busy working.

He thought his happiness was complete when, as he meandered aimlessly along, suddenly he stood by the edge of a full-fed river. Never in his life had he seen a river before – this sleek, sinuous, full-bodied animal, chasing and chuckling, gripping things with a gurgle and leaving them with a laugh, to fling itself on fresh playmates that shook themselves free, and were caught and held again. All was a-shake and a-shiver – glints and gleams and sparkles, rustle and swirl, chatter and bubble. The Mole was bewitched, entranced,

fascinated. By the side of the river he trotted as one trots, when very small, by the side of a man, who holds one spellbound by exciting stories; and when tired at last, he sat on the bank, while the river still chattered on to him, a babbling procession of the best stories in the world, sent from the heart of the earth to be told at last to the insatiable sea.

As he sat on the grass and looked across the river, a dark hole in the bank opposite, just above the water's edge, caught his eye, and dreamily he fell to considering what a nice snug dwelling-place it would make for an animal with few wants and fond of a bijou riverside residence, above flood-level and remote from noise and dust. As he gazed, something bright and small seemed to twinkle down in the heart of it, vanished, then twinkled once more like a tiny star. But it could hardly be a star in such an unlikely situation; and it was too glittering and small for a glow-worm. Then, as he looked, it winked at him, and so declared itself to be an eye; and a small face began gradually to grow up round it, like a frame round a picture.

A brown little face, with whiskers.

A grave round face, with the same twinkle

in its eye that had first attracted his notice.

Small neat ears and thick silky hair.

It was the Water Rat!

Then the two animals stood and regarded each other cautiously.

"Hullo, Mole!" said the Water Rat.

"Hullo, Rat!" said the Mole.

"Would you like to come over?" inquired the Rat presently.

"Oh, it's all very well to *talk*," said the Mole, rather pettishly, he being new to a river and riverside life and its ways.

The Rat said nothing, but stooped and unfastened a rope and hauled on it; then lightly stepped into a little boat which the Mole had not observed. It was painted blue outside and white within, and was just the size for two animals; and the Mole's whole heart went out to it at once, even though he did not yet fully understand its uses.

The Rat sculled smartly across and made fast. Then he held up his fore-paw as the Mole stepped gingerly down. "Lean on that!" he said. "Now then, step lively!" and the Mole to his surprise and rapture found himself actually seated in the stern of a real boat.

"This has been a wonderful day!" said he, as the Rat shoved off and took to the sculls again. "Do you know, I've never been in a boat before in all my life."

"What?" cried the Rat, open-mouthed. "Never been in a – you never – well, I – what have you been doing, then?"

"Is it so nice as all that?" asked the Mole shyly, though he was quite prepared to believe it as he leant back in his seat and surveyed the cushions, the oars, the rowlocks, and all the fascinating fittings, and felt the boat sway lightly under him.

"Nice? It's the *only* thing," said the Water Rat solemnly, as he leant forward for his stroke. "Believe me, my young friend, there is *nothing* – absolutely nothing – half so much worth doing as simply messing about in boats. Simply messing," he went on dreamily: "messing – about – in – boats; messing – "

"Look ahead, Rat!" cried the Mole suddenly.

It was too late. The boat struck the bank full tilt. The dreamer, the joyous oarsman, lay on his back at the bottom of the boat, his heels in the air.

" – about in boats – or *with* boats," the Rat went on composedly, picking himself up with a pleasant laugh. "In or out of 'em, it doesn't matter. Nothing seems really to matter, that's the charm of it. Whether you get away, or whether you don't; whether you arrive at your destination or whether you reach somewhere else, or whether you never get anywhere at all, you're always busy, and you never do anything in particular; and when you've done it there's always something else to do, and you can do it if you like, but you'd much better not. Look here! If you've really nothing else on hand this morning, supposing we drop down the river together and have a long day of it?"

The Mole waggled his toes from sheer happiness, spread his chest with a sigh of full contentment, and leaned back blissfully into the soft cushions. "*What* a day I'm having!" he said. "Let us start at once!"

"Hold hard a minute, then!" said the Rat. He looped the painter through a ring in his landing-stage, climbed up into his hole above, and after a short interval reappeared staggering under a fat, wicker luncheon-basket.

"Shove that under your feet," he observed to the Mole, as he passed it down into the boat. Then he untied the painter and took the sculls again.

"What's inside it?" asked the Mole,

wriggling with curiosity.

"There's cold chicken inside it," replied the Rat briefly; "coldtonguecoldhamcoldbeefpickledgherkinssaladfrenchrollscressandwidgespottedmeatgingerbeerlemonadesodawater – "

"O stop, stop," cried the Mole in ecstasies. "This is too much!"

"Do you really think so?" inquired the Rat seriously. "It's only what I always take on these little excursions; and the other animals are always telling me that I'm a mean beast and cut it *very* fine!"

The Mole never heard a word he was saying. Absorbed in the new life he was entering upon, intoxicated with the sparkle, the ripple, the scents and the sounds and the sunlight, he trailed a paw in the water and dreamed long waking dreams. The Water Rat, like the good little fellow he was, sculled steadily on and forbore to disturb him.

"I like your clothes awfully, old chap," he remarked after some half an hour or so had passed. "I'm going to get a black velvet smoking-suit myself some day, as soon as I can afford it."

"I beg your pardon," said the Mole, pulling himself together with an effort. "You must think me very rude; but all this is so new to me. So – this – is – a – River!"

"*The* River," corrected the Rat.

"And you really live by the river? What a jolly life!"

"By it and with it and on it and in it," said the Rat. "It's brother and sister to me, and aunts, and company, and food and drink, and (naturally) washing. It's my world, and I don't want any other. What it hasn't got is not worth having, and what it doesn't know is not worth knowing. Lord! the times we've had together! Whether in winter or summer, spring or autumn, it's always got its fun and its excitements. When the floods are on in February, and my cellars and basement are brimming with drink that's no good to me, and the brown water runs by my best bedroom window; or again when it all drops away and shows patches of mud that smells like plum-cake, and the rushes and weed clog the channels, and I can potter about dry-shod over most of the bed of it and find fresh food to eat, and things careless people have dropped out of boats!"

"But isn't it a bit dull at times?" the Mole ventured to ask. "Just you and the river, and no one else to pass a word with?"

"No one else to – well, I mustn't be hard on you," said the Rat with forbearance. "You're new to it, and of course you don't know. The bank is so crowded nowadays that many people are moving away altogether. O no, it isn't what it used to be, at all. Otters, kingfishers, dabchicks, moorhens, all of them about all day long and always wanting you to *do* something – as if a fellow had no business of his own to attend to!"

"What lies over *there*?" asked the Mole, waving a paw towards a background of woodland that darkly framed the water-meadows on one side of the river.

"That? Oh, that's just the Wild Wood," said the Rat shortly. "We don't go there very much, we river-bankers."

"Aren't they – aren't they very *nice* people in there?" said the Mole a trifle nervously.

"W-e-ll," replied the Rat, "let me see. The squirrels are all right. *And* the rabbits – some of 'em, but rabbits are a mixed lot. And then there's Badger, of course. He lives right in the heart of it; wouldn't live anywhere else, either, if you paid him to do it. Dear old Badger! Nobody interferes with *him*. They'd better not," he added significantly.

"Why, who *should* interfere with him?" asked the Mole.

"Well, of course – there – are others," explained the Rat in a hesitating sort of way. "Weasels – and stoats – and foxes – and so on. They're all right in a way – I'm very good friends with them – pass the time of day when we meet, and all that – but they break out sometimes, there's no denying it, and then – well, you can't really trust them, and that's the fact."

The Mole knew well that it is quite against animal-etiquette to dwell on possible trouble ahead, or even to allude to it; so he dropped the subject.

"And beyond the Wild Wood again?" he asked. "Where it's all blue and dim, and one sees what may be hills or perhaps they mayn't, and something like the smoke of towns, or is it only cloud-drift?"

"Beyond the Wild Wood comes the Wide World," said the Rat. "And that's something that doesn't matter, either to you or me. I've never been there, and I'm never going, nor you either, if you've got any sense at all. Don't ever refer to it again, please. Now then! Here's our backwater at last, where we're going to lunch."

Leaving the main stream, they now passed into what seemed at first sight like a little land-locked lake. Green turf sloped down to either edge, brown snaky tree-roots gleamed below the surface of the quiet water, while ahead of them the silvery shoulder and foamy tumble of a weir, arm-in-arm with a restless dripping mill-wheel, that held up in its turn a grey-gabled mill-house, filled the air with a soothing murmur of sound, dull and smothery, yet with little clear voices speaking up cheerfully out of it at intervals. It was so very beautiful that the Mole could only hold up both fore-paws and gasp, "O my! O my! O my!"

The Rat brought the boat alongside the bank, made her fast, helped the still awkward Mole safely ashore, and swung out the luncheon-basket. The Mole begged as a favour to be allowed to unpack it all by himself; and the Rat was very pleased to indulge him, and to sprawl at full length on the grass and rest, while his excited friend shook out the table-cloth and spread it, took out all the mysterious packets one by one and arranged their contents in due order, still gasping, "O my! O my!" at each fresh revelation. When all was ready, the Rat said, "Now, pitch in, old fellow!" and the Mole was indeed very glad to obey, for he had started his spring-cleaning at a very early hour that morning, as people *will* do, and had not paused for bite or sup; and he had been through a very great deal since that distant time which now seemed so many days ago.

# Erich Kästner

# EMIL AND THE DETECTIVES

## *Illustrated by Walter Trier*

*Whilst asleep on a train journey to Berlin, Emil Tischbein's money is stolen from him by the man sharing his compartment. When the train arrives at the station, Emil decides to give chase.*

OF COURSE Emil would have liked to rush straight up to the man and shout, "Hand over my money!" But Grundeis did not look the type who would reply civilly, "With pleasure, my dear boy. Here it is. I'm terribly sorry. I'll never do such a thing again." No, it wouldn't be as easy as that.

The great thing was not to lose sight of him now he had found him, so Emil took cover behind a fat woman who was going in the right direction, but kept a sharp look-out from side to side. As he got nearer the bowler hat, he began to wonder what would happen next. When the man reached the main exit he stopped and looked back as though searching for someone in the crowd. Emil kept carefully out of sight, but the fat woman was getting near the exit too. He wondered if she would help him, but knew he could not really expect her to believe his story. Even if she did, the thief had only to say, "Madam, do I look so poor that I'd steal money from a child?" And everyone would start staring at Emil, and saying, "Disgraceful!

A boy like that making up such a story about anyone! Children are quite impossible nowadays." The mere thought set Emil's teeth chattering with fright.

At that moment the man turned away and stepped out into the street. Emil set down his bag, and dashed forward to see where he went. His arm ached like anything. That suitcase was a weight! He saw the thief cross the road slowly. Once he glanced back, then went on as though reassured.

A number 177 tram, made up of two cars linked together, drew up opposite the station. The man hesitated, and then got into the front part and sat down in a window seat.

Emil snatched up his case, put down his head, and plunged out into the street. He reached the tram just as it was going to start, but he had time to push his suitcase on to the platform of the rear part, and scrambled up after it – breathless but triumphant!

What next, he wondered? If the thief jumped off while the tram was going, he might as well give up the money as lost for

442

ever. It would be too dangerous to follow him, hampered as he was with the suitcase.

Motor cars rushed past with horns honking and screeching brakes. They signalled right-hand turns and left-hand turns, and swung off down side streets while other cars came swooping up behind them. The noise was indescribable, and on the pavements crowds of people kept hurrying by. Out of every turning vans and lorries, trams and double-decker buses swarmed into the main thoroughfare. There were newspaper stands at every corner, with men shouting the latest headlines. Wherever Emil looked there were gay shop windows filled with flowers and fruit, books, clothes, fine silk underwear, gold watches and clocks. And all the buildings stretched up and up into the sky.

So this was Berlin!

Emil wished he could stop and see everything properly, but there was not much chance of that. The man who had his money was sitting there, in the front part of the tram, and might get out at any moment and disappear into the crowds. If that happened, it would be the end of the matter. Emil was sure he could never follow him through all that traffic. Suddenly he got in a panic for fear the bowler hat might have got out already, and he shoved his head out to see. But it was no use, he just had to go on blind, not knowing whether the man had gone or was still sitting in the front car: not even knowing where the tram was taking him. And all this time, he supposed, his grandmother must be waiting for him by the flower stall at the Friedrich Street station! What would she say if she knew that her grandson was travelling round Berlin on a number 177 tram, alone, and in such trouble?

The tram stopped just then for the first time. Emil kept his eye on the car in front, but no one got out though a great many more people got on. They had to push past Emil to get to the seats, and one man complained about his blocking up the gangway.

"Other people want to get home as well as you," he growled.

The conductor, who was taking fares inside, rang the bell and the tram moved off. Emil got pressed back into a corner and someone trod on his foot. Then, all of a sudden, he remembered that he'd no money for the fare, and the conductor was on his way to him. "I'll be turned off if I can't pay," he thought. "Then I shall be done for!" He looked at the other passengers standing all round him and wondered if any of them would lend him the money to pay for his ticket. But they were all deeply engrossed in their own concerns; one reading a newspaper, two others discussing a big bank robbery.

"They dug a tunnel," one of them was saying, "and got inside the bank that way. They cleared everything out of the safe deposits. Thousands of pounds gone they say."

"It would be very difficult to prove what was in some of those safes," observed the other. "Apparently no one's obliged to tell the bank what they deposit in them."

"I suppose," said his friend, "people could claim to have diamonds worth thousands of pounds there when all they had really was a lot of worthless bonds or a few plated spoons!" They both laughed at that.

"That's what will happen to me," thought Emil. "No one will believe that Mr Grundeis stole seven pounds from me. He'll say I'm telling stories and that he only took half a crown. Oh dear, what a mess to be in."

By this time the conductor had got to the platform where Emil was, and called out,

"Any more fares?"

The passengers round him handed over their money and in exchange got long white strips of paper punched with holes. When the conductor reached Emil, he said:

"What about yours?"

"Please, I've lost my money," Emil told him, feeling sure the man would never believe it had been stolen.

"Lost it, eh? I've heard that tale before. And how far might you be going?"

"I...I...I don't know yet," Emil stammered.

"Well you can just get out at the next stop and make up your mind."

"Oh I can't do that!" Emil cried. "I *must* stay on – for a bit. Please let me."

"When I tell you to get off, off you get," said the conductor. "Understand?"

"Oh, give the boy a ticket," said the man who had been reading the paper, and he produced the money.

Emil got his ticket, but the conductor said, "You wouldn't believe how many kids get on every day and pretend they've lost their money. They're only trying it on. I've heard them laugh the moment my back was turned. They think it's a good joke."

"I don't think this one will," said the man.

"Oh no, I won't," Emil assured him, as soon as the conductor had gone inside the tram again. "Thank you very much, sir."

"That's all right," said the man, and returned to his paper.

Then the tram stopped again, and Emil had to lean out to see whether the man in the bowler hat was getting off, but he was not.

"Please will you give me your address?" Emil asked the man with the

newspaper when the tram moved on again.

"Why?"

"So that I can pay you back when I have some money again. I'm going to stay in Berlin for a week, so I could bring it round to you. My name is Emil Tischbein, I come from Neustadt."

"Oh, don't bother," said the man. "The fare's paid, and that's all there is to it. Do you want any more money?"

"Oh no thank you," Emil replied quickly. "I shouldn't like to take any more."

"Just as you like," said the man and went back to his paper.

The tram moved on, stopped, and went on again. Emil discovered that the fine broad street they were in was called Kaiser Avenue, but of course he had no idea where that was. The thief was still in the front compartment, and for all he knew there might be thieves all round him. No one seemed interested, one way or the other. A strange man had paid his fare, but had gone on reading again without even asking why he had no money. Emil felt very small among them all, in that big, busy city. Nobody cared about his having no money, or that he didn't know where he was going. There were four million people in Berlin at that moment, and not one of them cared what was happening to Emil Tischbein. No one has time for other people's troubles in a city. They've all troubles enough of their own. They may listen for a moment, and perhaps say how sorry they are, but they are probably thinking, "Oh, for goodness' sake, don't bother me about it!"

It was awful to feel so alone, and Emil wondered what would happen to him.

# Charles Dickens

# A CHRISTMAS CAROL

## The Christmas Pudding

*Three ghosts visit the miser Scrooge: the ghosts of Christmas Past, Christmas Present and Christmas Future. Through them, he sees Victorian London and his own life as never before. Here, unseen, he visits the home of his poor clerk, Bob Cratchit.*

THEN UP ROSE MRS CRATCHIT, Cratchit's wife, dressed out but poorly in a twice-turned gown, but brave in ribbons, which are cheap and make a goodly show for sixpence; and she laid the cloth, assisted by Belinda Cratchit, second of her daughters, also brave in ribbons; while Master Peter Cratchit plunged a fork into the saucepan of potatoes, and getting the corners of his monstrous shirt-collar ( Bob's private property, conferred upon his son and heir in honour of the day) into his mouth, rejoiced to find himself so gallantly attired, and yearned to show his linen in the fashionable Parks. And now two smaller Cratchits, boy and girl, came tearing in, screaming that outside the baker's they had smelt the goose, and known it for their own; and basking in luxurious thoughts of sage-and-onion, these young Cratchits danced about the table, and exalted Master Peter Cratchit to the skies, while he (not proud, although his collars nearly choked him) blew the fire, until the slow potatoes bubbling up, knocked loudly at the saucepan-lid to be let out and peeled.

"What has ever got your precious father then," said Mrs Cratchit. "And your brother, Tiny Tim! And Martha warn't as late last Christmas Day by half-an-hour!"

"Here's Martha, mother!" said a girl, appearing as she spoke.

"Here's Martha, mother!" cried the two young Cratchits. "Hurrah! There's *such* a goose, Martha!"

"Why, bless your heart alive, my dear, how late you are!" said Mrs Cratchit, kissing her a dozen times, and taking off her shawl and bonnet for her, with officious zeal.

"We'd a deal of work to finish up last night," replied the girl, "and had to clear away this morning, mother!"

"Well! Never mind so long as you are come," said Mrs Cratchit. "Sit ye down before the fire, my dear, and have a warm, Lord bless ye!"

"No no! There's father coming," cried the two young Cratchits, who were everywhere at once. "Hide Martha, hide!"

So Martha hid herself, and in came little Bob, the father, with at least three feet of comforter exclusive of the fringe, hanging down before him; and his threadbare clothes darned up and brushed, to look seasonable; and Tiny Tim upon his shoulder. Alas for Tiny Tim, he bore a little crutch, and had his limbs supported by an iron frame!

"Why, where's our Martha?" cried Bob Cratchit looking round.

"Not coming," said Mrs Cratchit.

"Not coming!" said Bob, with a sudden declension in his high spirits; for he had been Tim's blood horse all the way from church, and had come home rampant. "Not coming upon Christmas Day!"

Martha didn't like to see him disappointed, if it were only in joke; so she came out prematurely from behind the closet door, and ran into his arms, while the two young Cratchits hustled Tiny Tim, and bore him off into the wash-house, that he might hear the pudding singing in the copper.

"And how did little Tim behave?" asked Mrs Cratchit, when she had rallied Bob on his credulity and Bob had hugged his daughter to his heart's content.

"As good as gold," said Bob, "and better. Somehow he gets thoughtful, sitting by himself so much, and thinks the strangest things you ever heard. He told me, coming home, that he hoped the people saw him in the church, because he was a cripple, and it might be pleasant to them to remember upon Christmas Day, who made lame beggars walk and blind men see."

Bob's voice was tremulous when he told them this, and trembled more when he said that Tiny Tim was growing strong and hearty.

His active little crutch was heard upon the floor, and back came Tiny Tim before another word was spoken, escorted by his brother and sister to his stool beside the fire; and while Bob, turning up his cuffs – as if, poor fellow, they were capable of being made more shabby – compounded some hot mixture in a jug with gin and lemons, and stirred it round and round and put it on the hob to simmer; Master Peter and the two ubiquitous young Cratchits went to fetch the goose, with which they soon returned in high procession.

Such a bustle ensued that you might have thought a goose the rarest of all birds; a feathered phenomenon, to which a black swan was a matter of course: and in truth it was something very like it in that house. Mrs Cratchit made the gravy (ready beforehand in a little saucepan) hissing hot; Master Peter mashed the potatoes with incredible vigour; Miss Belinda sweetened up the apple-sauce; Martha dusted the hot plates; Bob took Tiny Tim beside him in a tiny corner at the table; the two young Cratchits set chairs for everybody, not forgetting themselves, and mounting guard upon their posts, crammed spoons into their mouths, lest they should shriek for goose before their turn came to be helped. At last the dishes were set on, and grace was said. It was succeeded by a breathless pause, as Mrs Cratchit, looking slowly all along the carving-knife, prepared to plunge it in the breast; but when she did, and when the long expected gush of stuffing issued forth, one murmur of delight arose all round the board, and even Tiny Tim, excited by the two young Cratchits, beat on the table with the handle of his knife, and feebly cried Hurrah!

There never was such a goose. Bob said he didn't believe there ever was such a goose cooked. Its tenderness and flavour, size and cheapness, were the themes of universal admiration. Eked out by the apple-sauce and mashed potatoes, it was a sufficient dinner for the whole family; indeed, as Mrs Cratchit said with great delight (surveying one small atom of a bone upon the dish), they hadn't ate it all at last! Yet everyone had had enough, and the youngest Cratchits in particular, were steeped in sage-and-onion to the eyebrows! But now, the plates being changed by Miss Belinda, Mrs Cratchit left the room alone – too nervous to bear witnesses – to take the pudding up, and bring it in.

Suppose it should not be done enough! Suppose it should break in turning out! Suppose somebody should have got over the wall of the back-yard, and stolen it, while they were merry with the goose: a supposition at which the two young Cratchits became livid! All sorts of horrors were supposed.

Hallo! A great deal of steam! The pudding was out of the copper. A smell like a washing-day! That was the cloth. A smell like an eating-house, and a pastry cook's next door to each other, with a laundress's next door to that! That was the pudding. In half a minute Mrs Cratchit entered: flushed, but smiling proudly: with the pudding, like a speckled cannon-ball, so hard and firm, blazing in half of half-a-quartern of ignited brandy, and bedight with Christmas holly stuck into the top.

Oh, a wonderful pudding! Bob Cratchit said, and calmly too, that he regarded it as the greatest success achieved by Mrs Cratchit since their marriage. Mrs Cratchit said that now the weight was off her mind, she would confess she had had her doubts about the quantity of flour. Everybody had something to say about it, but nobody said or thought it was at all a small pudding for a large family. It would have been flat heresy to do so. Any Cratchit would have blushed to hint at such a thing.

At last the dinner was all done, the cloth was cleared, the hearth swept, and the fire made up. The compound in the jug being tasted and considered perfect, apples and oranges were put upon the table, and a shovel-full of chestnuts on the fire. Then all the Cratchit family drew round the hearth, in what Bob Cratchit called a circle, meaning half a one; and at Bob Cratchit's elbow stood the family display of glass; two tumblers, and a custard-cup without a handle.

These held the hot stuff from the jug, however, as well as golden goblets would have done; and Bob served it out with beaming looks, while the chestnuts on the fire sputtered and crackled noisily. Then Bob proposed:

"A Merry Christmas to us all, my dears. God bless us!"

Which all the family re-echoed.

"God bless us every one!" said Tiny Tim, the last of all.

# Arthur Ransome
# SWALLOWS AND AMAZONS

*Illustrated by Jack McCarthy*

## The Amazons Attack

*In the holidays, John, Susan, Titty and Roger use their boat Swallow to go camping on an uninhabited island. Soon they see a strange pirate boat called Amazon and they meet the mysterious owner of a houseboat with a green parrot. Are they friends or enemies?*

AT THAT MOMENT something hit the saucepan with a loud ping, and ashes flew up out of the fire. A long arrow with a green feather stuck, quivering, among the embers.

The four explorers started to their feet.

"It's begun," said Titty.

Roger grabbed at the arrow and pulled it out of the fire.

Titty took it from him at once. "It may be poisoned," she said. "Don't touch the point of it."

"Listen," said Captain John.

They listened. There was not a sound to be heard but the quiet lapping of the water against the western shore of the island.

"It's him," said Titty. "He's winged his arrow with a feather from his green parrot."

"Listen," said Captain John again.

"Shut up, just for a minute," said Mate Susan.

There was a sharp crack of a dead stick breaking somewhere in the middle of the island.

"We must scout," said Captain John. "I'll take one end of the line, the mate the other.

Titty and Roger go in the middle. Spread out. As soon as one of us sees him, the others close in to help."

They spread out across the island, and began to move forward. But they had not gone ten yards when John gave a shout.

"*Swallow* has gone," he shouted. He was on the left of the line, and as soon as he came out of the camping ground he saw the landing-place where he had left *Swallow* when he came back with the milk. No *Swallow* was there. The others ran together to the landing-place. There was not a sign of *Swallow*. She had simply disappeared.

"Spread out again. Spread out again," said John. "We'll comb the whole island. Keep a look-out, Mister Mate, from your shore. She can't have drifted away. He's taken her, but he's still on the island. We heard him."

"Roger and I pulled her right up," said Titty. "She couldn't have drifted off."

"Spread out again," said Captain John. "Then listen. Advance as soon as the mate blows her whistle. A hoot like an owl means all right. Three hoots means something's up. Blow as soon as you're ready, Mister Mate."

The mate crossed the island nearly to the western shore. She looked out through the trees. Not a sail was to be seen on the lake. Far away there was the smoke of the morning steamer, but that did not count. Roger and Titty, half a dozen yards apart, were in the middle of the island. Captain John moved a little way inland, but not so far that anyone could be between him and the shore without being seen. They listened. There was not a sound.

Then, over the western side of the island, the mate blew her whistle.

The four began moving again through the trees and the undergrowth.

"Roger," called Titty, "have you got a weapon?"

"No," said Roger. "Have you?"

"I've got two sticks, pikes, I mean. You'd better have one."

She threw one of her sticks to Roger.

An owl hooted away to her left.

"That must be the captain," she said. She hooted back. Susan away on the right hooted in reply. And again they all listened. Then they moved forward again.

"Hullo," cried Roger, "someone's been here."

Titty ran to him. There was a round place where the grass and ferns were pressed flat as if someone had been lying there.

"He's left his knife," said Roger, holding up a big clasp knife that he had found in the grass.

Titty hooted like an owl three times.

The captain and the mate came running.

"He must be quite close to," said Titty.

"We've got his knife, anyway," said Roger.

Captain John bent down and felt the flattened grass with his hand.

"It's not warm," he said.

"Well, it wouldn't stay warm very long," said the mate.

"Spread out again and go on," said Captain John. "We mustn't let him get away with *Swallow*. He can't be far away, because we heard him. If he had taken *Swallow* to sea we should have seen her. He must have her here, somewhere, close along the shore."

At that moment there was a wild yell, "Hurrah, hurrah." But the yelling did not come from in front of them. It came from behind them, from the direction of the camp.

"Come on," said Captain John, "keep together. Charge!"

The whole party rushed back through the trees towards the camp.

Just as they came to the edge of the clearing there was a shout, but they could see no one.

"Hands up! Halt!"

The voice came from immediately in front of them.

"Hands up!" it came again.

"Flat on your faces," cried Captain John, throwing himself on the ground.

Susan, Titty, and Roger were full length on the ground in a moment. An arrow passed harmlessly over their heads.

They looked at their own camp, and did not at first see what Captain John had seen. In the middle of the camp a tall stick was stuck in the ground with a black pirate flag blowing from the top of it. But there seemed to be nobody there. Then, inside their own tents, they saw two figures, kneeling, one with a bow ready to shoot, the other fitting an arrow.

"It's not the houseboat man," said Titty. "It's the pirates from the pirate ship."

"And in our tents," said Susan.

"Let's take them prisoners," said Roger.

"Hands up," said the pirate girl from the *Amazon*, who was in the captain's tent.

"Hands up yourselves," cried Captain John, and made as if to leap to his feet. Both the pirates shot off their arrows.

"Now," shouted John, "before they load again. Swallows for ever!"

The four Swallows were up and halfway across the open space in a moment.

The red-capped Amazons leapt up out of the tents to meet them.

But they pointed their bows to the ground. "A parley," shouted the one who seemed to be the leader.

"Halt!" called Captain John.

The four explorers of the *Swallow* stood facing the two pirate girls from the *Amazon*. The Amazons were bigger than most of the Swallows. One of them was bigger than Captain John. The other was about the same size. If it had come to a fight, it might have been a very near thing.

But it did not come to a fight.

"Let's parley first and fight afterwards," said the leader of the Amazons.

"It's no good our parleying with you if the houseboat man has got *Swallow*," said John.

"The man from the houseboat?" said the younger Amazon. "But he's got nothing to do with it. He's a native, and very unfriendly."

"Well, he's unfriendly to us too," said John.

Susan pulled John by the sleeve. "If the houseboat man isn't with them," she whispered, "they must have taken *Swallow* themselves, and the only place they could put her is the harbour. Their own ship must be there too. So if they have got our tents we can take both ships."

"If he's unfriendly to you too, we had better parley at once," said the elder Amazon. "Where is *Swallow*?"

"She is a prize, and we have taken her into our harbour."

"It's our harbour," said John. "And anyhow that's not much good to you. You can't get out from this end of the island against the four of us. The harbour end of the island is in our hands, so that really it's the *Amazon* that's a prize, and we've got both ships. You've only got our tents."

Titty spoke. "Why have your arrows got green feathers? The pirate on the houseboat must have given them to you. You must be on his side."

The younger Amazon exclaimed, "But the green feathers are our trophies. We took them ourselves. He was keeping them to clean his pipes and we boarded his ship and took them."

The elder Amazon said, "We are all on the same side, and I don't see the good of fighting."

John said, "But why did you come to our island...?"

"Our island," said the Amazons together.

"How can it be your island? This is our camp!"

"It's been our island for years and years," said the Amazons. "Who built the fireplace? Who marked the harbour?"

"Who marked the harbour?" said John. "You mean putting a cross on a tree there. Anyone could put a cross on a tree."

The elder Amazon laughed. "That just shows it's our island," she said. "You don't even know how the harbour is marked."

"We do," said Roger.

John was silent. He knew that they did not.

At last he said, "Right, we'll parley. But you must put down your weapons, and so will we. You must take down your flag, because ours is in *Swallow*, so that we can't put it up beside it."

The elder Amazon said, "It seems a pity to take down the flag when there is such a good wind blowing it out. It isn't as if it was just hanging. One of you go to the harbour to get your flag from your ship, and then we can have both flags flying during the parley and everything will be proper."

"No fighting while one of us is going for it?"

"No. Peace. We'll put our weapons down now."

The Amazons put their bows on the ground. Roger and Titty put down their pikes. John and Susan had no weapons to put down.

"Mister Mate," said John, "will you send one of your men to the harbour to bring our flag from *Swallow*?"

"Skip along, Roger," said Mate Susan, and then, turning to the Amazons, "You swear the houseboat man is not there to take him prisoner?"

"Of course," said the Amazons. "But will you swear he does not do anything to our ship? We were very careful with yours, and we haven't done anything to your tents. We could have burnt them easily or razed them to the ground."

"We swear," said Captain John.

"Why not scuttle their ship and keep them prisoners?" said Titty.

"Until the parley is over it is peace," said Captain John. "Skip along, Roger, and get the *Swallow*'s flag, but don't touch anything else."

Roger ran off. "I've got their knife anyway," he shouted.

The elder Amazon turned to the other.

"Peggy, you donkey," she said. "Where's the ship's knife?"

Peggy, the younger Amazon, felt in the pockets of her breeches.

"Gone," she said. "We must have left it when we were in hiding in the bush."

"We don't want to take their knife," whispered Susan to John.

"We'll give you back your knife," said John to the Amazons. "As soon as our man comes back from the harbour he shall put it with the other weapons. We don't really want your knife. We have three knives on our ship."

"Besides the knives for cutting pemmican and bread and butter," said Susan.

"This knife was given us by Uncle Jim last year for polishing the cannon on the houseboat," said the elder Amazon.

"Is the man on the houseboat your uncle?" asked Titty. "I thought you said he was your enemy too."

"He is only our uncle sometimes," said the younger Amazon. "He was last year, but this year he is in league with the natives, and the natives are very unfriendly."

"Our natives are friendly," said Titty. "Everybody is friendly except the houseboat man...and you," she added. "And if he's your uncle you must be in league with him."

"We jolly well aren't," said the elder Amazon.

"Shut up, Titty, and wait for the parley," said Captain John.

Roger came back with Titty's flag from the *Swallow*.

"They've got a lovely boat," he whispered to Mate Susan.

"Hand over that knife," said John.

Roger handed it over and John cut a tall sapling from a hazel on the edge of the clearing. He made a sharp point at one end of it to stick in the ground. Then he fastened Titty's flag to the top of it, found a soft place, and planted his flagstaff firmly beside the pirate flag of the Amazons. Then he wiped the knife on the grass, shut it up, and put it with the bows and the pikes.

"Now for the parley," said he. He walked towards the Amazons and held out his hand.

"My name is John Walker," he said, "master of the ship *Swallow*. This is Susan Walker, mate of the *Swallow*. This is Titty, able-seaman. This is Roger, ship's boy. Who are you?"

The elder Amazon shook hands with him.

"I am Nancy Blackett, master and part owner of the *Amazon*, the terror of the seas. This is Peggy Blackett, mate and part owner of the same."

"Her real name isn't Nancy," said Peggy. "Her name is Ruth, but Uncle Jim said that Amazons were ruthless, and as our ship is the *Amazon*, and we are Amazon pirates from the Amazon River, we had to change her name. Uncle Jim gave us the ship last year. We only had a rowing boat before that."

Nancy Blackett scowled ferociously. "I'll shiver your timbers for you if you don't stop chattering, Peggy."

"They must be in league with the houseboat pirate," said Titty. "Didn't you hear how she said he gave them their ship?"

"That was last year," said Nancy. "He was friendly last year. This year he's worse than the natives."

"Hadn't we better sit down?" said Susan. "Shall I put a stick or two on our fire and warm up the kettle? It's still got some tea in it."

"We don't want any tea, thank you," said Nancy. "But use our fireplace if you want to."

"It's our camp," said Roger.

"Let's sit down," said Mate Susan.

The two parties sat on the ground by the fireplace where the fire was still smouldering. Susan was right. It is much more difficult to be fierce sitting down than standing up.

"First of all," said Nancy Blackett. "When did you come to these seas?"

"We discovered this ocean nearly a month ago."

"When did you first come to this island?"

"We have been on the island for days and days."

"Well," said Nancy Blackett. "We were born on the shores of the Amazon River, which flows into this ocean. We have been coming to this island for years and years."

"We used to come in a rowing galley until Uncle Jim gave us the *Amazon*," said Peggy. "We used to land at the place where we found your ship, until we discovered the harbour. We have made our camp here every year."

"Look here," said Nancy Blackett. "What is the name of the island?"

"We haven't yet given it a name," said John.

"It is called Wild Cat Island. Uncle Jim called it that, because it belonged to us. That shows you whose island it is."

"But it's our island now," said John. "It was uninhabited when we came and we put our tents up here, and you can't turn us out."

Titty broke in.

"Is your Uncle Jim a retired pirate?" she asked. "I said he was as soon as we saw him."

Nancy Blackett thought for a moment. "It's quite a good thing for him to be," she said at last.

"But," said Titty, "you are pirates too."

"That's why he hates us. He must be Captain Flint. He knows what pirates are. He knows the day will come when he will walk the plank off the deck of his own ship when we have captured it."

"We'll help," said Roger.

"He hates us," said Captain John. "He has been stirring up the natives against us."

"Let's be allies," said Nancy Blackett, "then it won't matter who the island belongs to. We will be allies against Captain Flint and all the natives in the world."

"Except our friendlies," said Titty.

"Let's be allies," said Peggy. "Really we wanted to be allies as soon as we saw your smoke on the island yesterday. We are sick of natives. And we wanted to be allies at once, if only we hadn't promised to be home for lunch. That was why we just sailed round the island and defied you with our flag. There wasn't time for anything else. Then we went home."

"We watched you from beyond the big islands by Rio," said Susan.

"Rio?" said Nancy. "Rio? Oh, well, if you'll agree to let the island go on being called Wild Cat Island, we'll agree to Rio. It's a good name."

"Wild Cat Island's a good name too," said John politely.

"But how could you see us beyond the islands by Rio when we left you here?" asked Peggy.

"We manned the *Swallow* and gave chase," said John.

"Thunder and lightning," said Nancy Blackett, "what a chance we missed. If we'd only known we'd have given you broadside for broadside till one of us sank, even if it had made us late for lunch."

Peggy Blackett went on. "We came here today to look at you again. We got up at sunrise and sailed close by the island and there was no smoke and we thought you had gone. Probably you were all asleep. Then we saw your ship at the landing-place. We sailed on to Tea Bay and had our second breakfast there, a real one with tea. The first was only cold porridge and sandwiches we got from cook last night. Then we crawled along the shore and saw one of you coming back from somewhere in your ship. The others were bathing. Then we saw you all disappear, and we crawled back to our ship and sailed straight into the harbour. There was nobody there. Then we came through the bush on the island, scouting, and saw you round your camp fire. We took away your ship and put her in the harbour. Then we came back and made our surprise attack. When you found your ship was gone and you all ran down to the landing-place we slipped past and took the camp, and Nancy was saying that somehow it was going to be difficult to be allies..."

"Avast there, Peggy, you goat," said Nancy Blackett. "Excuse my mate," she said to Captain John. "She does chatter so."

"Well, Nancy was saying that our surprise attack was such a good one that we'd have to go on being enemies, and I said I was sick of enemies, what with our natives and Uncle Jim being no good this year..."

"He's Captain Flint," said Nancy.

"Anyway, if she hadn't remembered about parleys you would have been natives too, for ever and ever," said Peggy.

"We couldn't be that," said Titty.

"Of course not," said Nancy Blackett; "it's

much more fun being sea-dogs and timber shiverers. I propose an alliance."

"I don't see why not," said Captain John.

"My idea," said Nancy Blackett, "is an alliance against all enemies, especially Uncle Jim – Captain Flint, I mean. But we want the sort of alliance that will let us fight each other if we want to."

"That's not an alliance," said Titty, "that's a treaty, a treaty of offence and defence. There are lots in the history book."

"Yes," said Nancy Blackett, "defence against our enemies and all sorts of desperate battles between ourselves whenever we want."

"Right," said Captain John.

"Have you got a bit of paper and a pencil?" asked Nancy.

"I have," said Titty, and ran into the mate's tent and brought out a leaf from her log and a pencil.

Nancy took it and wrote:

"I, Captain John of the ship *Swallow*, and I, Captain Nancy of the ship *Amazon*, do hereby make a treaty of offence and defence on behalf of our ships and our ships' companies. Signed and sealed at this place of Wild Cat Island in the month of August 1929."

She passed the paper to the others.

"It looks all right," said Captain John.

"It ought to be 'this month', not 'the'," said Titty. "And you haven't put in the lat. and long. They always put them in all over the place."

Nancy Blackett took the paper, crossed out "the" in front of the word "month" and put "this" instead, and after the word "Island" wrote in "Lat. 7 Long. 200."

"We ought to sign it in our blood," she said, "but pencil will do."

# Ruth Thomas
# THE RUNAWAYS

### Illustrated by Derek Brazell

## The Way to the Seaside

*Two children, Nathan and Julia, find a bag of money in a
deserted house. Everyone thinks they have stolen it. Terrified of the police,
school and their parents, they run away.*

"ARE WE NEARLY THERE?" Julia asked. "Shut up," said Nathan, scowling. "What you keep asking that for?"

The train slowed down and they saw it: EUSTON, in big letters. "What does that say?" asked Julia.

"Can't you read?" said Nathan, forgetting that indeed, she could not.

Julia blushed, and turned her head.

The station was quite different from the friendly sunlit one they had started from. This station was covered over, dark and gloomy and somehow forbidding. The children showed their tickets at the barrier, and walked up the long ramp to the entrance. The vast marbled hall they found themselves in amazed them – even Nathan, who had seen it before but forgotten how big it was. There was an appetising smell of frying food coming from somewhere.

"I'm hungry," said Nathan, who had had nothing to eat since lunch time, and Julia discovered that she was hungry too. They located a beefburger booth, one of several places in the station selling cooked food. They bought beefburgers and cans of Coke and looked for somewhere to sit down. There were very few seats, so they sat on the floor.

They ate ravenously, in silence. "I'm going to have another one," said Nathan. He was discovering the joy of having unlimited funds. You could have two beefburgers if you liked – three if you wanted them. Julia bought two bars of chocolate instead of another beefburger. She felt a little sick after she had stuffed them down, but she was beginning to enjoy herself. Running away was all right, she decided, though there was still a nasty sinking frightened feeling, somewhere in the depths of her stomach, nothing to do with the chocolate, when she remembered what an awful thing they were doing.

There were other people sitting on the floor besides Julia and Nathan. Some of them looked rather peculiar. "They been drinking too much beer," said Nathan, disapprovingly.

Those who had been drinking too much beer were taking no notice of Julia and Nathan. But one or two other people were beginning to give them funny looks. "Let's go now," said Julia. "Somebody might ask us what we're here for."

"All right. I'm tired now anyway."

"Where we going to sleep?"

"Dunno. Somewhere."

Until that moment it had not really

After that, they went to the little brick-built heating-house, at the end of the green-house, and Hatty set about opening that door for Tom. She was far too small to be able to reach the flat square of iron that latched the top of the door; but, standing on tiptoe and straining upward with her yew-twig, she was finally able to poke it aside. She opened the door, and they went down steps inside into darkness and the smell of rust and cold cinders – the weather was so warm that the stove for the greenhouse was not working. There was a small shelf with two or three books on it, that Hatty said belonged to Abel. The shelf was just out of reach, but they could see that the topmost book of the pile was a Bible. "Abel says the Bible must be above all the other books, like – like the Queen ruling over all England."

They went into the greenhouse, among the cacti and the creepers that swayed down from their roof-suspended cage-pots, and plants with strange flowers that could never be expected to live, like other plants, out of doors. Tom gasped for breath in the green-house, and wondered how they endured the stifling air. There was a Castor-oil Plant – Tom felt a little sick when Hatty named it. There was a Sensitive Plant, too, and Hatty showed Tom how, when she touched a leaf-tip, the whole frond drooped and shrank from her by folding itself together. The plant's sensitivity was something quite out of the ordinary; it seemed to feel even Tom's touch. He was so delighted that he worked his fingers over the whole plant, and left it in one droop of nervous dejection.

Then they leant over the water-tank and tried to see the goldfish – and tried to catch them. Hatty bared her arm, to plunge it in; and Tom laid his arm along hers and behind it, with his open hand behind hers, finger to finger. So, as with one arm and one hand, they dipped into the water and hunted. Tom could have done nothing by himself; but when Hatty very nearly caught a fish, Tom's hand seemed one with hers in the catching.

Then Hatty led Tom back to the doorway of the greenhouse and showed him the coloured panes that bordered the glass panelling of the upper half. Through each colour of pane, you could see a different garden outside. Through the green pane, Tom saw a garden with green flowers under a green sky; even the geraniums were green-black. Through the red pane lay a garden as he might have seen it through the redness of shut eyelids. The purple glass filled the garden with thunderous shadow and with oncoming night. The yellow glass seemed to drench it in lemonade. At each of the four corners of this bordering was a colourless square of glass, engraved with a star.

"And if you look through this one..." said Hatty. They screwed up their eyes and looked through the engraved glass.

"You can't really see anything, through the star," said Tom, disappointed.

"Sometimes I like that the best of all," said Hatty. "You look and see nothing, and you might think there wasn't a garden at all; but, all the time, of course, there is, waiting for you."

They went out into the garden again, and Hatty began to tell Tom about the yew-trees round the lawn. The one he had climbed and waved from was called the Matterhorn. Another tree was called the Look-out, and another the Steps of St Paul's. One tree was called Tricksy, because of the difficulty of climbing it: its main trunk was quite bare for some way up from the ground and could only be swarmed. Hubert and James and Edgar had

# Brian Jacques
# REDWALL

*Illustrated by Pete Lyon*

## Cluny's Army

*The mice in Redwall Abbey live at peace until they are besieged by
the terrible rat Cluny the Scourge and his army. Matthias, a young mouse,
soon finds his dream of becoming a warrior is a grim reality.*

CLUNY'S ARMY HALTED at the sound of the Joseph Bell. As the dust settled, Fangburn looked to his leader for approval.

"They're ringing that big bell again, Chief. Ha! ha! Maybe they think it'll frighten us off."

The Warlord's eye rested balefully on his scout. "Shut your mouth, fool. If you'd done as I ordered and come right back to report, the way Cheesethief did, we might have been inside that Abbey by now!"

Fangburn slunk back into the ranks. He hoped Cluny had forgotten, but Cluny rarely forgot anything on a campaign. The element of surprise had been lost: now he must try another ploy, the show of force. The mere sight of a fully armed horde had worked before, and he had little doubt it would prove effective now. Ordinary peaceful creatures were usually panic-stricken at the sight of Cluny the Scourge at the head of his army. The rat was a cunning general, except during the times when his mad rage took control of him, but what need of berserk fits for a bunch of silly mice?

Cluny knew the value of fear as a weapon.

And Cluny was a fearsome figure.

His long ragged black cloak was made of batwings, fastened at the throat with a mole skull. The immense war helmet he wore had the plumes of a blackbird and the horns of a stag beetle adorning it. From beneath the slanted visor his one eye glared viciously out at the Abbey before him.

Matthias's voice rang out sharp and clear from the high parapet, "Halt! Who goes there?"

Redtooth swaggered forward and took up the challenge in his Chief's name, as he called back up at the walls, "Look well, all creatures. This is the mighty horde of Cluny the Scourge. My name is Redtooth. I speak for Cluny our leader."

Constance's reply was harsh and unafraid, "Then speak your piece and begone, rats."

Silence hung upon the air while Redtooth and Cluny held a whispered conference. Redtooth returned to the walls.

"Cluny the Scourge says he will not deal with badgers, he will only speak with the leaders of the mice. Let us in, so that my Chief may sit and talk to your Chief."

Redtooth dodged back as his request was greeted by howls of derision and some loose pieces of masonry from the ramparts. These plump little mice were not as peaceful as they first looked.

## Robert Louis Stevenson
# TREASURE ISLAND

*Illustrated by N. C. Wyeth*

## In the Apple Barrel

*This is the famous story told by young Jim Hawkins of how he finds a treasure map belonging to the notorious pirate, Captain Flint. Jim and Squire Trelawney and Dr Livesey set out in the* Hispaniola *to find Treasure Island. The ship's cook is a very clever, capable man called Long John Silver, whom they all trust.*

THE COXSWAIN, ISRAEL HANDS, was a careful, wily, old, experienced seaman, who could be trusted at a pinch with almost anything. He was a great confidant of Long John Silver, and so the mention of his name leads me on to speak of our ship's cook, Barbecue, as the men called him.

Aboard ship he carried his crutch by a lanyard round his neck, to have both hands as free as possible. It was something to see him wedge the foot of the crutch against a bulkhead, and, propped against it, yielding to every movement of the ship, get on with his cooking like someone safe ashore. Still more strange was it to see him in the heaviest of weather cross the deck. He had a line or two rigged up to help him across the widest spaces – Long John's earrings, they were called; and he would hand himself from one place to another, now using the crutch, now trailing it alongside by the lanyard, as quickly as another man could walk. Yet some of the men who had sailed with him before expressed their pity to see him so reduced.

"He's no common man, Barbecue," said the coxswain to me. "He had good schooling in his young days, and can speak like a book when so minded; and brave – a lion's nothing alongside of Long John! I seen him grapple four, and knock their heads together – him un-armed."

All the crew respected and even obeyed him. He had a way of talking to each, and doing everybody some particular service. To me he was unweariedly kind; and always glad to see me in the galley, which he kept as clean as a new pin; the dishes hanging up burnished, and his parrot in a cage in one corner.

"Come away, Hawkins," he would say; "come and have a yarn with John. Nobody more welcome than yourself, my son. Sit you down and hear the news. Here's Cap'n Flint – I calls my parrot Cap'n Flint, after the famous buccaneer – here's Cap'n Flint predicting success to our v'yage. Wasn't you, cap'n?"

And the parrot would say, with great rapidity, "Pieces of eight! pieces of eight! pieces of eight!" till you wondered that it was not out of breath, or till John threw his handkerchief over the cage.

"Now, that bird," he would say, "is, maybe, two hundred years old, Hawkins – they lives for ever mostly; and if anybody's seen more wickedness, it must be the devil himself. She's sailed with England, the great Cap'n England, the pirate. She's been at Madagascar, and at Malabar, and Surinam, and Providence, and Portobello. She was at the fishing up of the wrecked Plate ships. It's there she learned 'Pieces of eight', and little wonder; three hundred and fifty thousand of 'em, Hawkins! She was at the boarding of the *Viceroy of the Indies* out of Goa, she was; and to look at her you would think she was a babby. But you smelt powder – didn't you, cap'n?"

"Stand by to go about," the parrot would scream.

"Ah, she's a handsome craft, she is," the cook would say, and give her sugar from his pocket, and then the bird would peck at the bars and swear straight on, passing belief for wickedness. "There," John would add, "you can't touch pitch and not be mucked, lad. Here's this poor old innocent bird o' mine swearing blue fire, and none the wiser, you may lay to that. She would swear the same, in a manner of speaking, before chaplain." And John would touch his forelock with a solemn way he had, that made me think he was the best of men.

In the meantime, squire and Captain Smollett were still on pretty distant terms with one another. The squire made no bones about the matter; he despised the captain. The captain, on his part, never spoke but when he was spoken to, and then sharp and short and dry, and not a word wasted. He owned, when driven into a corner, that he seemed to have been wrong about the crew, that some of them were as brisk as he wanted to see, and all had behaved fairly well. As for the ship, he had

taken a downright fancy to her. "She'll lie a point nearer the wind than a man has a right to expect of his own married wife, sir. But," he would add, "all I say is we're not home again, and I don't like the cruise."

The squire, at this, would turn away and march up and down the deck, chin in air.

"A trifle more of that man," he would say, "and I should explode."

We had some heavy weather, which only proved the qualities of the *Hispaniola*. Every man on board seemed well content, and they must have been hard to please if they had been otherwise; for it is my belief there was never a ship's company so spoiled since Noah put to sea. Double grog was going on the least excuse; there was duff on odd days, as, for instance, if the squire heard it was any man's birthday; and always a barrel of apples standing broached in the waist, for anyone to help himself that had a fancy.

"Never knew good come of it yet," the captain said to Dr Livesey. "Spoil foc's'le hands, make devils. That's my belief."

But good did come of the apple barrel, as you shall hear; for if it had not been for that, we should have had no note of warning, and might all have perished by the hand of treachery.

This was how it came about.

We had run up the trades to get the wind of the island we were after – I am not allowed to be more plain – and now we were running down for it with a bright look-out day and night. It was about the last day of our outward voyage, by the largest computation; some time that night, or, at latest, before noon of the morrow, we should sight the Treasure Island. We were heading S.S.W., and had a steady breeze abeam and a quiet sea. The *Hispaniola* rolled steadily, dipping her bowsprit now and then with a whiff of spray. All was drawing alow and aloft; everyone was in the bravest spirits, because we were now so near an end of the first part of our adventure.

Now, just after sundown, when all my work was over, and I was on my way to my berth, it occurred to me that I should like an apple. I ran on deck. The watch was all forward looking out for the island. The man at the helm was watching the luff of the sail, and whistling away gently to himself; and that was the only sound excepting the swish of the sea against the bows and around the sides of the ship.

In I got bodily into the apple barrel, and found there was scarce an apple left; but, sitting down there in the dark, what with the sound of the waters and the rocking movement of the ship, I had either fallen asleep, or was on the point of doing so, when a heavy man sat down with rather a clash close by. The barrel shook as he leaned his shoulders against it, and I was just about to jump up when the man began to speak. It was Silver's voice, and, before I had heard a dozen words, I would not have shown myself for all the world, but lay there, trembling and listening, in the extreme of fear and curiosity; for from these dozen words I understood that the lives of all the honest men aboard depended upon me alone.

"No, not I," said Silver. "Flint was cap'n; I was quartermaster, along of my timber leg. The same broadside I lost my leg, old Pew lost his deadlights. It was a master surgeon, him that ampytated me – out of college and all – Latin by the bucket, and what not; but he was hanged like a dog, and sun-dried like the rest, at Corso Castle. That was Roberts's men, that was, and comed of changing names to their ships – *Royal Fortune* and so on. Now, what a ship was christened, so let her stay, I says. So it was with the *Cassandra*, as brought us all safe

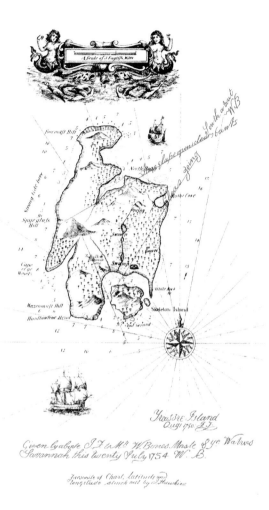

home from Malabar, after England took the *Viceroy of the Indies*; so it was with the old *Walrus*, Flint's old ship, as I've seen a-muck with the red blood and fit to sink with gold."

"Ah!" cried another voice, that of the youngest hand on board, and evidently full of admiration, "he was the flower of the flock, was Flint!"

"Davis was a man, too, by all accounts," said Silver. "I never sailed along of him; first with England, then with Flint, that's my story; and now here on my own account, in a manner of speaking. I laid by nine hundred safe, from England, and two thousand after Flint. That ain't bad for a man before the mast

– all safe in bank. 'Tain't earning now, it's saving does it, you may lay to that. Where's all England's men now? I dunno. Where's Flint's? Why, most of 'em aboard here, and glad to get the duff – been begging before that, some on 'em. Old Pew, as had lost his sight, and might have thought shame, spends twelve hundred pound in a year, like a lord in Parliament. Where is he now? Well, he's dead now and under hatches; but for two year before that, shiver my timbers! the man was starving. He begged, and he stole, and he cut throats, and starved at that, by the powers!"

"Well, it ain't much use, after all," said the young seaman.

"'Tain't much use for fools, you may lay to it – that nor nothing," cried Silver. "But now, you look here: you're young, you are, but you're as smart as paint. I see that when I set my eyes on you, and I'll talk to you like a man."

You may imagine how I felt when I heard this abominable old rogue addressing another in the very same words of flattery as he had used to myself. I think, if I had been able, that I would have killed him through the barrel. Meantime, he ran on, little supposing he was overheard.

"Here it is about gentlemen of fortune. They lives rough, and they risk swinging, but they eat and drink like fighting-cocks, and when a cruise is done, why, it's hundreds of pounds instead of hundreds of farthings in their pockets. Now, the most goes for rum and a good fling, and to sea again in their shirts. But that's not the course I lay. I puts it all away, some here, some there, and none too much anywheres, by reason of suspicion. I'm fifty, mark you; once back from this cruise, I set up gentleman in earnest. Time enough too, says you. Ah, but I've lived easy in the meantime; never denied myself o' nothing heart desires, and slep' soft and ate dainty all my days, but when at sea. And how did I begin? Before the mast, like you!"

"Well," said the other, "but all the other money's gone now, ain't it? You daren't show face in Bristol after this."

"Why, where might you suppose it was?" asked Silver derisively.

"At Bristol, in banks and places," answered his companion.

"It were," said the cook; "it were when we weighed anchor. But my old missis has it all by now. And the 'Spy-glass' is sold, lease and goodwill and rigging; and the old girl's off to meet me. I would tell you where, for I trust you; but it 'ud make jealousy among the mates."

"And can you trust your missis?" asked the other.

"Gentlemen of fortune," returned the cook, "usually trusts little among themselves, and right they are, you may lay to it. But I have a way with me, I have. When a mate brings a slip on his cable – one as knows me, I mean – it won't be in the same world with old John. There was some that was feared of Pew, and some that was feared of Flint; but Flint his own self was feared of me. Feared he was, and proud. They was the roughest crew afloat, was Flint's; the devil himself would have been feared to go to sea with them. Well, now, I tell you, I'm not a boasting man, and you seen yourself how easy I keep company; but when I was quartermaster, *lambs* wasn't the word for Flint's old buccaneers. Ah, you may be sure of yourself in old John's ship."

"Well, I tell you now," replied the lad, "I didn't half a quarter like the job till I had this talk with you, John; but there's my hand on it now."

"And a brave lad you were, and smart, too," answered Silver, shaking hands so heartily that all the barrel shook, "and a finer figurehead for a gentleman of fortune I never clapped my eyes on."

By this time I had begun to understand the meaning of their terms. By a "gentleman of fortune" they plainly meant neither more nor less than a common pirate, and the little scene that I had overheard was the last act in the corruption of one of the honest hands – perhaps of the last one left aboard. But on this point I was soon to be relieved, for Silver giving a little whistle, a third man strolled up and sat down by the party.

"Dick's square," said Silver.

"Oh, I know'd Dick was square," returned the voice of the coxswain, Israel Hands. "He's no fool, is Dick." And he turned his quid and spat. "But, look here," he went on, "here's what I want to know, Barbecue: how long are we a-going to stand off and on like a blessed bumboat? I've had a'most enough o' Cap'n Smollett; he's hazed me long enough, by thunder! I want to go into that cabin, I do. I want their pickles and wines, and that."

"Israel," said Silver, "your head ain't much account, nor ever was. But you're able to hear, I reckon; leastways, your ears is big enough. Now, here's what I say: you'll berth forward, and you'll live hard, and you'll speak soft, and you'll keep sober, till I give the word; and you may lay to that, my son."

"Well, I don't say no, do I?" growled the coxswain. "What I say is, when? That's what I say."

"When! by the powers!" cried Silver. "Well, now, if you want to know, I'll tell you when. The last moment I can manage; and that's when. Here's a first-rate seaman, Cap'n Smollett, sails the blessed ship for us. Here's

this squire and doctor with a map and such – I don't know where it is, do I? No more do you, says you. Well, then, I mean this squire and doctor shall find the stuff, and help us to get it aboard, by the powers. Then we'll see. If I was sure of you all, sons of double Dutchmen, I'd have Cap'n Smollett navigate us half-way back again before I struck."

"Why, we're all seamen aboard here, I should think," said the lad Dick.

"We're all foc's'le hands, you mean," snapped Silver. "We can steer a course, but who's to set one? That's what all you gentlemen split on, first and last. If I had my way, I'd have Cap'n Smollett work us back into the trades at least; then we'd have no blessed miscalculations and a spoonful of water a day. But I know the sort you are. I'll finish with 'em at the island, as soon's the blunt's on board, and a pity it is. But you're never happy till you're drunk. Split my sides, I've a sick heart to sail with the likes of you!"

"Easy all, Long John," cried Israel. "Who's a-crossin' of you?"

"Why, how many tall ships, think ye, now, have I seen laid aboard? and how many brisk lads drying in the sun at Execution Dock?" cried Silver, "and all for this same hurry and hurry and hurry. You hear me? I seen a thing or two at sea, I have. If you would on'y lay your course, and a p'int to windward, you would ride in carriages, you would. But not you! I know you. You'll have your mouthful of rum tomorrow, and go hang."

"Everybody know'd you was a kind of a chapling, John; but there's others as could hand and steer as well as you," said Israel. "They liked a bit o' fun, they did. They wasn't so high and dry, nohow, but took their fling, like jolly companions every one."

"So?" says Silver. "Well, and where are they now? Pew was that sort, and he died a beggar-man. Flint was, and he died of rum at Savannah. Ah, they was a sweet crew, they was! – on'y, where are they?"

"But," asked Dick, "when we do lay 'em athwart, what are we to do with 'em, anyhow?"

"There's the man for me!" cried the cook, admiringly. "That's what I call business. Well, what would you think? Put 'em ashore like maroons? That would have been England's way. Or cut 'em down like that much pork? That would have been Flint's or Billy Bones's."

"Billy was the man for that," said Israel. "'Dead men don't bite,' says he. Well, he's dead now hisself; he knows the long and short on it now; and if ever a rough hand come to port, it was Billy."

"Right you are," said Silver, "rough and ready. But mark you here: I'm an easy man – I'm quite the gentleman, says you; but this time it's serious. Dooty is dooty, mates. I give my vote – death. When I'm in Parlyment, and riding in my coach, I don't want none of these sea-lawyers in the cabin a-coming home, unlooked for, like the devil at prayers. Wait is what I say; but when the time comes, why, let her rip!"

"John," cries the coxswain, "you're a man!"

"You'll say so, Israel, when you see," said Silver. "Only one thing I claim – I claim Trelawney. I'll wring his calf's head off his body with these hands. Dick!" he added, breaking

off, "you just jump up, like a sweet lad, and get me an apple, to wet my pipe like."

You may fancy the terror I was in! I should have leaped out and run for it, if I had found the strength; but my limbs and heart alike misgave me. I heard Dick begin to rise, and then someone seemingly stopped him, and the voice of Hands exclaimed:

"Oh, stow that! Don't you get sucking of that bilge, John. Let's have a go of the rum."

"Dick," said Silver, "I trust you. I've a gauge on the keg, mind. There's the key; you fill a pannikin and bring it up."

Dick was gone but a little while, and during his absence Israel spoke straight on in the cook's ear. It was but a word or two that I could catch, and yet I gathered some important news; for, besides other scraps that tended to the same purpose, this whole clause was audible: "Not another man of them'll jine." Hence there were still faithful men on board.

When Dick returned, one after another of the trio took the pannikin and drank – one "To luck"; another with a "Here's to old Flint"; and Silver himself saying, in a kind of song, "Here's to ourselves, and hold your luff, plenty of prizes and plenty of duff."

Just then a sort of brightness fell upon me in the barrel, and, looking up, I found the moon had risen, and was silvering the mizzen-top and shining white on the luff of the foresail; and almost at the same time the voice of the look-out shouted, "Land ho!"

482

## *William Blake*
# THE TYGER

TYGER! Tyger! burning bright
In the forests of the night,
What immortal hand or eye
Could frame thy fearful symmetry?

In what distant deeps or skies
Burnt the fire of thine eyes?
On what wings dare he aspire?
What the hand dare seize the fire?

And what shoulder, and what art,
Could twist the sinews of thy heart?
And when thy heart began to beat,
What dread hand? and what dread feet?

What the hammer? what the chain?
In what furnace was thy brain?
What the anvil? what dread grasp
Dare its deadly terrors clasp?

When the stars threw down their spears,
And water'd heaven with their tears,
Did he smile his work to see?
Did he who made the Lamb make thee?

Tyger! Tyger! burning bright
In the forests of the night,
What immortal hand or eye,
Dare frame thy fearful symmetry?

# T. H. White

# THE SWORD IN THE STONE

*Illustrated by Virginia Mayo*

## King Pellinore Fights Sir Grummore

*Magically transported to the Forest Sauvage, Merlyn the
Magician and the Wart – the young King Arthur – witness a jousting
match between King Pellinore and Sir Grummore.*

A S SOON AS THEY WERE READY, the two knights stationed themselves at each end of the clearing and then advanced to meet in the middle.

"Fair knight," said King Pellinore, "I pray thee tell me thy name."

"That me regards," replied Sir Grummore, using the proper formula.

"That is uncourteously said," said King Pellinore, "what? For no knight ne dreadeth for to speak his name openly, but for some reason of shame."

"Be that as it may, I choose that thou shalt not know my name as at this time, for no askin'."

"Then you must stay and joust with me, false knight."

"Haven't you got that wrong, Pellinore?" inquired Sir Grummore. "I believe it ought to be 'thou shalt'."

"Oh, I'm sorry, Sir Grummore. Yes, so it should, of course. Then thou shalt stay and joust with me, false knight."

Without further words, the two gentlemen retreated to the opposite ends of the clearing, fewtered their spears, and prepared to hurtle together in the preliminary charge.

"I think we had better climb this tree," said Merlyn. "You never know what will happen in a joust like this."

They climbed up the big beech, which had easy branches sticking out in all directions, and the Wart stationed himself towards the end of a smooth bough about fifteen feet up, where he could get a good view. Nothing is so comfortable to sit in as a beech.

To be able to picture the terrible battle which now took place, there is one thing which ought to be known. A knight in his full armour of those days, or at any rate during the heaviest days of armour, was generally carrying as much or more than his own weight in metal. He often weighed no less than twenty-two stone, and sometimes as much as twenty-five. This meant that his horse had to be a slow and enormous weight-carrier, like the farm horse of today, and that his own movements were so hampered by his burden of iron and padding that they were toned down into slow motion, as on the cinema.

"They're off!" cried the Wart, holding his breath with excitement.

485

Slowly and majestically, the ponderous horses lumbered into a walk. The spears, which had been pointing in the air, bowed to a horizontal line and pointed at each other. King Pellinore and Sir Grummore could be seen to be thumping their horses' sides with their heels for all they were worth, and in a few minutes the splendid animals had shambled into an earth-shaking imitation of a trot. Clank, rumble, thump-thump went the horses, and now the two knights were flapping their elbows and legs in unison, showing a good deal of daylight at their seats. There was a change in tempo, and Sir Grummore's horse could be definitely seen to be cantering. In another minute King Pellinore's was doing so too. It was a terrible spectacle.

"Oh, dear!" exclaimed the Wart, feeling ashamed that his blood-thirstiness had been responsible for making these two knights joust before him. "Do you think they will kill each other?"

"Dangerous sport," said Merlyn, shaking his head.

"Now!" cried the Wart.

With a blood-curdling beat of iron hoofs the mighty equestrians came together. Their spears wavered for a moment within a few inches of each other's helms – each had chosen the difficult point-stroke – and then they were galloping off in opposite directions. Sir Grummore drove his spear deep into the beech tree where they were sitting, and stopped dead. King Pellinore, who had been run away with, vanished altogether behind his back.

"Is it safe to look?" inquired the Wart, who had shut his eyes at the critical moment.

"Quite safe," said Merlyn. "It will take them some time to get back in position."

"Whoa, whoa, I say!" cried King Pellinore in muffled and distant tones, far away among the gorse bushes.

"Hi, Pellinore, hi!" shouted Sir Grummore. "Come back, my dear fellah, I'm over here."

There was a long pause, while the complicated stations of the two knights readjusted themselves, and then King Pellinore was at the opposite end from that at which he had started, while Sir Grummore faced him from his original position.

"Traitor knight!" cried Sir Grummore.

"Yield, recreant, what?" cried King Pellinore.

They fewtered their spears again, and thundered into the charge.

"Oh," said the Wart, "I hope they don't hurt themselves."

But the two mounts were patiently blundering together, and the two knights had simultaneously decided on the sweeping stroke. Each held his spear at right angles towards the left, and, before the Wart could say anything further, there was a terrific yet melodious thump. Clang! went the armour, like a motor omnibus in collision with a smithy, and the jousters were sitting side by side on the green sward, while their horses cantered off in opposite directions.

"A splendid fall," said Merlyn.

The two horses pulled themselves up, their duty done, and began resignedly to eat the sward. King Pellinore and Sir Grummore sat looking straight before them, each with the other's spear clasped hopefully under his arm.

"Well!" said the Wart. "What a bump! They both seem to be all right, so far."

Sir Grummore and King Pellinore laboriously got up.

"Defend thee," cried King Pellinore.

"God save thee," cried Sir Grummore.

With this they drew their swords and rushed together with such ferocity that each, after dealing the other a dint on the helm, sat down suddenly backwards.

"Bah!" cried King Pellinore.

"Booh!" cried Sir Grummore, also sitting down.

"Mercy," exclaimed the Wart. "What a combat!"

The knights had now lost their tempers and the battle was joined in earnest. It did not matter much, however, for they were so encased in metal that they could not do each other much damage. It took them so long to get up, and the dealing of a blow when you weighed the eighth part of a ton was such a cumbrous business, that every stage of the contest could be marked and pondered.

In the first stage King Pellinore and Sir Grummore stood opposite each other for about half an hour, and walloped each other on the helm. There was only opportunity for one blow at a time, so they more or less took it in turns, King Pellinore striking while Sir Grummore was recovering, and vice versa. At first, if either of them dropped his sword or got it stuck in the ground, the other put in two or three extra blows while he was patiently fumbling for it or trying to tug it out. Later, they fell into the rhythm of the thing more perfectly, like the toy mechanical people who saw wood on Christmas trees. Eventually the exercise and the monotony restored their good humour and they began to get bored.

The second stage was introduced as a change, by common consent. Sir Grummore stumped off to one end of the clearing, while King Pellinore plodded off to the other. Then they turned round and swayed backward and forward once or twice, in order to get their weight on their toes. When they leaned forward they had to run forward, to keep up with their weight, and if they leaned too far

backward they fell down. So even walking was complicated. When they had got their weight properly distributed in front of them, so that they were just off their balance, each broke into a trot to keep up with himself. They hurtled together as it had been two boars.

They met in the middle, breast to breast, with a noise of shipwreck and great bells tolling, and both, bouncing off, fell breathless on their backs. They lay thus for a few minutes, panting. Then they slowly began to heave themselves to their feet, and it was obvious that they had lost their tempers once again.

King Pellinore had not only lost his temper but he seemed to have been a bit astonished by the impact. He got up facing the wrong way, and could not find Sir Grummore. There was some excuse for this, since he had only a slit to peep through – and that was three inches away from his eye owing to the padding of straw – but he looked muddled as well. Perhaps he had broken his spectacles. Sir Grummore was quick to seize his advantage.

"Take that!" cried Sir Grummore, giving the unfortunate monarch a two-handed swipe on the nob as he was slowly turning his head from side to side, peering in the opposite direction.

King Pellinore turned round morosely, but his opponent had been too quick for him. He had ambled round so that he was still behind the King, and now gave him another terrific blow in the same place.

"Where are you?" asked King Pellinore.

"Here," cried Sir Grummore, giving him another.

The poor King turned himself round as nimbly as possible, but Sir Grummore had given him the slip again.

"Tally-ho back!" shouted Sir Grummore, with another wallop.

"I think you're a *cad*," said the King.

"Wallop!" replied Sir Grummore, doing it.

What with the preliminary crash, the repeated blows on the back of his head, and the puzzling nature of his opponent, King Pellinore could now be seen to be visibly troubled in his brains. He swayed backward and forward under the hail of blows which were administered, and feebly wagged his arms.

"Poor King," said Wart. "I wish he would not hit him so."

As if in answer to his wish, Sir Grummore paused in his labours.

"Do you want Pax?" asked Sir Grummore.

King Pellinore made no answer.

Sir Grummore favoured him with another whack and said, "If you don't say Pax, I shall cut your head off."

"I won't," said the King.

Whang! went the sword on the top of his head.

Whang! it went again.

Whang! for the third time.

"Pax," said King Pellinore, mumbling rather.

Then, just as Sir Grummore was relaxing with the fruits of victory, he swung round upon him, shouted "Non!" at the top of his voice, and gave him a good push in the middle of the chest.

Sir Grummore fell over backwards.

"Well!" exclaimed the Wart. "What a cheat! I would not have thought it of him."

King Pellinore hurriedly sat on his victim's chest, thus increasing the weight upon him to a quarter of a ton and making it quite impossible for him to move, and began to undo Sir Grummore's helm.

"You said Pax!"

"I said Pax Non under my breath."

"It's a swindle."

"It's not."

"You're a cad."

"No, I'm not."

"Yes, you are."

"No, I'm not."

"Yes, you are."

"I said Pax Non."

"You said Pax."

"No, I didn't."

"Yes, you did."

"No, I didn't."

"Yes, you did."

By this time Sir Grummore's helm was unlaced and they could see his bare head glaring at King Pellinore, quite purple in the face.

"Yield thee, recreant," said the King.

"Shan't," said Sir Grummore.

"You have got to yield, or I shall cut off your head."

"Cut it off then."

"Oh, come on," said the King. "You know you have to yield when your helm is off."

"Feign I," said Sir Grummore.

"Well, I shall just cut your head off."

"I don't care."

The King waved his sword menacingly in the air.

"Go on," said Sir Grummore. "I dare you to."

The King lowered his sword and said, "Oh, I say, do yield, please."

"You yield," said Sir Grummore.

"But I can't yield. I am on top of you after all, am I not, what?"

"Well, I have feigned yieldin'."

"Oh, come on, Grummore. I do think you are a cad not to yield. You know very well I can't cut your head off."

"I would not yield to a cheat who started fightin' after he said Pax."

"I am not a cheat."

"You are a cheat."

"No, I'm not."

"Yes, you are."

"No, I'm not."

"Yes, you are."

"Very well," said King Pellinore. "You can jolly well get up and put on your helm and we will have a fight. I won't be called a cheat for anybody."

"Cheat!" said Sir Grummore.

They stood up and fumbled together with the helm, hissing, "No, I'm not" – "Yes, you are," until it was safely on. Then they retreated to opposite ends of the clearing, got their weight upon their toes, and came rumbling and thundering together like two runaway trams.

Unfortunately they were now so cross that they had both ceased to be vigilant, and in the fury of the moment they missed each other altogether. The momentum of their armour was too great for them to stop till they had passed each other handsomely, and then they manoeuvred about in such a manner that neither happened to come within the other's range of vision. It was funny watching them, because King Pellinore, having already been caught from behind once, was continually spinning round to look behind him, and Sir Grummore, having used the stratagem himself, was doing the same thing. Thus they wandered for some five minutes, standing still, listening, clanking, crouching, creeping, peering, walking on tiptoe, and occasionally making a chance swipe behind their backs. Once they were standing within a few feet of each other, back to back, only to stalk off in opposite directions with infinite precaution, and once King Pellinore did hit Sir Grummore with one of his back strokes, but they both immediately spun round so often that they became giddy and mislaid each other afresh.

After five minutes Sir Grummore said, "All right, Pellinore. It is no use hidin'. I can see where you are."

"I am not hiding," exclaimed King Pellinore indignantly. "Where am I?"

They discovered each other and went up close together, face to face.

"Cad," said Sir Grummore.

"Yah," said King Pellinore.

They turned round and marched off to their corners, seething with indignation.

"Swindler," shouted Sir Grummore.

"Beastly bully," shouted King Pellinore.

With this they summoned all their energies together for one decisive encounter, leaned forward, lowered their heads like two billy-goats, and positively sprinted together for the final blow. Alas, their aim was poor. They missed each other by about five yards, passed at full steam doing at least eight knots, like ships that pass in the night but speak not to each other in passing, and hurtled onward to their doom. Both knights began waving their arms like windmills, anti-clockwise, in the vain effort to slow up. Both continued with undiminished speed. Then Sir Grummore rammed his head against the beech in which the Wart was sitting, and King Pellinore collided with a chestnut at the other side of the clearing. The trees shook, the forest rang. Blackbirds and squirrels cursed and wood-pigeons flew out of their leafy perches half a mile away. The two knights stood to attention while one could count three. Then, with a last unanimous melodious clang, they both fell prostrate on the fatal sward.

"Stunned," said Merlyn, "I should think."

"Oh, dear," said the Wart. "Ought we to get down and help them?"

"We could pour water on their heads," said Merlyn reflectively, "if there was any water. But I don't suppose they would thank us for making their armour rusty. They will be all right. Besides, it is time that we were home."

"But they might be dead!"

"They are not dead, I know. In a minute or two they will come round and go off home to dinner."

"Poor King Pellinore has not got a home."

"Then Sir Grummore will invite him to stay the night. They will be the best of friends when they come to. They always are."

# Michael Palin
# LIMERICKS

### Illustrated by Tony Ross

A brave taxi driver called Clive,
Once found a Black Mamba alive.
Though they said, "Shoot it dead!"
He decided instead
To take it round town for a drive.

A deep-water sailor called Rod
Used to dive in and rescue live cod.
He wasn't a fool
Who thought nets were cruel,
But he certainly was pretty odd.

## Patricia Wrightson

# THE NARGUN AND THE STARS

*Illustrated by Joan Saint*

## The Stone Moves

*This story is set in Australia. When his parents are killed in a car crash,
Simon comes to Wongadilla to live with his cousins, Charlie and Edie. Simon discovers the
Potkoorok and the Turongs, ancient creatures who were there before humans arrived, as they
revenge themselves on a bulldozer and a grader sent to cut down trees and
build a new road. But up on the ridge lurks something infinitely
older and more frightening – the Nargun.*

THERE WAS UTTER STILLNESS in the scrub. Delighted with himself, Simon went running down the root terraces into the sunlight. The song of frogs lay over the swamp. At the far end, sitting on the bank with its legs in the water, sat the green-skinned golden-eyed swamp-creature eating an apple.

Simon stood still while excitement fluttered in his veins. The swamp-thing stayed peacefully where it was. Simon took the second apple from his pocket and went slowly to the bank and sat down. The swamp-creature gave him a comical look. They sat side by side on the bank, both chewing apples and Simon swelling with delight. After a while he ventured to speak.

"What's your name?" It was a stupid thing to say to a swamp-thing, but how else could you start?

The swamp-creature made a sound like the calling of frogs.

"Eh?" said Simon.

The creature made the sound again: "Potkoorok."

"Is that your own name? Or is it what you are?"

"That is my name that I am," said the creature a little grandly. "You are Boy. I am Potkoorok." It put the last bit of apple into its froglike mouth and crunched away. Juice ran out of the corners of its mouth. "Good," it said, turning its head towards Simon.

"Pot-koo-rok," said Simon. The creature chuckled. "And what are *they*? The ones in the trees?"

"Turongs. Tu-rongs. Their name that they are is Turongs." It was watching Simon with sly attention.

"Turongs," repeated Simon thoughtfully. " – *Hey!*"

He had lost his apple. A green hand with flattened webbed fingers had plucked it lightly from his own hand while he spoke. The Potkoorok chuckled with glee and munched

the remains of the apple. Simon supposed that if you wanted to be friends with it you would have to put up with that sort of thing.

"There's a lot more Turongs up there now, aren't there?" he said. "Did they come from the other scrub when the trees were cut down?" The Potkoorok's wide mouth turned down and it looked at him sadly. "Why do they throw sticks and chase the sheep? *We* didn't cut down their trees."

"They play jokes," said the Potkoorok reproachfully. "On hunters – not so good as fishermen. They can't help it; they are Turongs, not Potkooroks. They play jokes good enough for hunters. If there are no hunters, what can they do? They play tricks on sheep."

"*You* played a trick on *them* last night," said Simon. "You made them pinch the wrong machine."

"No trick. The Turongs want to sink the wrong machine. It is wrong for them too. The yellow machine is a wrong trouble, killing frogs and trees."

"But that was two different machines! This one killed the frog, the other one killed the trees. The Turongs wanted to get rid of the other one."

The Potkoorok gave him an offended look. "The Turongs brought the yellow machine," it said huffily.

"Both of them were yellow! You just wait – the other one will go on killing trees on the mountain."

The Potkoorok turned its golden eyes along the mountain and looked far off. "The Boy tricks the Potkoorok," it said dryly. "I see no yellow machine on the mountain."

As it happened, the bulldozer was not working that morning, so Simon was not able to prove his point. In any case, the Potkoorok

seemed upset and that was a bad way to begin a friendship. He set out to soothe its ruffled feelings.

"What happened to the machine, anyhow? I looked in the water and it's gone. You can't see anything at all."

This was evidently the right thing to say, for the creature chuckled like the lapping of water. "You can't see anything at all? You look now," it said.

Simon stood up and looked into the pool. Clearly through the brown water he could see a yellow shape: a wheel, and part of a frame. While he was looking the water grew dark again. Nothing showed.

"Hey!" said Simon. "Would you believe that?"

The Potkoorok was chuckling away when the sound of a motor came from the road. Still chuckling and without a splash the creature slid into the water and was gone. Simon was almost relieved. It had been a tremendous excitement, but a strain too. He wanted time to think about it and grow used to it.

He guessed that the motor would be Charlie's, driving home after the search had been given up, so he went to the bend of the road to wait for it. But it was not the station-wagon that came round the curve of the mountain. It was a blue car, much newer and smarter, driven by a stocky young man wearing a navy singlet. He stopped the car when he saw Simon, and leaned through the window to speak.

"Nice day after the storm…Haven't seen a bulldozer about, have you?"

It was the driver of the bulldozer, and he too was looking for his machine.

The disappearance of the bulldozer as well as the grader caused a fuss that took up the rest of that day. It began at the telephone in

Charlie's small study where drivers rang up their bosses and the police, and the police rang up other police, and neighbours and townspeople, to help in the search. Edie was kept busy making tea for them and listening to their telephone conversations.

From there the fuss spread all round Wongadilla. Cars nosed along roads and tracks, four-wheel-drive vehicles charged into gullies; the whining and grinding of their motors hung round the hills all day. There were constant meetings between men who exchanged theories, agreed with each other, massaged their heads, and lapsed into puzzled silence. Only the grader man was sure of anything, and he grew more certain every moment that the brake of the grader had been fully on.

There were times when Simon, following them about, wondered whether he ought to tell about the grader. But he was sure they would not believe him if he did, and somehow just as sure that people should not interfere with the creatures of the country. Besides, he had no idea what could have happened to the bulldozer. Perhaps, after he had run home last night, the wild crowd of Turongs had gone on across the mountain and carried off the bulldozer too. Yet he didn't believe this. The Potkoorok would have known and boasted about it, instead of being huffy when he mentioned two machines.

Late in the afternoon Charlie extricated himself and Simon from the search, telling the searchers to help themselves to the telephone if they needed it and that he had to check up on some sheep. By that time the searchers were ready to give up in any case, and began to drive away. The final theory was that thieves or practical jokers had driven the two machines off last night, unheard in the storm, and that

the police must look for them miles away from Wongadilla.

Simon and Charlie came into the kitchen where Edie was already pouring their tea. She looked at Charlie with a questioning face. "Not a sign," he told her. "They'd have to be *somewhere*, they couldn't vanish."

"It won't do any good," said Edie in a vexed way, pushing the sugar basin towards him. "There'll be another bulldozer up there inside a week."

"Anyhow, this one's nowhere on Wongadilla. They reckon it's been stolen, and I'd say they're right. A wasted day, and too late to get around the sheep tonight – best I can do is have a look at their camp. I wish these machine men could look after their own stock. Eh, Simey?"

Simon didn't really hear. He was listening, at last, to the silence with its clear, frail sounds. He was tired of interruptions and strangers and excitement. Now he wanted to be alone with the silence and the windy heights of Wongadilla, letting them restore to him the small old creatures of the land. Later, though he sat between Charlie and Edie, he was alone with the fire; and he thought of the Potkoorok stealing his apple, and smiled and hugged himself. Then he was alone between the white walls of his room, hearing the pine whisper and a fox call; and he thought of spidery grey shadows climbing round trunks. He went to sleep thinking of the Turongs' dance, and woke deciding to spend the day alone on the mountain.

Charlie was going to muster the sheep and look them over, as he had meant to do yesterday. "I could do with a hand," he told Simon, "that's if you've got nothing better to do." When Simon stammered that he thought he might go and look at the place where the bulldozer had been, Charlie said quickly, "That's right, you look around while you've got the chance. You wouldn't want to go through the fence, of course – one of those trees could make a mess of you if it happened to fall on you." He helped Simon to catch Pet while Edie cut lunch for them both, and watched Simon ride off alone without seeming to mind at all. He only shouted after him: "If you see any sheep send 'em down!" And Simon waved in reply and then forgot. Perhaps a cicada feels as Simon did when it crawls out of the earth in its tight shell.

He rode first to the foot of the steepest slope and reined in near the fence; the screen of forest had been cleared from there, and he could see what the bulldozer had done. Before it disappeared it had flattened about half the forest on that side of the fence. No one was working there today.

Someone would come and finish the job, he supposed. Someone would load and cart away the trimmed logs, and perhaps burn the others. Grass would grow in time, and bracken, and a few new trees. Then it would look like any other ridge. Now it looked barer and uglier than the rocks that rose above it at the end of the mountain.

Standing in the stirrups and switching at Pet's rump with his stick, he forced her up the trail that had frightened him that first time. Whenever the trail turned and she was faced with the need to clamber higher, Pet stopped dead until Simon shouted and switched. They came at last to the ledge, and he got off and tethered her where Charlie had. He walked to the fence and looked down, as he had that other day. There was no place down there to hide a bulldozer except in the forest itself; even the Turongs couldn't have done it. The bulldozer must have gone out by the way it came

in, as the searchers had said. He went back to the ledge and looked down at Wongadilla.

There it was, plunging down, with blue heights swinging up beyond. There was the glinting green of the swamp, and the white shoebox house. Some tiny sheep were collected on the flat; he could hear Charlie's shouts, and the answering yelps of the dogs. Next time, he thought, he would have to give Charlie a hand – when he had sorted out the things he wanted to think about.

Now it must be nearly "time for a cup". He took an apple from his lunch bag: Edie had given him two. Simon suddenly knew that Edie would always give him two apples, since yesterday when he had asked for one. He took the apple across the steep slope to that little gully where he had been before; last time he had climbed into it from high up the mountain, and he had climbed out again at about this level.

It was very quiet and alone in there, just as he remembered. He could look down the gully over Wongadilla, but no one there would see him, leaning back against the side like this. He sat there eating his apple and feeling the strength of the mountain surging behind him. He felt the earth rolling on its way through the sky, and rocks and trees clinging to it, and seas and the strands of rivers pressed to it, and flying birds caught in its net of air. And though he didn't know what the Potkoorok and the Turongs were, still he knew they were part of the earth and this mountain. People might come and go, he thought, but those others belonged here; and he thought they had belonged here always. There was something old and innocent in the way the Turongs danced, and in the sly teasing of the Potkoorok. There was something that didn't care – something free and old like the mountain, and elusive like the blue shadows of distance. Simon could not have explained it, but he knew it.

His breath came quicker when he faced the question of what these old creatures *were*. For the only words that came to him were "elf" and "magic" – and surely those meant something different? He put the question away again and thought of the Turongs: "If there are no hunters, what can they do? They play tricks on sheep." Once they had played their tricks on dark-skinned hunters, he thought; and they had lived hidden in a wide world of forests instead of fleeing from one small scrap to the next...

BRENT, said the gully silently.

Simon frowned. No one could have spoken his name up here. Nothing interrupted the silence. He went back to his thoughts.

BRENT, said the gully.

Simon shifted in an irritated way. He looked, and saw his name scratched on a small rock – he must have been seeing it for some time without really seeing. It made him jump at first, until he remembered scratching it there himself the other time he was here. He must be sitting in almost the same spot as he was that day.

BRENT, said the gully, speaking urgently. He shrugged, trying to forget it. He frowned and looked about, then sat up straight, frowning again.

Where was SIMON?

He had scratched both names, on two rocks, side by side so that they made his whole name, SIMON BRENT. Here was BRENT; where was SIMON?

He began to look around, puzzled: it had been a big rock, very big, leaning against the wall of the gully with the smaller rock on its other side. He remembered quite well. The blue-green lichen in which he scratched his name had been bigger, too; it had caught his eye first, and started him off with his name-scratching. He had made the first name so big that there was no room left for the second. Idly, not really thinking much about it, he had looked for a place to scratch the second name and noticed the small rock with a smaller lichen. They had stood close, side by side, and made his whole name between them, even though the second name was smaller.

So where was SIMON?

"That's mad!" he said angrily, and got up to search. No one could have moved a big rock like that! Even in the storm, even a *torrent* of water rushing down couldn't have moved it... but perhaps it might have moved the smaller rock? Perhaps he wasn't in the same place at all but a little further down the gully? He went to examine the smaller rock.

He grasped it and wrenched at it, but it stayed firm. It was set in the earth; ferns and grass stood around its base and nothing had disturbed them...But there were crushed ferns and grass, and smeared moss, in a patch between the small rock and the gully wall. It didn't look as though a great rock had been torn from the ground where it belonged – but something very heavy *had* been moved.

He looked for more crushed ferns and moss, and saw a patch on rocks six feet higher up the gully. From there he saw, higher still, a deep groove ploughed into soft soil; and beyond that a scraped muddy mark on a flat rock. From sign to sign, he traced a trail up the gully between walls that grew steeper and closer as he went.

*Up* the gully!

"It's mad!" cried Simon angrily again.

Then he hit on a solution to the mystery, and wondered why he hadn't thought of it before. The Turongs, of course. He couldn't guess why or how they had moved a great boulder up this little gully, but they must have done it; and who knew how or why the Turongs did anything? Greatly relieved he came to a sharp elbow in the gully and stopped.

Ahead, he could see, the gully was choked with blackberry. In front of this screen, and leaning against the wall of the gully, was a great unevenly-shaped boulder that called to him silently: SIMON. He took a step towards it – and stopped again.

It had a queer crouching shape that looked as if it were pressing itself against the side of the gully, hiding its face. It was stone, dark with age and heavy and still as stone; if you saw it suddenly in the moonlight would it move, a very little and very slowly, towards you? Simon began to back carefully away, watching it. That was not a blunt muzzle pressed against the rock; it was only stone. That cavity was not an eye full of darkness; it saw nothing. He backed away round the elbow of the gully, then turned and began to scurry down.

When he came to the stone marked BRENT he did not climb out of the gully but hurried past. He didn't want the slow trouble of getting Pet down the mountain; he wanted to reach the Potkoorok. The little gully shallowed and widened, merging into the mountain's broad lap. Just inside its mouth he came on something very ugly: a sheepskin, mangled and torn, with flies buzzing about it and small hoofs still attached. The hoofs were crushed and flattened as if something heavy had smashed them. He took his eyes away from it with a shiver and began running hard along the mountain.

When he got to the swamp there was no sign of the swamp-creature. He had no idea how to summon it and no apple to offer it. He tried calling.

"Potkoorok!"

No sign. Of course it wouldn't come when it knew he wanted it; it would hide, and try to surprise him. But he called again urgently:

"Potkoorok!"

When it didn't come he grew desperate and shouted a mixture of pleading and command: "I gave you apples – I didn't tell about the grader – I picked up the frog – I *need* you! Come!"

It came out of the water at his feet and sat on a tuft of bull-grass, looking slightly offended as if Simon's manners displeased it; but when it saw that he was desperately serious it grew uneasy instead.

"Listen!" said Simon, trying to breathe and talk evenly and slowly. "Up there on the mountain – there's a thing – a big stone. Did the Turongs move it?"

The Potkoorok stiffened. It spoke sternly. "They leave it alone. It doesn't belong here. It is the Nargun."

"Go on," Simon demanded. "Does it move by itself, then? Is it another one – like you? Is it good?"

"Good?" said the Potkoorok. "What is good? It is the Nargun. It came from a long way south. It should go back."

"Does it – hurt things? Would it – kill a sheep?"

The Potkoorok blinked its old-looking eyes and turned its head away. It scooped up a water-spider in its webbed fingers and held it up with a coaxing smile for Simon to admire.

"Would it hurt a person?" Simon persisted.

The Potkoorok gave him a huffy look and slipped off the tuft of grass into the water. It was gone.

# Kit Wright
# OBJECTION
*Illustrated by Posy Simmonds*

MY feelings towards my little brother
Would soften
If only, once every so often,
He'd blow his nose.

He's not without style.
Why won't he, just once in a while,
Do you suppose?

As things are,
I just can't stick it.
Why can't he blow it
Instead of pick it?

# Robert Westall
# THE KINGDOM BY THE SEA

*Illustrated by Tony Kerins*

## The Bombs Fall

HE WAS AN OLD HAND at air raids now. As the yell of the siren climbed the sky, he came smoothly out of his dreams. Not scared. Only his stomach clamped down tight for action, as his hands found his clothes laid ready in the dark. Hauled one jumper, then another, over his pyjamas. Thrust both stockinged feet together through his trousers and into his shoes. Then bent to tie his laces thoroughly. A loose lace had tripped him once, in the race to the shelter. He remembered the smashing blow as the ground hit his chin; the painful week after, not able to eat with a bitten tongue.

He grabbed his school raincoat off the door, pulling the door wide at the same time. All done by feel; no need to put the light on. Lights were dangerous.

He passed Dulcie's door, heard Mam and Dulcie muttering to each other, Dulcie sleepy and cross, Mam sharp and urgent. Then he thundered downstairs; the crack of light from the kitchen door lighting up the edge of each stair-tread. Dad was sitting in his warden's uniform, hauling on his big black boots, his grey hair standing up vertically in a bunch, like a cock's comb. Without looking up, Dad said, "Bloody Hitler! Four bloody nights in a row!"

There was a strong smell of Dad's sweaty feet, and the fag he had burning in the ashtray.

That was all Harry had time to notice; he had his own job; the two objects laid ready in the chair by the door. The big roll of blankets, wrapped in a groundsheet because the shelter was damp, done up with a big leather strap of Dad's. And Mam's precious attaché case with the flask of hot coffee and insurance policies and other important things, and the little bottle of brandy for emergencies. He heaved the blankets on to his back, picked up the case with one hand and reached to unlock the back door with the other.

"Mind that light," said Dad automatically. But Harry's hand was already reaching for the switch. He'd done it all a hundred times before.

He slammed the door behind him, held his breath and listened. A single aircraft's engines, far out to sea. *Vroomah, vroomah, vroomah*. A Jerry. But nothing to worry about yet. Two guns fired, one after another. Two brilliant points of white, lighting up a black landscape of greenhouse, sweet-pea trellises and cucumber-frames. A rolling carpet of echoes. Still out to sea. Safe, then.

He ran down the long back garden, with his neck prickling and the blankets bouncing against his back comfortingly. As he passed the greenhouse the rabbits thumped their heels in alarm. There was a nice cold smell of dew and

500

cabbages. Then he was in through the shelter door, shoving the damp mould-stinking curtain aside.

He tossed the things on to Mam's bunk. Found the tiny oil-lamp on the back girder, and lit it and watched the flame grow. Then he lit the candle under the pottery milk-cooler that kept the shelter warm. Then he undid the bundle and laid out the blankets on the right bunks and turned back to the shelter door, ready to take Dulcie from Mam. He should be hearing their footsteps any second now, the patter of Mam's shoes and the crunch of Dad's hobnailed boots. Dad always saw them safe in the shelter, before he went on duty. Mam would be nagging Dad – had he locked the back door against burglars? They always teased Mam about that; she must think burglars were bloody brave, burgling in the middle of air raids.

God, Mam and Dad were taking their time tonight. What was keeping them? That Jerry was getting closer. More guns were firing now. The garden, every detail of it, the bird-bath and the concrete rabbit, flashed black, white, black, white, black. There was a whispering in the air. Gun-shrapnel falling like rain…they shouldn't be out in *that*. Where were they? Where *were* they? Why weren't they tumbling through the shelter door, panting and laughing to be safe?

That Jerry was right overhead. *Vroomah. Vroomah. Vroomah.*

And then the other whistling. Rising to a scream. Bombs. Harry began to count. If you were still counting at ten, the bombs had missed you.

The last thing he remembered was saying "seven".

His back hurt and his neck hurt. His hands scrabbled, and scrabbled damp clay, that got under his fingernails. The smell told him he was still in the shelter, but lying on the damp floor. And a cautious, fearful voice, with a slight tremble in it, was calling out:

"Is anybody down there?"

Somebody pushed the curtain across the shelter door aside, and shone a torch on him. The person was wearing a warden's helmet, the white "W" glimmering in the light of the torch. He thought at first it might be Dad. But it wasn't Dad. It had a big black moustache; it was a total stranger.

The stranger said, to somebody else behind him, "There's only one of them. A kid."

"Jesus Christ," said the somebody else. "Ask him where the rest are. There should be four in this shelter."

"Where's the rest, son? Where's your Mam and Dad?"

"In the…I don't know."

"D'you mean, still in the house, son?"

The voice behind muttered, "Christ, I hate this job." Then it said, with a sharp squeak of fear, "What's that?"

"What's *what*?"

"Something soft under me foot. Shine your light."

"'S only a rabbit. A dead rabbit."

"Thank God. Hey, son, can you hear me? Can you get up? Are you hurt?"

Why didn't the man come down and help him? What was he so *frightened* of?

Harry got up slowly. He hurt nearly all over, but not so badly that he couldn't move. The man gave him a hand and pulled him up out of the shelter. Harry peered up the garden. He could see quite well because the sky to the west was glowing pink.

There was no greenhouse left.

There was no house left. The houses to each side were still standing, though their windows had gone, and their slates were off.

"Where's our house?"

There was a silence. Then the man with the moustache said, "What's yer name, son?" Harry told him.

"And what was yer Dad's name? And yer Mam's?" He wrote it all down in a notebook, like the police did, when they caught you scrumping apples. He gave them Dulcie's name, too. He tried to be helpful. Then he said, "Where *are* they?" and began to run up the garden path.

The man grabbed him, quick and rough.

"You can't go up there, son. There's a gas leak. A bad gas leak. Pipe's fractured. It's dangerous. It's against the law to go up there."

"But my Mam and Dad're up there…"

"Nobody up there now, son. Come down to the Rest Centre. They'll tell you all about it at the Rest Centre."

Harry just let himself be led off across some more gardens. It was easy, because all the fences were blown flat. They went up the path of Number Five. The white faces of the Humphreys, who lived at Number Five, peered palely from the door of their shelter. They let him pass, without saying anything to him.

In the road, the wardens who were leading him met two other wardens.

"Any luck at Number Nine?"

"Just this lad…"

There was a long, long silence. Then one of the other wardens said, "We found the family from Number Seven. They were in the garden. The bomb caught them as they were running for the shelter . . ."

"They all right?"

"Broken arms and legs, I think. But they'll live. Got them away in the ambulance."

Harry frowned. The Simpsons lived at Number Seven. There was some fact he should be able to remember about the Simpsons. But he couldn't. It was all…mixed up.

"Come on, son. Rest Centre for you. Can you walk that far?"

Harry walked. He felt like screaming at them. Only that wouldn't be a very British thing to do. But something kept building up inside him; like the pressure in his model steam-engine.

Where *was* his steam-engine?

Where was Mam, who could cuddle him and make everything all right?

Where was Dad in his warden's uniform, who would sort everything out?

Next second, he had broken from their hands, and was running up another garden path like a terrified rabbit. He went through another gate, over the top of another air-raid shelter, through a hedge that scratched him horribly…on, and on, and on.

He heard their voices calling him as he crouched in hiding. They seemed to call a long time. Then one of them said, "That wasn't very clever."

"It's the shock. Shock takes them funny ways. You can never tell how shock's going to take them."

"Hope he's not seriously hurt, poor little bleeder."

"Kid that can run like that…?"

And then their voices went away, leaving him alone.

So he came to his house, slowly, up his garden.

He found his three rabbits; they were all dead, though there wasn't a mark on them. Where the greenhouse had been was a tangle of wrecked tomato plants, that bled green, and gave off an overpowering smell of tomato.

The house was just a pile of bricks. Not a very high pile, because everything had fallen down into the old cellar.

There was a smell of gas; but the gas was burning. Seeping up through the bricks and burning in little blue points of flame, all in the cracks between the bricks. It looked like a burning slag-heap, and he knew why the wardens had given up hope and gone away.

He knew he must go away too. Before anybody else found him, began to ask him questions, and do things to him. Because he felt like a bomb himself, and if anyone did anything to him, he would explode into a million pieces and nobody would ever be able to put him back together again.

Especially, he mustn't be given to Cousin Elsie. Cousin Elsie, who would clutch his head to her enormous bosom, and sob and call him "poor bairn" and tell everybody who came all about it, over and over and over again. He'd seen her do that when Cousin Tommy died of diphtheria. Cousin Elsie was more awful than death itself.

No, he would go away. Where nobody knew him. Where nobody would make a fuss. Just quietly go away.

Having made his mind up, he felt able to keep moving. There were useful things to do. The blankets in the shelter to bundle up and take with him. The attaché case. All proper, as Mam and Dad would have wanted it.

It seemed to take him a long time to get the blankets bundled up exactly right and as he wanted them.

In the faint light before dawn, he even managed to find Dad's spade and bury his three rabbits. They had been his friends; he didn't want anybody finding them and making a meal of them. He even found some wooden seed markers, and wrote the rabbits' names on them, and stuck them in for tombstones.

Then he went, cutting across the long stretch of gardens and out into Brimble Road, where hardly anybody knew him.

He looked dirty, tear-stained, and exactly like a refugee. His face was so still and empty, nobody, even Cousin Elsie, would have recognised him.

He felt...he felt like a bird flying very high, far from the world and getting further away all the time. Like those gulls who soar on summer thermals and then find they cannot get down to earth again, but must wait till the sun sets, and the land cools, and the terrible strength of the upward thermal releases them to land exhausted. Only he could not imagine *ever* coming to earth again, ever. Back to where everything was just as it always had been, and you did things without thinking about them.

He supposed he would just walk till he died. It seemed the most sensible thing to do.

He must have wandered round the town all day, in circles. Every so often, he would come to himself, and realise he was in Rudyerd Street, or Nile Street.

But what did Rudyerd Street *mean*? What did Nile Street *mean*? Sometimes he thought he would go home, and Dulcie would be swinging on the front gate, shouting rude things at the big boys as they passed, but running to the safety of Mam's kitchen if they made a move to attack her. And Mam would be doing the ironing, or putting the stew in the oven.

But the moment he turned his steps towards home, the truth came back to him; the burning pile of bricks. And he would turn his steps away again.

The last time he came to himself, he was somewhere quite different.

On the beach. The little beach inside the harbour mouth, that didn't have to be fenced off with barbed wire because it was under the direct protection of the Castle guns.

He suddenly felt very tired and sat down with a thump on the sand, with his back against a black tarry boat. He closed his eyes and laid back his head; the warmth of the sun smoothed out his face, like Mam had often done with her hands. He smelt the tar of the boat and it was a nice smell; it was the first thing he'd smelt since the burning gas, and it was a comforting smell. The sun warmed his hands as they lay on the sand, and his knees under his trousers, and in a very tiny world, it was nice, nice, nice. It felt as if somebody *cared* about him, and was looking after him.

On the edge of sleep, he said, "Mam?" questioningly. And then he was asleep.

He dreamed it was just a usual day at home, with Dulcie nagging on, and Mam baking, and Dad coming in from work and taking his boots off with a satisfied sigh. He dreamed he shouted at them, "*There* you all are! Where have you *been*?"

And they all laughed at him, and said, "Hiding, silly!" And it was all right.

The all-rightness stayed with him when he woke; a feeling they were not far away. He lay relaxed; as he remembered lying relaxed in his pram when he was little and watching the leaves of trees blowing, whispering and sunlit overhead. As long as he didn't move he knew the bubble of happiness would not break. But if he moved, he knew they would go away and leave him again.

So he lay on, dreamily. The sun still shone, though it was setting, and the shadows of the cliff were creeping out towards him. And that he knew was bad. When the shadow reached him the sun would be gone, the world would turn grey, a cold breeze would blow.

And it would be time to go home. Like the three girl bathers who were walking up the beach towards him, chattering and laughing and feebly hitting each other with wet towels.

They had a home; he had no home. There was a sort of glass wall between people who had a home and people who hadn't.

He watched them pass and get into a little black car that was waiting to pick them up. He thought, with a twinge of resentment, that *some* people could still get petrol for cars even in wartime. Black market. It would serve them right if the police caught them.

Then the car moved off with a puff of blue smoke, and he felt even more lonely. The shadow of the cliff grew nearer. And nearer.

"Please help," he said to the soft warm air, and the dimming blue sky. "Don't leave me." He felt the approach of another night alone as if it was a monster.

The shadow of the cliff was only a metre away now. He reached out his arm and put his hand into it; it felt cold, like putting your hand in water, icy water.

And yet still he hoped, as the shadow crept up his arm.

He closed his eyes and felt the shadow creeping, like the liquid in a thermometer. Only it wasn't recording heat, it was recording cold.

And then he heard an explosive snort, just in front of him. Sat upright, startled, and opened his eyes.

It was a dog. A dog sitting watching him. A dog who had been in the sea, because its black fur was all spikes. A dog who had been rolling in the sand, because the spikes were all sandy. The dog watched him with what seemed to be very kind eyes. But then most dogs had kind eyes.

The dog held its paw up to him, and hesitantly he took it. The dog woofed twice, softly, approvingly, then took its paw back.

Was this his miracle? He looked round swiftly, for an owner, before he let himself hope.

There was no one else on the beach, just him and the dog.

But lots of dogs came down to the beach on their own and made friends with anybody, for an afternoon. And there was a medal on the dog's collar.

Not breathing, not daring to hope, he pulled the dog to him by the collar, and read the medal.

The dog was called Don, and lived at 12 Aldergrove Terrace.

Harry shut his eyes, and he couldn't even have told himself whether he closed them in gladness or horror.

Aldergrove Terrace had been a very posh and very short terrace. Three weeks ago, Aldergrove Terrace had been hit by a full stick of German bombs. Anybody in Aldergrove who was still alive was in hospital... permanently.

He opened his eyes, and looked at his fellow survivor. The dog was a sort of small, short-legged Alsatian. It looked quite fit, but rather thin and uncared-for. It certainly hadn't been combed in a long time, and people had combed their dogs in Aldergrove every day. It had been that sort of place.

He pulled the dog towards him again, almost roughly. It willingly collapsed against his leg and lay staring out to sea, its mouth open and its tongue gently out. He stroked it. The sandy fur was nearly dry, and he could feel the warmth of its body seeping out damply against his leg.

They stayed that way a long time, a long contented time, just being together. Long ago, they'd had a dog at Number Nine, but it had got old and died. It was good to have a dog again, and the way the dog delighted in his hand, he knew it was glad to have found somebody as well. He dreamily watched the little waves breaking on the sand; glad he

wasn't alone any more.

And then the dog stood up, and shook itself, and whined, watching him with those warm eyes. It wanted something from him.

"What is it, boy?" The sound of his own voice startled him. He hadn't spoken to anybody since he ran away from the wardens. "What do you want, boy?"

The dog whined again, and then nudged with its long nose at the bundle of blankets, sniffing. Then it turned, and nosed at the attaché case, pushing it through the sand.

The dog was hungry. And he had nothing to give it, nothing in the world. And suddenly he felt terribly hungry himself.

It threw him into a panic of helplessness. It was getting dark as well, and he had nothing to eat and nowhere to sleep. He put his face in his hands, and rocked with misery. And then he remembered his father's voice saying, angrily, "Don't flap around like a wet hen. Think, son, *think*."

It was the boat he noticed first; the boat he had been leaning against. The owner had turned it upside down, to stop the rain getting in, like they always did. But that had been a long time ago. This boat hadn't been used for years; the black, tarry paint was splitting, peeling, blistering. There was a half-inch crack, where the stern met the side. That meant...

Safety. A hiding place. A roof for the night, if it started to rain. There was a gap on this side, between the boat and the sand. Only six inches, but he could make it bigger. He began to scrabble at the sand with his hands. The sand came easily; it was soft and dry. Soon he managed to wriggle through the hole he had made. Inside, it was dark, apart from the cracks in the stern, where some light came in. But it smelt sweetly of the sea and old tar, and dry wood. The dog wriggled through to join him, licking his face, sure it was a game. He pushed it away and reached out and dragged in the bundle of blankets and the attaché case. There was plenty of room; it was a big boat, a fishing boat. He squatted by the entrance, like an Indian in his wigwam. He'd solved one problem, and it gave him strength.

Now, food. He racked his brains. Then remembered there had always been a big fish and chip shop in Front Street. It wouldn't sell much fish now, because the trawlers were away on convoy-escort. But it still sold chips and sausages cooked in batter. All the fish and chip shops did.

But…money.

He searched desperately through his pockets for odd pennies and ha'pennies.

And his fingers closed on the milled edge of a big fat two-shilling piece. Yesterday had been Thursday, and Dad had given him his week's pocket-money as usual. It all seemed so very far away, but there was the big fat florin in his hand. He rubbed the edge in the dim light, to make sure it was real, not just a penny.

He took a deep breath, and wormed out through the hole again, followed by the dog. He was in a hurry now; his stomach was sort of dissolving into juice at the thought of the battered sausages. He didn't like the idea of leaving his blankets and the precious attaché case behind, but he couldn't carry them and the chips as well. Besides, they would make him look conspicuous. They would have to take their chance, as Dad always said, when he and Harry planted out tiny seedlings, watered them, and left them for the night. Harry shook his head savagely, to shake away the memory, and the sting of hot tears that pricked at his eyes suddenly. He smoothed back the sand to conceal the hole he had dug, and set off for Front Street, the dog running ahead and marking the lamp-posts as if this was an ordinary evening stroll along the sea front.

Even a hundred metres away, the breeze carried the appetising smell to his nostrils. The shop wasn't shut then; he felt full of triumph. There was a crowd of people in the shop and they hadn't drawn the blackout curtains yet.

He pushed open the door, and the dog nosed past him eagerly, nostrils working. The owner of the shop, a tall bald man in a long greasy white apron, looked over the heads of his customers and saw them, and Harry instantly knew he was a very nasty man indeed, even before he opened his mouth.

"Get that dirty great animal out of here! This is a clean shop, a food shop!"

Covered with confusion, blushing furiously, Harry grabbed the dog's collar, and dragged him out. He pushed the dog's bottom to the pavement, and shouted, "Sit! Sit!" The dog looked at him trustingly, wagging his tail, and Harry dived back into the shop again, before the dog changed his mind. He joined the back of the queue which was about six people long.

"Filthy great beast," said the man, to no one in particular. "I don't know what this town's coming to." He shovelled great mounds of golden chips into newspaper and said to the woman helping him, "More batter, Ada," equally nastily.

Harry heard the shop door open again, and the next second, Don was beside him, leaping up at the glass counter with eager paws, and leaving dirty scratch-marks on the glass.

"I told you, get that bloody animal out of here! I won't tell you again!"

Harry grabbed Don a second time. He could feel tears starting to gather in his eyes. He hauled him out, as two more people passed him to join the queue inside. He had lost his place in the queue. And every time somebody else came, Don would come in with them, and he'd always lose his place in the queue, and *never* get served.

He looked round desperately. There was a lamp-post, with two sandbags attached, for use against incendiary bombs. They were tied to the lamp-post with thick string... Harry hauled Don over, undid the string, and slipped it through Don's collar, tied a knot, and fled back into the shop.

"Messing with our sandbags, now?" said the man savagely. He seemed to have eyes everywhere but on his own business. "Don't live round here, do you?"

Harry's heart sank. Not living round here was important; he mightn't get served at all, now. Shopkeepers looked after their own, these days of rationing.

"And it's a while since yer face saw soap an' water. Or yer hair a comb. Where yer from? The Ridges?"

The Ridges was the slummiest council estate in the whole town; it was a downright insult, to anyone who came from the Balkwell.

"No. From the Balkwell," he said stoutly.

"Well, you get back to the Balkwell chip shop, sonny Jim. We've only got enough chips for Tynemouth people in this shop. An' take that damned dog with you. Stolen him, have you? He looks a bit too grand for the likes of you. I've a mind to phone for the poliss."

The tears were streaming down Harry's face by that time. One of the women in the queue said, "Steady on, Jim. The bairn's upset. What's the matter, son?"

Something gave way inside Harry. It was all too much. He said, "I've been bombed out."

He heard a murmur of sympathy from the assembled customers, so he added, "Me Dad was killed." He said it like he was hitting the man with a big hammer.

There was a terrible hush in the shop. Everyone was looking at him, pale and open-mouthed. Then the woman said, "Serve him first, Jim. He can have my turn. What do you want, son?"

Harry had only meant to have one portion, to share with the dog. But the wild triumph was too sweet. The dog would have his own; and they'd have one each for breakfast in the morning, too. And he was thirsty.

"Four sausage and chips. And a bottle of Tizer."

Viciously, the man scooped up the portions. Harry thought he tried to make them mingy portions, but all the customers were watching him. So he suddenly doubled-up the number of chips, far more than he should have given. Then he banged the big newspaper parcel on the counter, and the bottle of Tizer with it. "Two shillings and fourpence!"

Harry gazed in horror at the two-shilling piece in his hand.

He'd over-reached himself with a vengeance, and he hadn't another penny on him. He stared around panic-stricken at the staring faces.

Then the woman took his two shillings off him, added fourpence of her own, and gave it to the man, saying, "Run along, son. Yer Mam could do with those chips while they're hot."

"Ta," he said, staring at her plump kindly face in wonder. Then he was out of the shop, with the burning packet of chips against his chest and the Tizer bottle on the pavement as he untied Don.

He walked back to the boat in a whirl. So much had happened so quickly. But he'd gone to get chips, and he'd done it. Made a terrible mess of mistakes, but he'd *done* it.

He spread the dog's share on the sand, on its newspaper, so the dog wouldn't eat any sand by mistake. The dog wolfed the sausage first, then all the chips, and nosed the folds of paper for every last crumb of batter. Then came to scrounge off Harry. It must have been really starving. Well, now, it was full, and he himself had seen to that. He felt obscurely proud. The dog was his, and he'd fed it. And found it a place to sleep.

He stretched his legs out and lay against the boat, relaxed, and swigged Tizer. He couldn't give the dog any Tizer. He hadn't a bowl. But the dog loped off to where a little freshwater stream trickled down the sand from the Castle cliff and lapped noisily. Another problem solved.

He watched the little waves coming in to the beach from the darkening river. Little lines of whiteness coming out of the dark. This time last night they'd all been sitting down to supper, Mam, Dad, Dulcie...

He let himself cry then. Somehow he could afford to, with his belly full, and his new home against his back, and his new friend the dog snuffling at his raincoat, still looking for crumbs of batter. He cried quite a long time, but he cried very quietly, not wanting anyone to hear him, in case they came across to find out what was the matter. The dog licked his tears with a huge wet tongue, and he hugged it to him.

And yet, even as he was crying, he was thinking. Hard. So many things going round in his mind, like a squirrel in a cage.

He must keep himself clean and tidy somehow. A dirty face got you into trouble. He must comb his hair. He must keep his shoes polished and his raincoat clean. And he must get a leash for Don. And he must stay near fresh water to drink... And...

He reached for Don's collar in the

dark, twisted off the medal and threw it as far down the beach as he could. That medal was Don's death-sentence. The police caught dogs who'd lost their owners in air raids, and had them put down on an electrified plate at the police station. They dampened the dog's coat, then they electrocuted it. That was what Dad had said had happened to their old dog, when he got too old. He said they did it to some lovely dogs, it was a shame.

Don was his dog now.

As the last tinge of light faded, far out over the sea, he dug under the boat again, crawled in and called the dog in after him. It wouldn't do to be on the beach after dark. People might ask questions.

He spread the blankets neatly, wishing he had a candle to see by. That was something else he'd have to lay his hands on.

He had the sand-hole neatly filled in again when his need to pee caught him in the groin like a knife. Swearing to himself, he dug the hole again, and got outside only just in time. He crawled back, thinking he had an awful lot to learn. He'd always had Mam until now, saying do this, do that, till you could *scream*. Now he had to say do this, do that, to himself.

Still, he was snug. He had enough blankets to make two into a pillow and give one to the dog. Except the dog snuggled up close to him, and he let it in.

He gave one deep sigh, and was asleep. All night his breathing lay hidden under the greater breathing of the sea. He wakened once, to hear rain patting on the boat. But it only made things cosier.

509

# ACKNOWLEDGEMENTS

*The editor and publishers would like to thank the following for permission to include copyright material in this collection. The publishers have made every effort to contact all copyright holders but apologise if any source remains unacknowledged. We would be grateful to be informed of any omissions so that corrections can be made at the earliest opportunity.*

NICOLA BAYLEY'S BOOK OF NURSERY RHYMES Published by Alfred A Knopf, an imprint of Random House, Inc © illustrations Nicola Bayley 1975
QUENTIN BLAKE'S NURSERY RHYME BOOK Published by HarperCollins Children's Books USA © illustrations Quentin Blake 1983
I WANT MY POTTY Published by Kane-Miller © Tony Ross 1986
A DARK, DARK TALE Published by Dial Books for Young Readers, a division of Penguin Books USA Inc © Ruth Brown 1981
'Pat-a-Cake, Pat-a-Cake', 'Hickory, Dickory, Dock', 'Twinkle, Twinkle, Little Star' and 'I'm a Little Teapot' from A DAY OF RHYMES Published by The Bodley Head © Sarah Pooley 1987
HALLO! HOW ARE YOU? Published by Philomel Books as 'Where's My Daddy?', a division of the Putnam Grosset Group © text Shigeo Watanabe 1979 © illustrations Yasuo Ohtomo 1979
KING ROLLO AND THE NEW SHOES Published by Andersen Press © David McKee 1979
MR GUMPY'S OUTING Published by Henry Holt & Co Inc © John Burningham 1970
ALFIE'S FEET Published by Lothrop, Lee & Shepard Books, a division of William Morrow & Co Inc © Shirley Hughes 1982
IN THE ATTIC Published by Henry Holt & Co Inc © text Hiawyn Oram 1984 © illustrations Satoshi Kitamura 1984
THE SNOWY DAY Published by Viking Children's Books USA © Ezra Jack Keats 1962, copyright renewed © Martin Pope 1990
THE WIND BLEW Published by Simon & Schuster Books for Young Readers © Pat Hutchins 1974
WILLY AND HUGH Published by Alfred A Knopf, an imprint of Random House, Inc © A. E. T. Browne & Partners 1991
'Granny Granny Please Comb My Hair' from I LIKE THAT STUFF Published by Cambridge University Press © Grace Nichols
MR RABBIT AND THE LOVELY PRESENT Published by HarperCollins Children's Books USA © text Charlotte Zolotow 1968 © illustrations Maurice Sendak 1968
IT'S YOUR TURN, ROGER! Published by Dial Books for Young Readers, a division of Penguin Books USA Inc © Susanna Gretz 1985
'Geraldine Giraffe' from THE BEST OF WEST Published by Hutchinson Children's Books © Colin West 1990
THE VELVETEEN RABBIT © illustrations Maggie Glen 1995
DR. XARGLE'S BOOK OF EARTHLETS Published by Dutton Children's Books USA, a division of Penguin Books USA Inc © text Jean Willis 1988 © illustrations Tony Ross 1988
'The Silent Ship' from THE BEST OF WEST Published by Hutchinson Children's Books © Colin West 1990
OLD BEAR Published by Philomel Books, a division of the Putnam Grosset Group © Jane Hissey 1986
THE WHALES' SONG Published by Dial Books for Young Readers, a division of Penguin Books USA Inc © text Dyan Sheldon 1990 © illustrations Gary Blythe 1990